THE SCARLET OAK

The Scarlet Oak

Murder, Spies, and Spirits

Jerry Aylward

Wild Lion Publishing

Copyright © 2022 by Jerry Aylward

First Wild Lion Publishing paperback edition July 2022

Library of Congress Cataloging-in-Publishing Data

Names: Aylward, Jerry, author.

Title: The scarlet oak : murder ,
spies , and spirits : a novel / Jerry Aylward.
Description: Huntington, NY: Wild
Lion Publishing, 2022.
Identifiers: LCCN: 2022905809 |
ISBN: 979-8-9859052-0-5 (paperback) | 979-8-9859052-1-2 (ebook)
Subjects: LCSH Time travel--Fiction. | Murder--Investigation--Fiction. | New York (State)--History--Revolution, 1775-1783--Fiction. | United States--History--Revolution, 1775-1783--Fiction. | Long Island (N.Y.)--Fiction. | Mystery fiction. | Historical fiction. | BISAC FICTION / Mystery & Detective / General | FICTION / Historical / Mystery & Detective | FICTION / Historical / Colonial America & Revolution

Classification: LCC PS3601 .Y59 S33 2022 | DDC 813.6--dc23

FOR KATE

Contents

One

AN ODD COOLNESS SWEPT across Finn's back as he stood at the edge of the empty road. Though it was barely noticeable, it did cause him to glance over his left shoulder toward the roadway, half expecting to see a passing car and feeling somewhat surprised he didn't. Yet, there was no mistaking that ethereal chill he felt against his skin as if he had, or the scant sent of a pleasing fragrance that seemed to follow. He rubbed the few standing hairs at the nape of his neck, quickly dismissing the uncanny coldness, knowing the infrequency with which cars drove on Mill River Road at this hour of the morning. Diligently, he returned his investigative focus back to the emergency-service cop who was less than 150 feet away in the trampled grass of the private horse pasture, the last of the police support units responding to his crime scene. Finn's concentration drifted while he eyed the cop working the hydraulic control levers of the flatbed that guided the dead boy's car onto the police transport, in preparation for the trip to the evidence garage.

A few hours earlier, the local fire department's emergency medical service crew was first to arrive at the scene, and quickly realized they weren't needed. As did the police paramedics, who remained only long enough to make the official death pronouncements.

Doctor Collier from the county medical examiner's office was just as quick, though he did, after staggering like a big-footed clown through the ankle-high pasture grass to his waiting car, provide his professional street-level diagnosis to Finn. Lowering his driver's door window and avoiding direct eye contact with Finn, Collier managed an inebriated slur of the obvious. "They're both dead, Detective! Call for the wagon and basket, tag'em and bag'em, have them shipped to the shop, I'll do both autopsies first thing..." He trailed off, as if he had suddenly thought of something more important. Collier started the car's engine and wove back onto the empty roadway, his vehicle soon absorbed into the night's darkness, the taillights fading from view.

He shook his head. Collier's elusive response to the teenage bodies wasn't something new for Finn, Collier had a history of struggling with the obvious.

A hardened, ten-year veteran of the county police department, Finn joined shortly after completing a highly active, three-year stint with the U.S. Army as an airborne ranger. Two extended combat deployments earned him numerous decorations for bravery. His six-foot frame balanced a steady weight of 165 pounds on a solid, well-toned athletic body. Thick, mahogany brown hair complemented a steady, no-nonsense glare from a set of slate grey eyes that added to his determined look. His soft cheekbones were in contrast to the ever-present spear-shaped piece of wood barely visible in the little crease at the corner of his lip.

To many, that toothpick was symbolic of Finn's hard-boiled detective character, intensified by an indifferent attitude toward just about everyone and everything, living or dead. But they'd be wrong, only to a degree. The toothpick didn't make him hard-boiled, or indifferent, it was a coping tool of sorts. That tiny sliver of wood was part of Finn's well-being, his physical crutch for managing a life of anxiety. Safer than smoking, though just as addictive. Without his toothpick he'd be just another one-legged contestant in some nameless ass-kicking contest.

Standing at an elevated perch on the road's edge, next to the uneven, rocky gravel of the shoulder, Finn eyed the shadowed silhouette of the lone uniformed police officer standing guard on the southbound lane, waving his flashlight, guiding the crime scene unit's van inside the protected space, just short of the inclining curve of the road behind the strategically placed orange pylons.

Both youthful-looking techs were clad in the department's official one-piece royal blue work coveralls, with the identifying white block letters CSU affixed to the back. Finn watched as they exited their van and casually glanced in the direction of the four large LED flood lights that illuminated the dead kid's car and the two cold, lifeless bodies in the vacant pasture. Neither bothered to cross over the dry ravine or up to the broken horse fence for the slightest glimpse of a professional observation, or even for a curious peek at the bodies. He overheard one of them loudly claim, "It's clearly just an accident, if anything, this scene belongs to the Fatal Accident Reconstruction Team!"

"Maybe you'd like to examine the scene before you classify it?" Finn said sternly.

"Must be a slow night in homicide!" the first crime scene cop remarked to the other, before he shot Finn a cynical eye and a shitty smile.

"Why is homicide interested in a car accident?" the second tech asked Finn as they swaggered slowly up the darkened roadway toward him.

"Who said it was a car accident?" Finn responded, sending a quick blast of blinding light from his flashlight into their eyes.

"What, you think it's something different?" the first tech volleyed back, shielding his eyes from the glaring illumination with an open palm.

"We don't even need to inspect the car. Any rookie can see from here that the driver was going too fast, lost control, crashed through the fence, landed in that field, then hit that giant tree. Case closed!" he added with a salty smirk before turning again to his partner as they broke out in laughter in unison.

"I need you guys to process this scene," Finn declared.

"It's only an accident, Finn!" the first tech replied, pointing at the broken fence.

Finn coaxed them into taking a few photos. They reluctantly complied, but only as a courtesy, and without leaving the roadway. Finishing with a cluster of useless blacked-out photos that could have very well been taken from inside of a lightless broom closet, instead of the required array of photos necessary for a double-homicide investigation. Grudgingly, after being ordered by Finn again, the two techs submissively yielded a couple quick, triangular measurements of the road's elevated surface in relation to the sharply curved arc of the roadway, calculated against the height of the damaged horse fence, before they sped off to give some other detective their unsolicited crime-solving advice, or to finish the rest of their shift in the coop.

The warming rays of the early-morning September sun, beginning its slow climb to the top of the giant blue spruces along the roadside, adjacent to the open horse pasture, were welcome against his tired face. Evenly spaced giant Colorado evergreens, intentionally planted as saplings many years before, now served as a privacy barrier from the passing vehicle traffic, while also serving as a relief from the hot summer sun and the cold, wet winters of Long Island's North Shore for the rare and priceless thoroughbreds that occasionally roamed that side of the private horse pasture. The western side of the pasture was bordered by unpassable, barbed-wire-sharp thorny branches of dense thickets, set before a row of tall sycamores, that lay just beyond the wooden fence line. The southern end of the pasture was tightly sealed with thick, tall, English-style pivot hedges that ended at the southwest corner of the pasture, providing just enough room for the wide-swinging, metal-tubed paddock gate that led from the estate's stable into the pasture.

The rising eastern sun gradually burned away a thin, curling layer of morning mist that coated the tips of the remaining undisturbed sweet grass in the horseless pasture. And only now returning to an autumn of clean, crisp, cool air, following a night of controlled chaos with the many different emergency responders and their wailing sirens converging from every possible direction, while Finn watched from a safe distance on the other side of the roadway. Their vehicles illuminated the entire crime scene with mesmerizing red and blue wigwags, and sending blinding strobes of fiery white daggers into the endless darkness. Finally, leaving a lone Emergency Service Unit officer with his flatbed tow truck to crush and twist the ankle-high sweetgrass into crude field art as it maneuvered over and around the tire impressions made by the dead boy's car.

Nearing an end to a mentally exhausting night, Finn's tired eyes deliberately scanned every inch of the crime scene. After he'd watched the night bagman from the morgue tag, bag, and remove the lifeless bodies from the serene horse pasture, while trying to imagine what had taken place earlier to these two kids. He was unable to suppress the nagging suspicion, deep within his restless gut, that this secluded horse pasture wasn't your everyday bucolic horse pasture, that it was concealing more secrets then it revealed.

He'd gone over everything in and around the pasture and roadway not once or twice, but three times. Still, he couldn't come up with even a basic explanation of what caused the car to leave the roadway, let alone who could have wanted these kids dead?

This was one of those times he'd wished he could shake some magical evidence tree for a rock-solid lead, or jog loose an anonymous eyewitness that would give the investigation a little traction. The longer he studied the crime scene, the more he wondered if this was all he was going to get. Though he knew all murder scenes concealed their own special kind of secrets, they just needed to be exposed. He had nothing—no trace evidence, and no known witnesses. There was only the obvious: one car, one giant tree, and two murdered teenagers in a vacant private horse pasture in the middle of an affluent area on the North Shore of Long Island.

Two

MILL RIVER ROAD WAS dangerous to navigate at any time of the day, in the best of weather, with its treacherous switchback design and harrowing hairpin turns. Which is why it was seldom used, except by those who either lived near the road or by locals who resorted to using it out of frustration from the perpetual buildup of heavier traffic on the more commonly used four-lane Pine Hollow Road just two hills over to the east.

Finn was familiar with both roads. He knew Mill River Road started less than a quarter mile away from where he stood, as it branched off Lexington Avenue and traced south along the east side of a small, shallow freshwater pond that long ago had been fed by the narrow, fast-moving Mill River.

As a teenager Finn navigated this road countless times, in daylight and dark, and in all the seasonal weather. Though it'd been a long time since he had physically walked or even stood on any part of this road.

The landscape around the crime scene took on a clearer focus as the day began to brighten. It also resurrected memories of his past that slowly seeped into his thoughts as he gazed around at the dangerously blind curve of the now-empty roadway, with thoughts back to his youth, to Saint Xavier's.

Remembering the claustrophobic shock that physically froze him in place as Father Dom closed the thick wooden door of the alter box squarely behind him with a solid echoing thud, sending prickly little vibrating waves of fear throughout his small body. Followed by another wave of terror as the loud metallic click of the thick, medieval-style bronze padlock was heard on the other side of the wooden door.

Even now, he could vividly hear Father Dom's voice, in his barely distinguishable English. *I do this, my child, for your own good. This will build your character. It will give you strength. It will make you mentally strong. You'll need this, I promise you, because you are the Final One.*

The horse pasture along the seldom-used rural roadway finally lay quiet and peaceful in the early autumn morning. The landscape was so picturesque that it could have very well graced the front cover of one of Long Island's most popular equestrian magazines. And it probably had, he thought.

The area had not changed much over the years, not that he could remember, from his obligatory after-school walks to his part-time job. Father Dom saw to it that every one of his boys had a job, and Finn's was at the top of Mill Hill, at the Whitney estate.

Standing on the road that was so familiar to him, his thoughts unwittingly shifted focus from the crime scene back to his youth, a time in his life he so desperately tried to forget, to block from his memory. A time he wanted to consider nothing more than one of life's misfortunes, though it somehow always seemed to linger just below the surface, waiting to be resurrected by some unforeseen event or jostled loose by one of his senses, forcing him again to come face to face with those wounds.

At times, like this morning, as he stood at the side of the road, he consciously admitted to himself that he missed the pleasant scent of sweetgrass blending with the fresh, rich, damp earth as it wafted from the vacant horse pasture, mixing with a warming autumn sun. It woke one of the few enjoyable thoughts of his past that he remembered so vividly.

Those reflective flashes from his youth only rekindled the telling and imperious images of Father Dominic Fabiano of Saint Xavier's Home for Boys, Finn's home. Father Dom, as he insisted on being called, never cared much for the people in the little hamlet of Oyster Bay referring to Saint Xavier's as an orphanage, while others simply regarded it as an asylum for boys, some even referring to it as "that group home on the hill." There never were any girls housed there, leaving Father Dom to proudly insist on calling Saint Xavier's simply a home for boys.

Given that no child had ever been offered for adoption, it never really qualified as an orphanage. Father Dom, their patriarch, was a tall, thin, lanky, middle-aged Jesuit priest with a milk-toned complexion and a long, narrow, oval-shaped face. When closed, his paper-thin lips gave his face the appearance that his lips had mysteriously slipped away from the space just below the long splinter of a nose. His short, straight white hair blended well with his aged complexion, contrasted against the small birdlike piercing dark eyes that were shaded by unusually thick dark bushy eyebrows.

Father Dom carried himself with a pious gait, slow and deliberate, but his speech was laced with a thick, heavy Italian accent. Causing his expressed commands or requests to be misunderstood or misdirected by most of the boys in the home. Many of the older boys, the tougher ones, would just flash the priest a bewildered stare as they cocked their heads to one side, like an attentive dog.

On first impressions, to most outsiders, Father Dom was simply a warm and spiritually inviting member of the clergy. But, to Finn and the rest of the boys at the home, he was more than just a life's provider and spiritual leader, he was also their savior, their protector, their guiding father.

The mere thought of Father Dom's unique method of character building caused Finn's mind to unintentionally return to one sunny afternoon at Saint Xavier's, when he had just barely turned eight years old. It was the first time Father Dom locked him inside the smelly, dank, subterranean human crate he referred to as his alter box—appropriately named for altering one's personality.

"Why, Father Dom? Did I do something wrong?" Finn *remembered asking shyly, his eyes lifted upward to see Father Dom's shadowed face through the thin crack of the wooden door.*

"No, my son, you haven't done anything wrong," Father Dom *replied.*

"Are you mad at me, then, Father Dom?" Finn *questioned, his lower lip beginning to quiver.*

"No, no, my son, I'm not mad at you either," Father *Dom said with a deep pain to his voice.* "You're too young now *to understand, but this will be a great benefit to you when you are older." adding "I have been blessed with the responsibility of guiding you in God's divine ways, in preparation for a most important, and noble, but extremely dangerous, task that you have*

been foreordained to endeavor. Together we will build your mental and emotional strength, so you will be skillfully prepared for the task that awaits you. Remember how I taught you to reflect?" Father Dom asked.

Finn nodded his head. "It's really dark in here, Father Dom!"

"This is your time to reflect, to pray. It will make you strong in so many ways. Your life will depend on this someday, I promise you. When your time comes to leave Saint Xavier's, you will witness the devil's work, the evils of this world, and you will be guided on a righteous path. Your time here in the alter box will help you chart that course."

The sound of the padlock's shackle being latched before it fell with a hollow thud against the heavy wooden door, was the last thing he remembered hearing for two solid days. Save for Father Dom's rigid footsteps as they faded through the hollowed subterranean passageway, away from the modified coal bin hidden deep within the crypt of the home's damp, cold stone building.

Finn would never admit, even to himself, that he was scared. He'd never been alone— really alone—before, and he was beyond confused. Why had Father Dom designed such a scary method to develop and guide him against the evils of the devil? What was this lesson? He didn't like being in the dark. Even at this early age he believed things could happen in the dark that would never happen in the light.

That was Finn's first frightful experience in the blackened alter box. Over the next ten years he would spend many more lonely days and nights of imposed reflection in that box. His recollection of it was so vivid that he would pulverize the wooden toothpick lodged in his mouth at the mere thought of being locked in that smelly, damp subterranean abyss.

It left scars, invisible scars, though none deeper than his paralyzing claustrophobia. Now he never slept without a night light, or with his bedroom door closed.

Three

THE PROTECTED LITTLE NORTH Shore harbor had a mixture of pristine tidal saltwater with just the right amount of fresh natural spring water that was so clean and pure it produced an uncommon but succulent scalloped oyster. So fiercely desirable were these prized little oysters that their popularity created an unexpected economic boost to the tiny hamlet that so proudly took the name Oyster Bay.

Finn had been told years before that when the first families settled in the area, long before they even had roads, the narrow Mill River coursed free and clear as it emptied into the Mill Pond. While the water on the north end of the small pond was captured in a hand-dug, tapered race that flowed fast to power the large wooden paddles of the hamlet's only flower grist mill. The overflow water from the mill emptied into the west side of Oyster Bay's fertile bay.

He enjoyed the stories told by old Joe Labinsky, who had labored as a caretaker on the vast Whitney estate for more than fifty years, and whose family could trace their roots in Oyster Bay back to before the start of the American Revolution. He'd also remembered old Joe telling him that the Mill River was not really a river at all, but a series of many different artesian wells that dotted the landscape along an untouched mile-and-a-half stretch of virgin

woods south of Mill Pond, that percolated to the surface along
the forest floor. Over time, the individual wells eventually joined
a common flow that carved out a narrow but shallow waterway. In
the beginning, old Joe said, the Mill River and the Mill Pond were
the only source of fresh drinking water for all the residents of the
tiny hamlet, and they fiercely guarded it.

Along the first curve on the tree-lined Mill River Road, past
the southernmost tip of Mill Pond, was the secluded pasture—a
mere five-acre parcel of a larger 75-acre private estate that had, in
turn, once been part of a much larger tract of 400 acres—that had
now become Finn's crime scene. The land had been bequeathed
by Britain's King George III in 1780 to James Barrington Cook,
in recognition for his loyal dedication to the Crown, for his valued
contributions to the King's royal troops as they fought the rebels
during the American Revolution. And it had remained in the
Cook family for those 238 years.

The original owner of that same tract of land was Jacob
Blair, who had been singled out by the local commander of
the invading army and forced to pay exorbitant land taxes to
King George III. Blair's family was one of the original 1653
founding families of Oyster Bay. He also happened to be one of the
few outspoken and loyal American patriots—mostly moderates
and Quakers—residing there. Then, one night Blair and all six
members of his immediate family had mysteriously disappeared,
vanishing without a trace.

The entrance to the lavish Cook estate, along with the proper
entrance to the horse pasture and Finn's crime scene, was set off
the road, just past the first deadly curve. Its opulent wrought-iron

entrance gate was obscured from view beyond the giant blue spruces and thick pivot hedges.

Finn continued to inspect the grassy incline that separated the roadway from the closest edge of the pasture for anything out of the ordinary, for anything relevant to his crime scene. Aside from the emergency-service cop fixing his temporary aluminum ramps over the dry ravine for access to the horse pasture and the dead kid's car, there was nothing unusual, no skid marks to indicate that the kid had tried to stop his car to avoid another car or the sudden appearance of an animal in the roadway.

It hadn't rained, so the road wasn't wet, and the thin veil of night fog didn't begin to settle over the field or roadway until around 3:00 a.m. Nor were there any tire tracks or marks in the uncut grass by the road's edge to indicate the initial path of the car. Just the mangled inkberry holly shrubbery in front of the shattered wood fence, broken in the exact outline of the kid's car. Finn did notice, though, that the car's tire tracks didn't appear on the ground until it was on the inside of the horse fence, before coming to a stop at the base of the giant tree, roughly 150 feet from the road's edge. Which he thought could be explained if the car had left the road at a high rate of speed, gone airborne over the ravine, then crashed through the fence before continuing into the horse pasture.

There was one little troubling thought with that scenario though. As Finn's eyes focused on the damaged shrubbery in front of the horse fence. He couldn't be sure, do to all the recent foot traffic from the emergency responders, but there seemed to be more shards of splintered wood from the broken fence on the roadside of the fence. Plus, he thought, some of the shrubbery appeared to have been bent back toward the roadway, away from the pasture. That could be explained as well, he thought.

If the force of the car passing over the shrubbery, then through the fence created a reactionary result from the speed and weight of the car moving in one direction over the tops of the shrubbery and bending them so far back from their original planted position, that the final resting place of the shrubbery was caused by a whiplash effect. But without any forensic support, he'd just have to follow the facts as he found them and draw his own inference.

The sharp curve of the narrow road left little shoulder. The grassy incline to the dry riverbed started at the edge of the road, right at the thin strip of loose gravel, before it inclined to the shallow, dry ravine. A natural separation between the roadway and the horse fence, that had lain largely undisturbed for more than two centuries, except for the occasional summer grass mowers, and, up until a few hours ago, from the dead kid's car.

Sensing the discomforting sensation through the soles of his shoes in the rough, rocky crunch of the uneven gravel, while he walked along the edge of the roadway as he examined every angle of the crime scene. He'd finally glanced down at his cordovan wingtips and noticed a thin layer of gray gravel dust from his all-night pacing along the thin apron. An impeccable dresser, Finn wore only the finest business suits and most comfortable-fitting size 11 wingtip shoes, buffed to a high gloss every day.

Obsessed with being squared away was a compulsive habit carried over from his days at Saint Xavier's and then enhanced during his time in the military. Glaring at his gravel-dusted wingtips, he felt an immediate need to clean them. He couldn't imagine continuing the remainder of the day with unpolished shoes, in his mind a reflection of his character.

He quickly grabbed ahold of the only thing close by, an early morning air chilled tubular metal signpost at the edge of the narrow shoulder. Lightly, he rubbed the gravel-dusted wingtips against the calves of his pant legs. He hadn't really noticed or paid much attention to the signpost before, thinking he must have missed it in the dark, or maybe he overlooked it as something that didn't factor into the crime scene. After wiping his shoe tops clean, he took a slight step backward to read the sign, seeing it was one of New York State's Department of Transportation's rectangular, blue cast iron historical markers with embossed yellow lettering announcing.

In 1780 King George III's 400 Queen's Rangers led by Colonel John G Simcoe bivouacked at this site.

The distance from the road's edge over the dry ravine to the top of the wooden horse fence was exactly 67 feet. Finn also had the crime scene cops measure the height of the fence against the angle height at the middle of the road surface, which was exactly 77 feet, and the travel portion of the southbound lane was ten feet at its widest, less at the apex of the curve.

These measurements would only square with the scene if the car was traveling at a high rate of speed, went airborne from the highest point in the curve of the road, crossed over the ravine, then crashed through the fence before landing in the grass of the pasture. One of the crime scene techs had gloated as much; Finn found this highly unlikely. The daylight view confirmed that was physically impossible, providing that the oral statements made by the dead kid's friends and parents were truthful, all stating they were definitely on their way home. If so, their car should have been traveling in the northbound lane, which was at a lower angle of the road's surface, and never meeting the elevated apex of the road's curve of the southbound lane. And without leaving the slightest trace of tire marks or impressions on the road surface, or any visible damage to the car. Or was it possible that the kid was traveling on the wrong side of the road, at a high rate of speed?

The winding bed of Mill River ran unbroken for almost two miles, except for a few affluent driveway aprons that were paved out of the rarest of imported stones. There it ran underneath.

The first estate on Mill River Road, heading south, was the Cook estate, with its towering double-wide wrought-iron gates at its entrance anchored by elaborate stone columns. The jet-black iron gates were electronically controlled through a 4″ x 4″, unbreakable, weather-resistant, glass bio-metric security touch screen, mounted on a free-standing decorative stone pedestal accessible from a driver's side window, or, if needed, activated from inside the property.

Most of the estates on Mill River Road, if not all, were equipped with column-mounted multidirectional motion-activated camera nests, or clusters, some complete with heated lenses. The Cook estate was no different. They even had a closed-circuit, military-grade, encrypted Wi-Fi security camera system that was further equipped with state-of-the-art facial recognition, including an extremely sensitive pan, tilt and zoom (PTZ) capability. The rich could well afford the latest bells and whistles in security technology, Finn thought, but most were blind to the obvious vulnerability of the column-mounted instruments, with their easy access to the passing public.

He'd already witnessed the up-close, horrendous nighttime view a few short hours before, when he found the boy's lifeless body not ten feet in front of his own car, sprawled against the only tree in the pasture. Slumped in a lethargic sitting position with both shoulders resting against the base of the giant tree. His head was angled slightly to the rear as his fully dilated, dark brown sightless eyes gave a conquered skyward stare, a familiar look that reminded Finn of what he had witnessed many times before on the faces of dead soldiers, in the rugged mountains of Afghanistan.

The boy's face was almost completely masked by his own coagulated dark blood, thick droplets webbing off his swollen cheeks before cascading into a small pool of syrup-thick fluid on his chest. His arms were extended at his sides, palms up, in a gesture of surrender. The boy's body was muscular and fit, his nut-brown hair neatly cut short in military style. He was wearing light khakis that appeared to have been recently pressed with a sharp military crease down the center of each pant leg, with a dark brown, nondescript leather belt. On his upper half he wore a collared light blue Tommy Hilfiger shirt under a shredded dark blue V-neck, long-sleeve sweater. His feet displayed brightly polished plain dark brown oxford shoes.

Finn noticed numerous, long lengths of deep, razor-thin, V-shaped lacerations across the front of his torso, some wider than others. There were also a few of the V-shaped lacerations across the front of both legs, though not as deep. Both forearms had similar clean-cut lacerations from the shoulders to the elbows. His skull exposed a laceration running across his entire forehead, along with a severed left ear. Finn thought there appeared to be an unusual amount of blood on the boy's torso, with much more pooling on the ground beneath his body, slowly being sucked into the base of the tree. A strong copper smell filled Finn's nostrils as he examined the boy's body up close.

The large amount of blood loss told Finn that the boy hadn't died quickly, it appeared he'd bled to death over a period of time. How much time Finn couldn't tell, but the boy had suffered a long, painful death, possibly after having been tortured in some manner, before his strong young heart pumped out all its life fluid.

At first glance, when he cast the beam of his flashlight over the body, Finn thought the kid looked like a dead, out-of-uniform military warrior. What was puzzling were the traces of random-sized blood spatter above his head, on the tree. How was there blood spatter that high up on the tree? There was no evidence the boy had been ejected from the car and his body thrown against the tree. Finn thought he couldn't have been ejected from the car if he had his seatbelt on, even if the car's airbags had failed to deploy, which had been known to occur. Plus, there was no obvious evidence of the car hitting any object with enough force that would have ejected any occupant, anyway.

The blood spatter on the tree appeared in equal amounts both to the left and to the right of a silhouetted outline of the boy's body, as though he had been standing with his back up against the tree. Finn shone his flashlight back across the front of the car, and saw no visible damage, not a scratch, not even a cracked or broken window, or the half-deflated pillow from a deployed airbag.

Finn had started a slow, circular examination from the tree and the boy's body outward, around to the passenger's side of the car, when he came upon the young girl. She lay on her back in the damp, thick sweetgrass, her arms folded across her chest meeting at the wrists, her fingers interlaced peacefully and resting on her stomach. Shinning his beam of light over her body, he saw she was dressed in dark brown, pleated, soft flannel slacks, a Louis Vuitton cream-colored, long-sleeve collared blouse, and black leather flats.

Struck by the frightened, frozen stare on the girl's face, Finn knelt next to her in the grass and gently pushed her long, light brown hair aside. At first glance, he thought she was just unconscious, until he felt for a pulse at the left carotid artery. The absence of blood or external injuries suggested to Finn that she may have died from internal injuries if she had also been ejected from the car. But he quickly ruled that out; there was no damage to the car on the passenger's side either, not a single dent or broken window, nor evidence that that side of the car had made contact with any fixed object. Finn rolled the girl onto her right side to examine her back. Not seeing anything unusual, he rolled her back over again. She looked as though she had been intentionally laid out in a respectful, peaceful position in the grass next to the dead boy's car, while the boy's body lay viciously butchered against the loan oak tree. "Well, this is no auto accident!" Finn muttered aloud.

Four

THE SHARP STING IN his nostrils from the overpowering stale urine smell was another memory that held him hostage to his past, remembering how long it took before his nose would finally accept the lingering foul odor of the lightless box, mixed with the rotten-egg smell of sulfur-laden coal dust, before his eyes would finally adjust to the total darkness.

He'd push one cheek up against the uneven vertical sliver between the sulfur-smelling boards of the wooden wall and door, peering out with statue stillness, alternating cheeks. Clearing his mind of wants or needs, partly to keep from crying, he'd sit in conditioned silence for hours at a time, watching the cuniculus movements of the home's indigenous rats, studying their habits, their behaviors, while learning their rodent hierarchy as they scurried along the damp stone floor to other parts of the blackened substructure.

The crudely modified, 8′ by 4′ rugged rectangular lightless chamber had two walls constructed of long, thick oak wood planks, stacked horizontally for strength from floor to ceiling. A heavy, wrought-iron-hinged, thick oak door hung from the smaller outer wall, where the worn stone floor hallway abruptly ended. The remaining two walls were cut from the cold, jagged granite of the building's foundation. Finn could visually recall the walls unreachable height, twelve feet. Though the room hadn't been used to store coal in many years, when jarred by movements from above, it would occasionally snow coal dust down from its exposed dark wooden rafters.

The alter box held a single, narrow wooden bed, low to the floor, with a thin, soiled, horsehair-stuffed canvas-covered mattress that rested on a thick burlap lattice mesh. It had been pushed tightly into the corner of the stone wall, farthest from the door, with one meager but tightly woven, stained wool blanket for warmth. A chipped and dented porcelain chamber pot, missing its cover, occupied the other corner. He remembered feeling that time had been suspended, that it somehow stopped just for him, and the world continued to turn outside the box while he'd been forgotten. Until Father Dom came to unlock the century-old, hand-forged bronze padlock with the heavy bronze key he kept tethered to a tightly braided hemp rope secured around his gaunt waist.

An older boy once told Finn that Father Dom held a distinct record in the Vatican, of being the only Catholic priest ever to be held prisoner by both the Nazis and the Japanese during the Second World War. First, he was held prisoner in his own country by Benito Mussolini and his tyrannical Fascist Party, who had allied with the Nazis. Until the American forces liberated Italy, and Father Dominic Fabiano had been given a special dispensation from the Vatican and approved by the American government to enter the United States, where he joined the ranks of the U.S. Army, becoming a chaplain in the Pacific Theater, as the American fight with the Japanese escalated. Father Dom was soon taken prisoner by the Japanese on a small, isolated atoll where he was caring for a group of young wounded and dying American soldiers. It was later said that Father Dom had momentarily abandoned the divinity of the cloth, and ferociously fought hand to hand against the torturous Japanese, though only after running out of ammo, while he tried to protect the dying American soldiers. He was rescued after a two-month bombardment of the tiny island by U.S. Navy gunships, but not before being subjected to starvation and extreme physical torture including being imprisoned in a sweltering, lightless metal box for days. Father Dom never spoke about the details of his short-lived military experience, nor would anyone even know by looking at him that he was a ferocious and protective warrior. Other boys maintained he wasn't even a real priest.

Finn had always thought of Father Dom as a model Jesuit, dressed in the Jesuit's traditional 33-buttoned, black, watered-silk cassock, with an ever-present thick gold crucifix dangling against his bony chest on a 24-karat gold linked chain. A Jesuit priest who lived a simple life in the image of Jesus, within the Jesuit's strict vow of poverty, all the while tending to the basic needs of children.

Father Dom had taken control of the 238-year-old Saint Xavier's Home for Boys right after the war ended, along with the aid of two other Jesuit priests who managed the run-down, two-story stone building that had been unconditionally donated by the New York Diocese of the Roman Catholic Church.

Saint Xavier's shared the same holy hill on Anstice Street as Saint Mary's Catholic Church and School. Though they remained separate, Saint Xavier's had always been independently funded by an anonymous donor, known only to Father Dom.

Anstice Street hill was the first of the four hills that spanned the tiny hamlet's topography from east to west. All sharing an unspoiled panoramic view of Oyster Bay's immaculate northern harbor. Saint Xavier's consisted of one isolated building on the west side, atop the highest point of the hill. Built of large, blocked charcoal-colored New Hampshire granite, with two solid core, 15-foot, hand-carved oak entrance doors that opened directly into the home's modest first-floor dining hall. An open-floor dormitory complete with military-style metal bunk beds ran the full length of the second floor. Each bunk was assigned an olive-drab double-door metal locker positioned against the outside wall, equipped with two full but worn hand-me-down Saint Mary's school uniforms, and a meager amount of personal clothes and effects. Every bunk was tightly fixed with the orderly olive drab wool coverings amongst the scantly but methodically arranged uniformed furnishings. An open-roomed bathroom with four small off-white sinks sat opposite four doorless commodes complete with a single on-again off-again working shower located at the far end of the second floor. The interior walls of both floors were bleak, and cold. The ceilings were a dingy whitewashed covering, with thick layers of peeling plaster wedged between massive hand-hewn dark oak beams, the floors made of hand-hewn, wide heart pine planks, worn smooth from years of children's foot traffic.

The first floor was mostly the unpretentious dining hall, with its four twenty-foot-long, rough-cut pine dining tables, polished daily by the small hands of many children, and accompanied by twenty-foot-long wooden bench seats worn to an irregular dullness. The dining hall was lit by a series of small, inadequate metal pendant lamps that dangled precariously above the diners from the exposed wooden beams. Eight massive, four-foot-wide, ten-foot-high stained-glass cathedral windows afforded little added light to the dining hall, while casting a prismatic-colored pattern across plates of the already distasteful food. Complete with the scent of 238 years of burnt incense and candle wax infused in the interior walls.

Every boy routinely attended Saint Mary's School. And at 6:00 a.m. every Sunday, every boy would be paraded, military style, down the hill to Saint Mary's Church for mass, Catholic or not. Saint Xavier's strict discipline policy prohibited any boy from joining or attending any extracurricular activities associated with the school or church, or from having any outside social contact with the children from Saint Mary's. Every boy worked, the youngest ones sweeping and cleaning in preparation for Father Dom's scrutinized inspections, while the older boys worked at after-school jobs within walking distance of the home, also arranged by Father Dom.

Again, Finn tried to refocus his drifting thoughts. He dragged his attention back to the police flatbed, and his crime scene. He couldn't afford to miss anything and continued closely scrutinizing the surrounding landscape for the slightest hint of anything relevant, knowing very soon everything would be removed, repaired, or cleaned up.

From a commanding view atop the apex of the curve in the roadway, he could make out the southern tip of Mill Pond in the distance. His mind spiraled back to earlier days, fishing for bass out of the fresh water. He smiled as he remembered getting caught by Father Dom. He hadn't even owned a fishing pole, the one he used belonged to an older brother of a classmate, the one who had invited him to go fishing. After all these years, Finn could still recall the guilt he felt for skipping work to go fishing, and the penance he suffered in the alter box because of it.

The Final One was the way Father Dom habitually referred to him, but with his thick Italian accent the pronunciation of the word *"final"* always sounded more like "Finn-ally," causing the other boys in the home to call him Finn. For as long as he could remember, he'd been known simply as Finn.

He was consistently pestering Father Dom with his inquisitive questions. "How did I get here? When did I get here? Where are my mother and father? Are my parents dead? Do I have any brothers or sisters? Do I have relatives?" Father Dom's consistent response was, "My son, you are the Finn-ally One," along with a twist of young Finn's cheek between his thumb and index finger, followed by a throaty laugh. Eventually, Finn stopped asking questions, spoke little, and pulled back from most human contact, thinking it was better if he never knew about his past. Less speculation, less doubt, less hurt.

Over time, he became an intent listener, with a keen sense of observation and deductive reasoning skills and a natural talent for solving complex riddles and intricate puzzles. He'd never married, believing he was incapable of any meaningful relationship with any woman, for longer than one night. Even though he knew a commitment was essential for a happy life. And he never stopped wondering who he was or where he came from.

Five

For Finn, the initial survey of a crime scene was essential, whether daylight or dark, rain or shine, in the heat of the day or the cold of the night. And he was extremely thorough, to a fault; many in the police department's Detective Division referred to it as overkill syndrome. He didn't care that he seemed compulsive, if it unlocked a hidden secret that might lead to the positive outcome of putting the guilty behind bars.

Finn made it a practice to visit his crime scenes personally before requesting any forensic assistance. Not all detectives did that. In fact, most detectives requested forensic assistance before they even left the office, if they went at all. Finn never had much trust for anyone else's eyes, no matter how long they had been in the police department, or how much training they had, or how many cases they'd bragged to have solved. He never left anything to chance. He knew time was of the essence when it came to collecting any physical evidence, especially in an outdoor environment. Water and fire were some of the surest ways to permanently destroy any crime scene evidence. Finn was also aware of another, more common method: destruction of relevant evidence by the collectors themselves, sometimes intentionally concealed or protected by those in charge. He believed that over time, cops, and saltwater, could destroy anything.

To Finn's amazement, possibly even to the amazement of physics itself, the kid's car had crashed through a fence and continued over a rutted horse pasture for almost 150 feet, before coming to an abrupt stop in front of the pasture's only standing fixed object: a majestic, 300-year-old deciduous scarlet oak that stood 100 feet tall, with its upper branches forming a pyramidal crown of bright autumn foliage.

After the boy's body had been removed from the base of the tree, Finn noticed that the dark brown bark, with its fine fissures and scaly ridges, showed signs of scarring. There were healing marks, as if from a knife's blade, on either side of an otherwise virgin midsection of the tree's trunk. Hack marks that seemed to run from just above the base of the trunk up to a height of about eight feet from the ground. He saw no clear evidence that the car had hit the tree; all that scarring must have been from another time. He entertained, and then dismissed, the speculation that maybe the bark had become gouged over years by horses rubbing against the tree.

He imagined it would take the outstretched arms of at least four grown men just to surround the circumference of the tree, which he'd only ever admired from the road. As he stood beneath it, gazing skyward, its branches seemed to first grow straight out from the colossal trunk before turning skyward, adding to the appearance that it was holding the weight of the cloudless azure sky. The lowest of the branches, one that was closest to Mill River Road, was about ten feet off the ground and somehow looked dwarfed under the scarlet canopy of the rest of the oak. It too had questionable-looking scars in its bark, prompting him to further examine the tree branch up close. Noticing two small cylindrical shapes, side by side, impressions embedded into both sides of the thick bark. They too were slowly being overtaken by time with the tree's growth. Moving in closer to study the branch, he observed in the center, on the pasture side between the two cylindrical markings, impressions reminding him of aged rope scars, was a small, concaved dimple, a hole, that was also overtaken by the growth of the tree. An old bullet hole, he wondered?

Trying to sort out the basic facts of this scene, the deaths of a seventeen-year-old boy and his seventeen-year-old girlfriend. Why would someone pick this horse pasture to commit a murder? Was it convenient or was there a significance? And why these two particular local teenagers? What had they done—or witnessed? Who had they pissed off? Was it road rage? It didn't appear to be a robbery gone bad; they had money, jewelry, even their cell phones. Without the slightest lead, any questions felt fruitless. Though he knew for certain this was a double homicide, plain and simple. Well, maybe not so simple, but it was plainly murder.

His suspicious eye was drawn back again to the car. Its condition, specifically on the interior, its appearance was too neat, too clean. The ignition key was in the off position, as was the headlights switch. The driver's seat was pushed completely back, as far as it could go, and the automatic transmission selector was in the park position.

Finn could read a crime scene like a radiologist could read an X-ray, revealing what had taken place during the commission of a crime. Though just as important, it could also tell him what hadn't occurred. And this scene was telling him that there were no signs of a struggle near or around the car, and no physical evidence to indicate anyone else had been present, aside from some old hoof impressions.

He'd never experienced death when he was young, though he had witnessed countless funeral processions come and go from in front of Saint Mary's. The only death that had had any real effect on him, was the sudden loss of Kate. She'd been as close to him as family. His time in the military, especially in battle, only cemented his impassive feelings. It was, after all, the golden rule of emotional survival in combat, at least for Finn: never get close to another GI, because they may not be around too long, leaving your vulnerable side exposed to the enemy. These two kids were no different. He felt no sorrow or empathy for life's unexpected endings. Death was inevitable. Everyone was going to die, some sooner than others. For Finn, there were only questions: how did they die, why did they die, and who was responsible for their deaths?

His job as a homicide detective was to investigate the intentional, suspicious, and sometimes undetermined death and to bring the perpetrator, if any, to trial. Nothing more, nothing less. Victim's families always looked for answers. That wasn't his job either. They wanted closure; Finn didn't give closure. To him that was a contrived term, a search for meaning by those who had suffered the sudden and unexpected loss of a loved one. Remembering when he first heard it, he thought of it as just another attention-grabbing term made up by some hungry news media types. Nothing more than a creative and politically correct utterance to grab the attention of some below average news viewers, keeping the ghoulish morons glued to their television sets, so the ratings seeking news media could boast, *"You saw it here first."* It was nothing more than a group of narcissistic Hollywood-type news reporters putting on a show for the emotional reactions of a grieving survivor, upon learning that the police had recovered their loved one's body or apprehended the one responsible for their loss.

What others called closure; Finn called satisfaction. If there was any possible way for anything to close a gaping hole in a grieving heart, it would probably take a miracle from God. And he knew that wasn't going to happen, from all his years at Saint Xavier's. Still, he could provide an ending, some satisfaction. He didn't give false promises of some magical feeling that would take away endless hurt and grieving. Satisfaction was his Band-Aid for a fractured heart. Plus, it was his sworn duty and life's commitment to serve as the victim's advocate.

There was one other obstacle that lay large between solving any homicide and apprehending the guilty party, and that obstacle was Lieutenant Thomas Hughes, Finn's boss. An impatient, demanding, intolerable man, who was commanding officer of the Homicide Squad. Hughes had risen quickly through the ranks in the police department, becoming a lieutenant in eight short years, and the police commissioner's first choice to command the elite investigative unit of the department's Homicide Squad, replacing the street-smart previous commander, who butted heads with the commissioner constantly over just about everything under the sun. Lieutenant Hughes had very little street experience—in fact, his street time in uniform could only be measured by his travel time from his station house at one of the slower North Shore precincts, where he had his short-lived rank-and-file street assignment, to police headquarters, maybe an hour away, if the traffic was heavy. Hughes always had his head buried in some police procedural manual, studying for the next promotion exam, while his counterparts struggled it out on the mean streets of the county in all elements, on family holidays, and on rotating shifts every weekend.

The lieutenant's world revolved around daily administrative rants that were never based on anything that remotely fit into the department's administrative policies or the rules on the laws of evidence or patterned from the criminal procedure law on murder investigations. Rants that would usually leave Finn shaking his head in total disbelief, forcing him to replenish one anxiety-gnawed toothpick for a fresh one, from his endless shirt-pocket stash. Hughes was more than just a clueless homicide commander; he was personally and professionally clueless to the evils of humanity.

Though not all death cases that passed through the Homicide Squad were classified as homicides—some were suicides, some were death by an unusual incidents, some were the results of fatal vehicle accidents, and some were simply undetermined—it was Hughes's job to question every aspect of suspicious deaths that occurred within his jurisdiction. Criminal deaths as determined by the county medical examiner with absolute medical and scientific certainty, that a death had been caused by the criminal deeds of another, would receive an appropriate murder case number, which prompted the highest level of criminal investigation by the detectives working for Lieutenant Hughes. And as that gatekeeper for any murder squad case number, Lieutenant Hughes was considered a miser, not merely for keeping the detectives' overtime to a rock-bottom low, but for keeping the county's homicide rate in check, if only on paper.

The lieutenant wanted his cases closed with a quick arrest; it mattered not if they lacked true probable cause or the required evidence for a successful prosecution. *"Convictions are problems for the district attorney and the courts,"* he would loudly rant, spewing a cloud of powdered confectioner's sugar into the atmosphere from a mouthful of doughnut. Before adding, *"The presumption of innocence and the preponderance of evidence isn't a problem for the police; it's a problem for the courts."* Hughes was what Finn considered to be the ultimate human barrier to any successful murder investigation, but the commissioner liked him.

It wasn't the image of the two dead seventeen-year-olds that Finn struggled with. His way of thinking, it was possible that the case could be ignored, fall between the cracks, misread by the powers that be, and go unsolved.

These weren't his first dead bodies, not even his first dead seventeen-year-olds. Never satisfied with any case that went unsolved, his personal thought was, if it's unsolved, it's incomplete, and if it's incomplete, someone is getting away with murder. Murders ebbed and flowed with the seasons, the economy, even the moon. In slower times Finn could be found randomly pulling dust-covered cardboard boxes of unsolved murders from a dust-covered shelf in the back closet of the Homicide Squad. They were cold cases, or, to Finn, the forgotten cases. Brushing the filth from the thick plastic binders containing useless, coffee-stained notes, pointless statements, and aging evidence, he'd meticulously comb through the abandoned cases in the hopes of finding an overlooked clue or a lead that could be developed from some new technology, or an unknown witness that could be flushed out. His most popular and rewarding endeavor was the unannounced revisit to an uncooperative person of interest from long ago, it never failed.

Six

By 8:00 a.m., the emergency-service cop pulled his flatbed truck loaded with the dead boy's car onto the vacant roadway, next to where Finn stood on the narrow shoulder of the road. He lowered the passenger's window of his truck and yelled to Finn, "My radio's out, so's my cell. Any special instructions, Detective?"

"Yeah, just make sure to place the car inside the garage, not in the outside lot, until it's been completely processed." Finn paused, then added, "Have the mechanic do a complete inspection of the car's undercarriage, drivetrain, all that. I don't want a quick once-over; I want the works. Oh yeah, and have Tony pull the crash box, and tell them I'll need prints all around, inside, and out."

"No problem. Anything else?" the cop asked.

"Yeah, tell him I need it ASAP!"

"Got it! Hey Detective, can I ask you why homicide is handling this, and not the Fatal Accident Reconstruction Team? They're going to want to know that back at the garage."

Finn thought that remark was odd, especially coming from a seasoned cop whose job was picking up vehicles for the evidence yard. Even he thought it was a fatal auto accident. Wasn't it obvious? Finn thought. Didn't he view of the scene? Did he not notice there wasn't any damage to the car? Finn wasn't in the mood to challenge him on indisputable facts.

"Yeah, you can tell them that the FART cops were called but didn't pick up their phone again, so I'm doing it," Finn shot back. "If they have any problems or questions with it, have them call me personally at the squad."

"You got it!" the cop said as he drove off.

Taking a final glance around the landscape before shutting down the crime scene and telling the uniformed officer to remove the yellow crime-scene tape before opening the road for traffic, he paused. For some reason, he had an eerie feeling that this horse pasture was no stranger to death.

Driving south on Mill River Road, he glanced over at the passenger's seat at the dead girl's pocketbook and the dead boy's wallet in the clear plastic evidence bags. The medical examiner would want to see all personal effects of the deceased; it was standard procedure. Finn had found the girl's pocketbook on the floorboard in front of the passenger's seat of their car. It revealed nothing suspicious; it'd still been zippered closed. The boy's wallet had been inside his right hip pocket.

Earlier in the night, Finn had the crime scene secured by a couple uniformed officers while he took a few minutes to drive the short distance into the village of Oyster Bay to make the preliminary death notifications to the kids' families, the most undesirable job in all the police department. The deceased were tentatively identified from their personal IDs found at the scene as Tom Buckley and Susanne White, both seventeen-year-old seniors at Oyster Bay High School.

Around 3:00 a.m. he'd pulled up in front of 300 Orchard Street, Susanne White's home. He couldn't miss her house; all the other houses on the street were understandably dark, but Susanne's was lit up like a Manhattan skyscraper. The family was apparently concerned, waiting for Susanne's safe return. As he parked, he noticed someone pushing aside the corner of a curtain and peering out from a front window. He proceeded up the walkway toward the front of the house. The front door opened, a thin middle-aged man and a heavy-set middle-aged woman stood backlit in the doorway. Both were wide-eyed as they watched Finn approach. The woman held a hand to her trembling lips. Her other hand tightly gripped her husband's limp arm. They clutched each other like they were watching their first horror movie. Before Finn reached the front stoop, he held up his badge. "Police," he announced. "Do you have a daughter named Susanne White?"

Moving closer, Finn could see that Mrs. White's knees were quivering like a bowl of overcooked pasta. Before he reached the first step of the porch, Mrs. White sank to her knees, her legs crumbling under the anticipated weight of grief. Both her arms crossed her heart and her eyes closed tight as she began to openly weep. Finn helped Susanne's father bring Mrs. White to her feet and back into the house, to a cushioned chair in the pleasantly furnished living room.

Twenty minutes later, Finn drove around the corner to 20 West Main Street, to the Buckley house, the only private house hidden amongst a city block of single-story shops that lined both sides of the street. The Buckley's house was the third structure on the north side of the street, just a few hundred feet west of South Street, the main road into and out of the hamlet of Oyster Bay. Few store fronts had night lights, but the haloed yellow glow from the corner streetlight helped to illuminate some of the deserted street.

The house was completely dark, which Finn would have expected at 3:30 a.m. on a Sunday. Peering up through the windshield, he noticed a faint light go on in the darkened house, somewhere toward the rear. Approaching the front door, he had a strange feeling of déjà vu, like he had been to this house before, but he couldn't remember when. Shaking it off, he thought maybe it was just from a lack of sleep, or maybe because he was about to give some unsuspecting parents the worst news they would hear in their lifetime. Finn gave a couple quick knocks on the door. A minute later a woman's voice questioned through the closed door, "What do you want?"

Finn unclipped his gold detective badge from his belt and dutifully held it up to the middle pane of the three small glass panels that were fixed high on the wooden exterior door. "Are you Mrs. Buckley?" he asked.

"Why? What do you want?" Suspicion clung to her voice. She asked again, this time softer. "Why are you here, Detective?"

Holding the screen door open with his foot and speaking into the doorjamb of the interior door, Finn said, "Mrs. Buckley, may I come inside? I have something to tell you. Is there a Mr. Buckley at home?" The sound of a heavy metallic click was heard as the dead-bolt lock was released. The door hinges creaked as the door opened slowly, a faint glow from a nightlight in the hallway shadowing the silhouette of a man standing directly behind the woman, in the open hallway. "I'm Mr. Buckley." the man said, almost like a question. "Please come in, Detective."

Dressed in thick white, matching cotton robes, the Buckley's, both in their early forties, Finn guessed, stood in the dimly lit hallway. Mr. Buckley wrapped a comforting arm around his wife's shoulder, pulling her close while they quietly but awkwardly stood back, waiting for Finn to enter the house and close the door. Once in the hallway, Finn took a quick glance around and noticed the living room was the first room off the hallway to the left. Addressing the Buckley's face to face, while gesturing toward the darkened living room, he said, "Do you mind if we all have a seat?" They said nothing. Finn motioned with an extended palm toward an oversized sofa in the tastefully decorated formal living room. They followed his command, and he stepped into the room behind them. They sat precariously at the edge of the sofa, like they were both waiting to fall off the edge of the earth. Turning the switch on a lamp that sat atop the end table nearest the sofa, Finn took a seat across from the Buckley's in a high-backed, tapestry-upholstered armchair. A thick, clear glass oval coffee table lay between them, with a finely cut emerald glass vase of fresh flowers that appeared to have been cut earlier the day before, filling out the center space of the coffee table. Peering past the sofa and beyond the Buckley's through the two double-hung windows that were smartly dressed in blue-and-white patterned, floor-length curtains, he could barely make out his car parked directly in front of the house, at the curb.

Finn shifted his weight forward in the upholstered armchair, and made direct eye contact with the Buckley's, calmly holding their full attention. His fingers clutched tightly at the closed leather-bound report writing pad that he held onto in his lap. "There was an auto accident up on Mill River Road a few hours ago, at the first curve," Finn started, then he abruptly stopped and started again. "Are either of you familiar with Mill River Road?"

"Yes!" Mr. Buckley answered.

"And the horse pasture?"

"Yes, we know where it is, Detective. Why do you ask?" Mrs. Buckley broke in. Then, softening her tone, she asked with a motherly concern, "Has something happened? Something to our Tom? Why are you here?" With her last question, Finn noticed they had moved closer together.

"Sometime just before midnight," Finn said, "it appears that a car lost control, went over the embankment, crashed through the horse fence, and came to rest in the field. There were two occupants of that car, the best we could determine, a young boy and a young girl." It wasn't what he really thought happened, but this wasn't the time to get into blind supposition on what actually occurred, plus he had no answers for them, because he didn't know himself, yet. They both appeared as if they had suddenly had the wind knocked out of them. Their faces pale and frozen, hanging on his every word.

He started to give them the standard police spiel of how he'd just happened to come across the accident, that everything was done that could have been done, but he stopped again, rethinking the department's bullshit policy of "*Tell them what they want to hear and get the hell out of there before they start asking questions ya can't answer.*" Mrs. Buckley's face had taken on a deer-in-the-headlights glare. Staring toward some distant place above and behind him, her pupils appeared unusually dilated even in the dimly lit room, while her husband kept his eyes locked on Finn, waiting for the real reason that brought him into their happy home.

Spinning a lie to the parents of a couple dead kids wasn't in his play book, but, in a way, he wasn't really lying. Because the car had gone off the road, or so it appeared, and both kids were dead, that wasn't a lie. It's how they died that he struggled with telling them, thinking it best for now that he didn't interject his cop's hunch that they were murder victims, especially with no physical evidence or any forensic foundation to support it.

Over the years he'd witnessed many different reactions from people who'd been abruptly awakened from a sound sleep, usually in the wee hours of the morning, by one of his death knocks. He finally said, "I'm sorry to inform you that your son, Tom, is dead." It usually took a second or two for any traumatized brain to completely process that kind of devastating shock. Surprisingly, Mrs. Buckley gave no immediate reaction. Finn thought he might have to repeat the news, until he noticed a single tear drop at the inner corner of her right eye grow larger and larger, then fall. Her bottom lip tightened, beginning a slow quiver, sending little waves of distress rippling across her grief-stricken face. An uncontrollable flood of tears rolled down her reddened cheeks before being sopped up by her cotton robe. "Tom is our only child, Detective! We're so proud of him. He never gives us a minute of trouble, never in his whole life. He's an honors student, a great athlete, a great son, with lots of friends. Everyone loves him." She said chokingly.

Suddenly, her body jerked rigidly upright. Wiping tears from her cheeks, with a little glimmer of hope revealed in her reddened eyes. "Detective! Are you sure you have the right Tom Buckley? Tom Buckley from Oyster Bay? Our Tom was driving the family

Toyota tonight, it's a dark green, four-door Camry. He was with his girlfriend, Susanne White. Maybe this is all just a terrible mistake."

"I'm sure, Mrs. Buckley," Finn said softly as he held out Tom's driver's license. While Mr. Buckley comforted his wife, Finn glanced around the elegantly furnished Victorian living room. There were lots of photos, many displayed in ornate silver and gold frames on built-in shelving, happier times with their young Tom. A large wedding photo of Mr. and Mrs. Buckley graced the center shelf. There were many photos of just Tom, others of Tom and his father, more of Tom with his mother and father together. But no other children that Finn could see.

The quiet was quickly disrupted by Mrs. Buckley saying, "I told you! I told you something like this would happen!" in a barely audible tone between sobs. She dabbed away her tears with a tissue she had removed from the pocket of her robe. "I'm sorry," Mr. Buckley answered quietly, without looking into her face. "I'm sorry!" he repeated as he grabbed his face in both hands and began to weep, his body involuntarily trembling with the grief.

Finn refrained from raising any suspicions or questions he couldn't answer. The autopsy needed to be performed first, and the news of the cause of death belonged to the medical examiner. Plus, Finn thought, as he studied the sobbing couple, he wasn't quite ready to rule either one of them out as suspects yet either. It wouldn't be the first time an angry parent wanted to see their child dead. The grieving husband moved his arm closer to his grieving wife, reaching for her hand. She quickly jerked it away.

"What about Susanne? Is she all right?" Mrs. Buckley asked.

"I'm sorry, no. Susanne didn't make it either."

"Our Tom is an Eagle Scout, Detective!" Mr. Buckley chimed in. Like it was something that needed to be said, that it would somehow change what Finn had already told them. "He doesn't drink, smoke, or do drugs, never has."

"Tom was just accepted to his dream school, West Point. He starts in June, right after high school graduation. See, Detective? Here's the letter. Tom just received it yesterday, on his seventeenth birthday." He proudly slid the official acceptance letter across the coffee table. "He's always wanted to be a soldier. That's all he's ever talked about. We've never encouraged him, but we've always supported him!" he added.

Finn picked up the letter and saw the official seal from the Department of the Army, United States Military Academy. He didn't bother to read any further than "Congratulations" at the opening sentence. He placed the letter back on the coffee table along with the phone number and address of the medical examiner's office, with written instructions for making the official identification later that afternoon.

Seven

FINN STOOD TO LEAVE, putting his business card on the coffee table, next to young Tom's West Point acceptance letter, and said, "Please feel free to call me with any questions, anytime."

Mrs. Buckley slowly stood up from beside her husband and turned, facing her husband. "It's this house! It's her! I've always said something's wrong with this place. This is why our Tom is dead. I've always had the feeling that something was going to happen; I could feel it!" she rambled between sobbing tears, before her grasping for air slowed her, then continuing with, "But how did she know?"

"What do you mean, Mrs. Buckley? Who is 'she'?" Finn asked.

"I've always had this feeling that something bad was going to happen, ever since we moved into this house seventeen years ago. Strange things are always happening here in this house!" she stated.

"What strange things?" Finn prompted.

"The detective doesn't want to hear that stuff, Laura," the father stated with a raised eyebrow.

"Yes, I do," Finn said in a matter-of-fact tone. "I want to hear everything you have to say." Wondering if a confession was forthcoming.

"We bought this house because we loved it, because it was the last historic eighteenth-century colonial house in the hamlet of Oyster Bay. The owners had to move and sold it at a considerable loss. Plus, it came furnished with all these beautiful antiques. We loved the peace and quiet and thought there wasn't a better place to raise our child. It was perfect, and it was affordable." She was slowly regaining her composure. "I was pregnant with Tom Junior, ready to give birth, that was seventeen years ago last week. Tom's seventeenth birthday was yesterday, the 23rd." She stopped to wipe away her tears as her sobs shortened and she gained control of her breathing. "Anyway, as soon as we moved in, while Tom Senior would be away at work, and I'd be home with the baby alone, I noticed strange things happening in the house."

"What sort of strange things?" Finn asked again before sitting back down in the upholstered chair. Mrs. Buckley subconsciously began to pace around the living room. "Like things being moved from one place to another, from where I had placed them."

"Things?" Finn asked.

"Like picture frames being turned around, to face the back of the shelf. Sometimes only one, other times all of them. Sometimes they were simply rearranged. Then a couple of times, the vase of fresh flowers I keep right here on the coffee table was moved behind a picture frames, always the same ones."

"Which pictures, Mrs. Buckley?"

"They were always pictures of Tom, from the time he was little, through to his most recent high school photo. We keep them all right here, on either side of the fireplace, as you can see," she said, pointing to the built-in shelves. "Sometimes lights would be turned on or turned off, or the toilet would flush. Nothing threatening, just odd things. But those things only happened to me," she said, gazing straight at Finn. "Only when I was alone, or if I was with our son, never when Tom Senior or anyone else was in the house. At first, I would get the strangest feeling that I was never alone, like I was being watched." She hugged herself as if to ward off the cold, eerie memory. "Then other times I would hear a door open or close in an upstairs bedrooms when I was downstairs. Or sometimes I'd hear soft footsteps, like a woman or a child was going up or down the stairs, when I knew I was the only one in the house."

"Did you ever think that maybe there was an explanation, like an open window on the second floor that blew the doors open or closed?" Finn offered.

"Of course I thought of that. I would check all the windows after hearing anything unusual upstairs."

"Did you tell your husband about these events?" Finn said.

"Sure, I did! I stopped after a while because he just thought I was nuts." She smirked and cocked her head toward him.

"I never heard, saw, or smelled anything that Laura did in all the years we've been here," Tom Senior added.

"Smelled?" Finn asked.

"Yes, a couple of years after it all started," Laura continued, "Sometimes I'd feel a cool breeze of air brush against me. It happened in all the rooms of the house, but mostly here in the living room, and only in the daytime. I'd have to admit, at times I could actually feel another person's energy in the room. Not their breathing or anything like that, just the swishing movements of moving air, like they had just walked past me. Over time, it felt like a strange woman was living with us. I even began to smell a slight scent in the air right after I felt her energy passing by me. It was a pleasant aroma, a fresh flower smell."

"A woman's perfume?" Finn questioned.

"Sort of, but not a commercial perfume" she said.

"Did you recognize the scent?"

"Yes, it was the scent of fresh lavender."

"Lavender isn't a perfume fragrance?" Finn said.

"It can be a perfume, but what I smelled wasn't as bold as a perfume oil, it was pleasant, more like freshly cut lavender. At first, I would feel a cool breeze at the nape of my neck, and then that strange energy of someone being in the room with me. After a while I would try to follow the lavender scent throughout the house, after I'd felt the cool breeze. One day, I was in the kitchen, I followed the lavender scent down the hall. It was coming from the living room. As I turned to enter the living room, the fresh scent of lavender greeted me head on. I was completely startled, to actually see someone, or the image of someone, in the room. I stopped so short I almost tripped on the edge of the living room carpet. A woman was just sitting there, in the chair. I could have reached out and touched her. I'd been following her scent for years, but I hadn't really prepared myself for seeing someone. All I could do was just stand there, frozen, gazing at her with my mouth wide open. I was even more surprised that my own presence didn't seem to bother her, because she just casually turned her head and smiled at me."

"You saw someone, a person?" Finn questioned with a raised brow.

"Well, it wasn't actually a person. It was more like a transparent image of a person."

"Like a ghost?" Finn stated with a skeptical nod.

"No! Not a ghost. Well, not in the sense of something scary. More like an apparition. It was the image of a young woman. She was dressed in a very elegant eighteenth-century, full-length overskirt in a soft rose color, with a bright flowered bodice, with long linen puffed sleeves that made a rustling noise when she moved her arms. Her hooped petticoat was a few shades darker, and she had a matching rose-colored bonnet, with sheer white embroidered lace around the outside edge. Her arms were slightly crossed, and her hands rested comfortably in her lap. she'd been gazing out the window toward the street, as if she were waiting for someone."

"Waiting for someone?"

"Yes, as if she was expecting someone."

"What happened after she saw you?" Finn asked, not sure where this was going.

"Nothing happened. The young woman turned toward me and gave me a warm smile. Then her image just faded, and she was gone."

"Can you describe her, tell me what she looked like?"

"She's young, maybe in her early twenties. She's petite and very pretty. Creamy-smooth skin, large, tropical-blue eyes with long eyelashes. She has a thin face, soft cheekbones, a delicate nose, perfectly sculpted lips, even teeth. Her hair is light brown, with long curls resting just past her shoulders."

"How many times have you seen her?

"Oh, I can't remember how many times. Too many to count. I think she lives here. She isn't afraid of me. We've seen each other so many times now that we've become comfortable with each other's presence."

"Have you ever tried speaking to her?"

"Yes, I once asked her what her name was. She just gave me that warm smile of hers, turned back toward the window. After a few seconds, she just disappeared."

"And she's never spoken to you in all these years?"

"No, never. Well, not until yesterday."

"Not until yesterday?" Finn said, then added, "You said she always sits looking out of the window?"

"Yes, and always in the same chair."

"Which one?"

Laura Buckley quickly looked at her husband, then back to Finn and said, "Why, Detective, the very one that you're sitting in right now. That's her chair!" Finn looked at the upholstered high-backed chair he was sitting in, then thought this was the strangest reaction he'd ever gotten from anyone in all the death knocks he'd made. Finally turning back to Laura, he said, "Why do you think this has anything to do with your son?"

"Because for the last seventeen years, this young woman has lived with us in our home. I thought only I could see her or feel her presence. But yesterday after our son came home from his Saturday-afternoon soccer game, he came running into the kitchen, waving his West Point acceptance letter in the air. He gave me a big hug and kissed my forehead and said he still couldn't believe it; he just couldn't put the letter down. I have never seen him this excited over anything, ever. Then as he was leaving the kitchen, he suddenly stopped, turned, and asked, 'Hey, Mom! Who's the woman in the living room?' 'What woman?' I asked. But he'd already run up the stairs to his room. I hurried down the hallway, but before I even got here, I could smell her fragrance. It was the strongest it had ever been. There she was, looking out the window, waiting, just like I have seen her so many times before. Only this time, Detective, she seemed upset. She didn't have the usual bright, warm, familiar smile on her face. She turned toward me, gave me a solemn stare, her eyes seemed softer, even sad. Then she said in a whisper, *Laura, I'm Sally, and I'm so very sorry for your loss! But I must take my leave of you now.* And just like that her image faded, and so did the scent of fresh lavender."

Eight

THE ONLY REAL FEELING of any nurturing love Finn had ever experienced while at Saint Xavier's began one day when he was not quite eight years old, the day Father Dom, in his broken English, directed him to go down to the rectory of Saint Mary's and see the cook, because she had some light chores for him. So off Finn went, down the hill, crossing the black-topped parking lot until he came to a two-story building next to Saint Mary's Chapel, one that seemed more like someone's private house than what he had imagined a holy church rectory should have looked like. After climbing the chipped and worn concrete steps, Finn knocked shyly at the kitchen door. A petite, mature woman with an inviting smile and silver hair opened the door. She had a magical twinkle in her bright sky-blue eyes, enhanced by delicate metal-framed eyeglasses that rested neatly atop her graceful nose. The colorful flower-patterned apron suspended from her neck, neatly tied in a bow at her waist, told Finn she was the cook.

"Oh my, who do we have here?" she exclaimed. Her voice carried a nurturing, spirited tone as she peered down at Finn.

"Father Dom sent me," Finn replied nervously, examining the worn tips of his secondhand, polished leather shoes.

"Oh yes, come in, come in. I've been expecting you," she said as she pushed the door wider and stepping aside to welcome Finn into her kitchen, and into her life. Upon entering the big, open kitchen, he was immediately overwhelmed by the delightfully sweet aroma of something he knew instantly he would like. He smiled.

"My name is Kate. And what would they be calling you, young fella?" she asked as she dried her delicate fingers against her apron.

"I'm Finn," he answered joyfully, still smiling. His eyes were drawn toward the tantalizing scent wafting from the oven of the large black stove.

"I'm so very glad to meet you, Finn!" she said.

Donning an old heat-stained, quilted oven mitt over her left hand, she removed a tray of hot cookies from the oven's top rack. "Before I tell you what I would like help with, would you like to have a couple of these warm cookies with a tall glass of cold milk? I've baked them especially for you." Watching as Kate maneuvered a well-used spatula to transfer the fresh-baked cookies from the hot tray onto a piece of waxed paper on the old porcelain kitchen tabletop.

"Yes! Thank you," Finn said, quickly taking a seat at the table as he eyed Kate's fresh-baked molasses cookies.

He was instantly attached to Kate's glowing warmth, her loving way, and secretly imagined her to be his mother. He always felt an inner peace when he was in her presence. From that moment on, he managed to sneak a few minutes away from Saint Xavier's at least two times each week for quick hellos, or to sample her most recently baked recipes, or just to chat. Kate and Finn became close, thoughtful of each other on birthdays and holidays. She would go out of her way to bake Finn his favorite cookies on his special occasions, to show him someone really did care for him. His visits with Kate always gave him a feeling he was part of a loving home, even if only for quick visits.

Years later, Finn knocked on the back door of the rectory kitchen. He'd been thinking of all the things he wanted to tell Kate as he approached the door, wanting to thank her, for all the ways she had been there for him over the years, what she really meant to him.

He was surprised when he saw an older priest, one he didn't recognize, peer out at him through a pane of glass in the door. "Can I help you?" the priest asked after opening the door, still grasping the doorknob.

"Is Kate working?" Finn asked, straining his neck to look beyond the priest into the kitchen.

"No, I'm sorry, she isn't," the priest said.

"But isn't she supposed to be working today?" Finn questioned.

"Yes, she is," the priest replied in a solemn voice. Then he asked, "What is your name?"

"Finn. I'm a good friend of Kate's," he said proudly, standing a little taller and flashing what he thought was a manly smile. "I'm sorry to tell you this, Finn, but Kate passed away last night," the priest said with a sadness in his hollowed eyes. Finn gasped loudly. "Passed away?" He said, taking a step backwards, as if he'd just absorbed an unexpected blow to the chest.

"Yes, Finn. She died last night."

"Oh," was the only thing Finn could offer. His shoulders slumped with the sudden realization. Slowly turning away from the open door without saying another word, he wavered toward the steps like an injured animal.

This was a foreign feeling he couldn't process. A deep sadness assumed control. Learning of Kate's death was like losing a mother, or so he imagined. The only person who had been so maternal, so kind, so thoughtful, and so nice to him for so many years, someone he genuinely loved. Overwhelmed with shock and disbelief, he slowly started down the concrete steps, seemingly alone again in the world.

"Wait a minute, Finn!" the priest called after him. I think there's something here with your name on it. From Kate." The priest disappeared back into the kitchen. Finn reluctantly turned around but didn't follow the priest. He didn't want to physically enter that kitchen, ever again, not without Kate being there. The priest picked up a white envelope off the kitchen table, the same table Finn had sat at so many times before with his Kate. He watched as the priest picked up a small paper plate piled high with molasses cookies covered in a clear plastic wrap. "I'm sure Kate meant these for you," he said, and offered them to Finn. "Is it your birthday, Finn?"

"Yes, today is my eighteenth birthday," Finn replied quietly. Without making eye contact, he took the envelope and cookies from the priest. The priest smiled. "Kate would only bake cookies for someone she loved."

There were times when Finn felt as if his memories had their own memories. But he knew any memory was merely a snippet in time, just a snapshot in his mind, and wondering if they could be flawed. He knew they could, even as he rolled the saliva-soaked wooden toothpick back and forth in his mouth, struggling to bring himself back to the scene of the two dead teenagers that mattered more than he would admit, away from Father Dom and Saint Xavier's. Spitting his toothpick out in disgust. Only to quickly replaced it with a fresh one.

Nine

RETURNING TO HIS CAR, Finn stopped at the curb. It finally dawned on him what he had been told about 20 West Main Street. Glancing back at the darkened house and narrowing his memory back to when he first joined the force, ten years ago. After graduating the police academy, every new recruit's first assignment was with an experienced field-training officer, who was responsible for providing an additional six months of practical street training. Finn was lucky enough to be assigned senior Police Officer Karl Stackhouse. Karl was the father of three children, a very patient and humble fifteen-year veteran police officer, a great training officer, and an even greater friend. Finn and Karl hit it off from the very start. They'd remained friends until two years ago, when Karl finally succumbed to the cancerous effects that lingered in his body for years, attributed to his time spent searching the rubble of the 9/11 terrorist attacks at the World Trade Center in New York City. Finn remained close with the Stackhouse children, fulfilling their father's dying request. He was especially close to the oldest son, Karl Junior. Finn had attended both his graduation from the police academy, as he followed in his father's footsteps, and his wedding to his childhood sweetheart.

Finn freshly recalled a decade earlier, when Stackhouse pulled the police cruiser up in front of 20 West Main Street and pointed out one of the inexplicable heartaches of a street cop's life. Seven years earlier, he'd had to do a death knock to the family that lived there, informing them that their only child had been killed upstate in a hunting accident in Saratoga on his seventeenth birthday. The kid wasn't even a hunter, Karl had remarked. He'd been out in a field with a group of friends from his high school Army Reserve Officers Training Corp, visiting an old Revolutionary War battlefield, when he was mysteriously shot and killed. His death was ruled an unfortunate hunting accident, which ended any further police investigation. Finn remembered Stackhouse saying, "Someday you'll have to make one of those death knocks." Little would he have believed that he'd do it at the very same house. Pulling away from the curb, he heard the echo of Stackhouse's voice. Stackhouse saying the dead boy's mother had blamed the house for her son's sudden death, but he couldn't remember why. What were the chances, he wondered, that the deaths of two high school youths, who had both resided in the same house though at different times, suddenly died violent, unexplained deaths on their seventeenth birthday?

Turning off the bustling six-lane Hempstead Turnpike into the parking lot of the county's medical center complex, to the medical examiner's office. A nondescript, standalone building adjacent to the county's nineteen-story winged-shaped hospital, intentionally secreted from public view. He parked his car in front of ME's office, and followed the sidewalk down a slight incline, along the side of the three-story red brick building that shared the entrance to the hospital's emergency room. Passing the heliport, he turned right, and walked down the damp, unlit concrete ramp into an underground cadaver drop-off, pick-up point. The same location where the police department's wagon discreetly unloaded its cargo of body bags.

The business end of the medical examiner's giant subterranean underbelly closely resembled the activity of a massive beehive, with a steady flow of drop-offs and pickups, some of whom had died of natural causes, some by accident, and some at the hands of others, many from reasons yet undetermined. The police departments unmarked white vans would return four or five times throughout the day, followed by a regular stream of black hearses from various funeral homes.

Finn pushed a small admittance buzzer next to a non-descript grey metal entrance door that adjoined the double overhead garage delivery doors. Within seconds, an electric door lock gave a loud click. Finn entered and stood silently in front of the receiving desk, while morgue attendant Carrie Major busied herself at her keyboard entering body notables into the morgue's database, her silky long blonde hair covering her downcast head. She glanced up in surprise. "Hey, Finn, what brings you here today?" An appealing smile revealed a perfect set of ultra-white teeth, set against a rosy, unblemished complexion.

He was amazed every time he saw Carrie dressed in her starched white medical smock, knowing she singlehandedly wheeled around all the cadavers between the slide-in coolers and the autopsy room all day long. Wondering why a beautiful woman in the prime of life would want to spend any time in the smelly basement of a hundred-year-old building, with a few ghoulish, eccentric doctors—and the newly dead—to keep her company.

"Hi, Carrie. Still at it, I see. How's Hollywood ever going to find you down here?" Finn said with a half-smile. The other half of his lips clutching the tip of his toothpick.

"This is Hollywood, isn't it, Finn?" Carrie said with a toothy grin.

"I'm looking for Dr. Collier," Finn said, glancing around and placing the two clear plastic bags of the kids' personal property on her desk.

"He's in the cutting room with the two kids from that auto accident up in Oyster Bay last night."

"He started already?"

"Yeah, about an hour ago. But why are you interested in them?"

"Just curious, I guess. I was at the scene last night. This is their property." Finn didn't feel like getting into the whole story with her, so he just removed his suit jacket, placed it on a coat hook, and took one of the disposable plastic smocks from the shelf on the wall, next to the cutting-room doors. He also selected a clear plastic face shield, and a pair of the thin blue latex gloves.

"I'll be joining him," Finn said as he pushed open the swinging doors, which swooshed as the tightly sealed rubber gasket of the doors released.

He was hit with the rushing stench of death as he entered the large autopsy room. After all these years, Finn had never managed to adjust to the unmistakable foul odor of decomposing bodies. He quickly dabbed a small amount of Vick's vapor rub in his nostrils, from a small bottle he carried when he knew he would be visiting the morgue. Despite its sometimes-euphoric side effects, it was better than the noxious odor of death, which could linger in his nose and on his clothes all day long if he didn't wear the smock or stick that little bit of vapor rub up his nostrils.

Finn started toward Dr. Collier's cutting station. Snapping the disposable smock closed, donning the plastic face shield, and forced his fingers into the cheap blue latex gloves as he walked. Two other doctors were busy performing their own separate postmortems. The buzzing sound from their bone saws filled the large room, sending shivers down Finn's spine as he walked past them.

Dr. Collier's back was to Finn as he approached the stainless-steel examining table, at the last of six autopsy stations in the crowded room. Dr. Collier had Tom Buckley's body laid out on his table, his chest cut open in the customary Y incision, with his rib cage spread open for easy access to his vital organs.

"What do you think, Doc?" Finn asked as he walked around the table to face Dr. Collier. Collier was a large man, 6'2', and no less than 300 pounds. His extended stomach tested the tensile strength of the fabric on his blood--and body fluid–stained white smock, giving him a giant sausage-like appearance, and preventing him from fully reaching across the autopsy table. His sandy, thinning hair matched his ruddy cheeks and swollen plum-colored nose, revealing an elaborate array of surface veins that was impossible to ignore. Dr. Collier rarely made eye contact with anyone and didn't acknowledge Finn's appearance. He continued to pull the boy's lacerated intestines from his open abdomen, placing them in the swinging stainless-steel base of the scale that hung suspended from the ceiling next to the cutting table.

"What do you think, Doc?" Finn repeated. "Have you ever seen anything like this from an auto accident?" Still no response. Finn watched patiently, letting Collier finish.

The ME systematically removed the boy's vital organs, taking the necessary little slices for pathology. He went throughout the entire chest cavity, collecting blood and DNA samples along the way. Finn watched as he made the customary incisions to the back of the head allowing him to peal the loose scalp from the top of the head down over the face, exposing the skull, then cutting the top of the skull open with the bone saw. Removing the boy's brain for another biopsy slice.

Only after Collier placed all the kid's vital organs into a red plastic biohazard bag, then stuffed the bag back into the hollowed-out chest cavity, did Finn speak again. "Have you ever seen injuries like this before, with all those deep lacerations?

"What are you asking, Detective?" Collier finally responded, without glancing up.

"From an auto accident, Doc! Have you ever seen so many lacerations on one body before? They look almost intentional, even surgical. They all have the same neat, clean V-shaped edges." Finn raised his voice, almost yelling at Collier. Colliers's early-morning Bourbon breath seeping from under his clear face mask. "I've seen worse from car accidents, Detective," Collier finally answered in a condescending tone.

"You've seen worse than this one?" Finn shot back. "It looks like this kids' body was pushed through a giant cheese grater! Can you at least give me a cause of death, Doc?"

"You'll have to wait until the toxicology and pathology reports are completed before I can give you an official cause of death, Detective."

"How about an unofficial one, then?"

"I'm not willing to do that either."

"Can you at least tell me if you think it's a suspicious death? And are you leaning toward it being a homicide?" Finn asked, knowing it was what he needed from the ME for the deaths to be classified, so he could officially open an investigation.

"I can't give you an answer either way, Detective, not without seeing the results from toxicology and pathology." He added, "But I will share something with you." He straightened up and reached over to pick up a small kidney-shaped, stainless-steel pan sitting near the stainless-steel sink. With a set of long-nosed stainless forceps, he removed a small, bloody piece of triangular-shaped metal and held it up for Finn to see. "Carrie found this on her initial X-ray examination. It was embedded in the front shaft of the fifth posterior rib of the thoracic cage..." Sending Finn a patronizing smile. "Or to put it more simply for you, Detective, the front part of fifth posterior rib, which is located just behind the heart."

Finn took the small piece of metal from Collier's forceps in his gloved fingers and held it up to the large operating light above the autopsy table.

"What do you make of that, Detective?"

"I'm not sure, but it looks like the broken tip of some sort of odd shaped knife blade." Finn stated as he studied the blood coated object.

"That would have to be an exceptionally long blade to enter his chest, pass through the anterior side of his thoracic cage, through his heart, and finally lodge deep in the shaft of the fifth posterior rib. That would be hard for any person to accomplish, no matter how strong they were. This boy's body is solid muscle."

"So, you think it's a homicide?" Finn questioned. "Did you find a laceration in the heart?" he added.

"I'm not prepared to make any classification until I have all the necessary reports, and actually, there were four lacerations in his heart, but only one passed completely through the muscle."

"Can you tell how long it's been there?"

"This piece of metal hasn't been there long, or the rib would have started to seal over with calcium. It doesn't take long for a healthy body like this one to start healing. But I'll know more when I get the results back from pathology," Collier said, holding up the kidney-shaped pan to Finn's face. "Perhaps it's a piece of chrome molding, as a result of the car accident," Collier added, smiling.

Finn dropped the metal shard back into the pan and Collier jerked it away. Collier hadn't changed a bit and was living up to the name other homicide cops had given him: Coddling Collier. He never make a summary classification of any death until he'd had all the supporting medical reports physically in his hand. At times he'd even asked for the crime-scene techs' reports before he made a final determination, which slowed any homicide investigation to a standstill.

Collier didn't like to classify any case as a homicide, even if the deceased was found with a couple hunting arrows lodged in his back, because then he'd have to go to court, he'd have to testify, and he'd be forced to look at the jurors' faces. Plus, they wouldn't let him drink in the witness box.

"One other thing, Doc. What's his stomach contents?" Finn asked.

"The stomach was almost empty. He hadn't eaten in...oh, I'd guess within the last six hours or so of his death. Everything had been pretty much digested and moved into the intestines." Collier busied himself with counting and cleaning his autopsy tools.

"What about the time of death—can you pinpoint that?"

"Yep, that was at exactly 12:33. I just can't say if that was a.m. or p.m., Detective," Collier said giving a wiseass chuckle.

"How do you know it was exactly 12:33?"

"The crystal on the kid's wristwatch was crushed at exactly 12:33."

"Are you really going to use that? That's your best medical evidence for time of death?" Finn said sarcastically.

Collier suddenly let out another belly chuckle, deeper and longer, causing him to break out in a fit of uncontrollable coughing that reminded Finn of a sick dog's bark. His round face flushed red as he spewed phlegm against the inside of his plastic face shield. Finn waited patiently. Once Collier had regained control, he said, "To answer your question, lividity is set, though it's minimal, and based on what little rigor there is, I'd place the time of death somewhere between three and four hours before you discovered his body in that field. The girl's time of death maybe one to two hours before his."

"That timeline doesn't make sense, Doc," Finn said, recalling the victim's friends telling him they had all eaten together at the diner and left the parking lot at around 11:10 p.m., in separate cars, to return to Oyster Bay.

Dr. Collier said, "The girl's stomach was partially empty as well, Detective. So, if they were on a dinner date, they must have eaten earlier, say around six o'clock or so."

"That's not what their friends are saying. They said they had finished eating at the diner about 11:00 p.m." He knew Collier had made some real medical blunders in the past, sharing that burden with Jack Daniels, but to make a mistake with the contents of the stomachs that were right in front of him, that was a little concerning to Finn. He didn't want to shut him down by questioning his medical observation, so Finn did what every other detective did: coddled him for answers.

"I finished her postmortem earlier," Collier said, then added, "Did you know that she didn't have any external or internal injuries?" Finn asked, "So, what was her cause of death?"

"She's a strange case," Collier said as he unraveled a short black hose from the sink and proceeded to spray down Tom's body. "Now, you must understand that I can't be absolutely positive until I get her toxicology results back. Normally, I wouldn't even share this with you, Detective, but her case seems medically cut and dry, although odd. I'm almost certain that she died from anaphylactic shock," continuing his wanton hose spraying water and body fluids off the body and the surface of the stainless-steel table onto the tile floor, where they circled the floor drain, but not before ricocheting off Finn's wingtips. Jumping back to avoid Collier's inattentive splashing, Finn asked. "Anaphylactic shock. How is that even possible?"

"Oh, it can happen."

"Was she on any drugs?"

"Her initial tox-screen didn't reveal the presence of any illicit drugs. Though it was the result of her bloodwork that made me look further." Collier rolled up the short hose and hung it back by the sink. Averting Finn's eyes, he continued. "There was an unusual amount of epinephrine in her blood, which, under normal conditions isn't suspicious or remarkable, as the body normally produces a certain amount of it. More so if one is under an unusual amount of stress. Epinephrine is a naturally produced hormone. But if for some reason the body goes haywire and produces too much, well, then it becomes toxic."

"Epinephrine?"

"Yes, you may recognize it as adrenaline. Anyway, it appears she had an allergic reaction to the unusual amount of epinephrine her system being so rapidly produced, resulting in an instantaneous shock to her organs. That's called anaphylactic shock, Detective."

"Any idea what would cause her body to produce a toxic amount of epinephrine?"

"Nope, that's your job."

"So, what you're saying is she was scared to death?" Finn said.

"That's absolutely correct, Detective. It's been known to happen."

"To a healthy, seventeen-year-old high school cheerleader?" Finn shot back.

"Well, no, that's a little unusual."

"Ya think!"

Finn was about to turn and leave Collier to finish up with the boy's body when he happened to notice a dark, thin circular abrasion to the boy's right wrist. Curious, Finn lifted the boy's arm at the elbow and noticed that the thin abrasion circled the entire wrist. Finn went around the table and lifted Tom's left arm and noticed an identical dark, thin abrasion around his left wrist.

"Dr. Collier." Finn questioned. "What are these marks on his wrists?"

"Oh yeah, I almost forgot to tell you." Standing at the stainless-steel sink with his back toward Finn, Collier said, "I found those thin contusions on both wrists. I won't know how they were made until pathology examines the skin tissue and a couple trace strands of a particle that I lifted from within the abrasions."

"One last question, Doc, then I'll get out of your way. When was the last time you performed an autopsy on a victim of an auto accident, who had had their hands restrained?"

Pushing open the double doors of the autopsy room, Finn removed his plastic smock, face shield, and latex gloves before discarding them in the closest trash bin, along with a gnawed toothpick. He waved to Carrie as he blew the vapor rub from his nose into his handkerchief and exited the morgue at the receiving-desk door. Finn was now convinced that Tom wasn't just brutally murdered, he'd been the victim of some bizarre homicidal sacrifice, with his body posed at the base of that tree by the killer or killers, who wanted to display their handiwork for whoever found him. It was a strange message, he thought as he replaced the discarded toothpick with a fresh one.

Driving home, Finn stopped at the nearest liquor store for his favorite memory blocker. He made another quick stop at a local grocery store for a frozen dinner and more toothpicks. Trying to remember back to the last time he'd had any real sleep. Knowing he'd need something extraordinarily strong to put him down and keep him down until the following morning. Finn wanted nothing more than to get home, open his bottle, lie back in his recliner, and sip his single malt while listening to his prized collection of classical mezzo soprano, losing himself to those angelic voices. Maybe he'd even get a couple of hours of sleep before he continued searching for the kids' killers.

Ten

TOSSING HIS BRIEFCASE ON the front passenger's seat of his car, Finn backed the unmarked black four-door Crown Victoria down his driveway and into the street, just missing the neighbor's garbage cans, which had been hurriedly left in the street by the collectors before moving on to the next pickup. The police radio crackled to life as various patrol cars were dispatched to locations throughout the county by a soft, authoritative female voice. He subconsciously listened as he drove the deserted three blocks on Renee Road to a busier Berryhill Road, where he made a left and followed the slowing traffic over the railroad tracks, adjacent to the rush of the Syosset train station. He continued south for two miles to the Long Island Expressway entrance, slipping into the legendary bumper-to-bumper traffic of the I-495 to the county seat. The daily trip to Police Headquarters taking longer and longer every year. What used to be a quick thirty-five-minute drive to headquarters was now an hour, if he was lucky, if it wasn't raining or snowing.

The only thing that mattered to Finn right now was how these three deaths could possibly be linked. The sudden, unexpected deaths of three healthy seventeen-year-old kids, seventeen years apart, from the same high school was beyond suspicious, by anyone's standards.

He knew where they died. He just needed to know how and why they died. All three shared a common denominator; all having attended the same high school, but two of them had lived in the same house seventeen years apart. There wasn't any evidence to indicate their families ever knew each other. And why Susanne? Where did she factor into this mess?

Finn hadn't planned on going into the office first thing this morning. It'd been over a week since he and Collier crossed paths in the cutting room, and he hadn't heard a thing from Collier or the pathology department. Wishing it wasn't Collier on call that night. Any one of the other ME's would have made the classification of homicide right at the scene, or first thing on the cutting table.

However, there was another trail Finn needed to navigate while he waited for someone to make up Collier's mind for him, that was an unfinished paper trail. He knew Hughes wouldn't approve any investigation until the deaths were classified as homicides, but he couldn't wait. Hughes didn't like Finn or any other detective in his squad spending time chasing "*ghosts*," a term he used when a detective couldn't explain any time they'd spent that wasn't a direct connection to a case or wasn't following up on a direct lead to an open red case on his murder board. That glossy white acrylic dry-erase board attached to the wall in his office. Homicide squad's scoreboard of sorts, listing all the current murder investigations in the county. Open investigations were written in a red marker, listing the victim's name followed by the date of the murder, the homicide case number, method of killing, and, finally, the detective assigned. If the case was solved, the red was changed to black, but remained on the board for that calendar year so Hughes could boast. If the name remained in red longer than Hughes thought it should, the only thing changed was the detective's name.

Parking his car in the lot behind headquarters, Finn walked right past the side entrance on Fifteenth Street, made a quick left onto Franklin Avenue, passing the old courthouse on the short block to Old Country Road, where he made a right and finished the twenty-minute trek to the county courthouse. It was a journey Finn would never make by car, if he needed to be in court before noon; the parking around the courthouse was worse than at police headquarters. Finn climbed the sprawling, pedestrian worn granite steps to the fifteen-foot-tall, bronze-framed glass doors of the three-story courthouse, built more than fifty years ago on the site of the old county fairgrounds. Once inside, he was greeted by two uniformed court officers conducting baggage searches at a conveyer belt that moved all visitors' carried items through the X-ray machine at the speed of a glacier. Each visitor passed through a set of arched mechanized detectors, the first was the customary metal detector, followed by a state-of-the-art explosive sniffer. Everyone had to follow this procedure, the defendants' families, their friends, trial jurors, even the witnesses for the prosecution, who more often than not were taunted and threatened by the accused's family and friends as they found themselves sandwiched in a slow-moving gauntlet of intimidation. Even defense attorneys packed the red-velvet-roped waiting lines like herded cattle, snaking back and forth from wall to wall in the echoing limestone rotunda.

Finn pushed his way through the crowded passageway at the entrance, waving his detective badge in the air above his head as he hugged the interior wall outside of the velvet rope, bypassing the security queue. One court officer recognizing him smiled, mouthed a hello, and waved him through. Finn followed along the limestone wall past the security machines to the first fluted Corinthian stone pillar, before turning into the large open stairwell. The heels of his wingtips clicked against the polished terrazzo floor, sending the rhythmic sound of his footfalls ricocheting off the towering, cold limestone walls. Finn counted the thirteen granite steps to the basement, as he had done so many times before in pre-trial murder cases, searching for documented evidence in the bowels of the county courthouse, home to the County Records Bureau. Once at the bottom of the stairs, Finn picked up his pace, hurriedly following the dimly lit tubular concrete tunnel to the middle of the courthouse building, gnawing feverishly at his toothpick.

The tunnel ended at an open wooden double doorway, revealing a forty-foot-by-forty-foot sparse, institutional room with its fifty-year-old bile-green colored squared tiled floor, and scuffed, dingy beige walls. Rows of inadequate yellowed florescent tube lighting buzzed continuously, fixed flush against a moisture ringed stained ceiling. The cramped, airless room gave off an odor of damp paper, mold, and body odor blending with inexpensive aftershave lotion and cheap perfume. A chest-high wooden counter lay at the far end. Beyond the counter, which most people never got to see, were all of Nassau County's property records dating back to 1899, when it was first established as one of New York State's sixty-four counties. Before that, Nassau County was the eastern part of Queens County, one of the five boroughs of New York City. Queens County, which was established in 1683, also annexed many of their archived records here as well.

The county records bureau was at its busiest in the early-morning hours, before most judges began any number of legal proceedings in their courtrooms on the floors above. The day usually started with defense lawyers and legal assistants pushing and shoving each other for their turn at one of the only two working computers in the records hall, both slower than molasses in January, searching the records database for that elusive silver bullet that would set their client free.

Both computer monitors were bolted to the back wall near the double entrance doors. A long, thin, frayed steel cable with one end fastened tight to the floor, tethered the worn, sticky keyboards precariously on a single piece of thick wood shelving that jutted out along two of the small office walls all the way to the clerk's counter. Here a haphazard line of people grew, waiting for hard copies of found documents and the lone cashier. The room filled quickly, as did tempers. With no clearly defined lines, confusion was the order of the day in the records bureau.

Finn witnessed one self-important male attorney trying to bump his way ahead of a female attorney with an excuse that fell on deaf ears. After a brief struggle of words, he found himself outside the double entrance doors, starting over.

Finn stood silently against the wall, the one closest to the clerk's counter, where he could see Kathleen, the only clerk working the busy counter. He felt he was in for a long wait. "It's like looking for a parking space at HQ," he murmured to himself, as he pushed the toothpick into the other corner of his mouth with his tongue.

Finn was well known at County Records, and liked, for the most part, at least by the people who worked there. Most times he came with a dozen fresh bagels, or some other form of baked goods as a token for the over-worked county employees. Today was different. Today he was just picking up information. The phone call he placed the past week to the only person at the County Records Bureau who would have an answer to his inquiries if there was an answer: Langdon Foster.

Langdon was only a volunteer at the County Records Bureau and had been for the past five years. It was a position the county provided just for him. Before volunteering, Langdon was the county's head record keeper for sixty-two years. Age forced his civil service retirement, but at 87, Langdon Foster had read most of the records in the Nassau/Queens County archives at one time or another and knew where to locate any document in the archives without the use of a computer. He knew stories, many told by his father and his grandfather, who had also been county record keepers, and he knew people. Thankfully, Langdon liked police officers, especially Finn.

Kathleen, the overworked records clerk at the counter, finally made eye contact with Finn. "Just a second, Detective. I'll get him," she said, holding up her index finger as she disappeared into the dimly lit rows of file cabinets and rusted shelving crammed with layer upon layer of dusty, dirty ledgers, books, maps, and other written county documents. Over the years the clerks had learned that Finn only conducted his business with Langdon. A couple minutes later, a thin old man appeared at the counter and lifted the heavy, hinged walk-through access section of the counter.

"Come into my office, Detective," Langdon said in a soft, barely audible librarian's whisper, as others in the room turned to see the man dressed in the funeral gray business suit receiving special attention. Langdon's turn-of-the-century wire-rimmed glasses were balanced at the forward edge of his sharply pointed nose. His emerald eyes rolled to the top of their sockets as he peered over top of the glasses. A full head of thick, snow-white hair fell over the collar onto a now oversized, well-worn tweed sports jacket that bore the shadow of the missing, once fashionable leather elbow patches.

"Detective," Langdon said in a soft murmur as he shook Finn's right hand with a grip amazingly strong for a man of his age. "It's nice to see you again. I see you still haven't gotten rid of that toothpick," he added with a friendly smile. "I don't see why you need a toothpick, it's not a very sanitary habit."

"I guess it's for the same reason why you need those old suspenders," Finn responded.

"Because they hold up my pants, Detective!" Langdon said with a little wink.

"Then why do you wear a belt?" Finn added. "And just for the record, Langdon, it's a different toothpick from the last time I was here."

Langdon carried that inevitable age bend at his waist. It was much more noticeable now to Finn as they walked side by side, between the maze of record racks toward Langdon's office. When Finn first met Langdon, they stood eye to eye at six feet. Now he shuffled along lower and slower and was much thinner.

Entering Langdon's small paper-cluttered office, the musty smell of moldy paper was overwhelming. Finn removed a stack of old, faded, and fragile folded paper maps from the dark-stained, heavy oak antique armchair facing Langdon's desk, sending a small cloud of dust swirling around his head. He placed them on the dirty vinyl floor next to the chair, then sat down. Gazing around the room, he felt dwarfed among the floor-to-ceiling piles of county records, books, and old documents that surrounded the room and Langdon's desk like paper stalagmites.

Langdon cautiously slid into his well-worn leather chair, pushing aside an uneven mound atop his desk of county records that blocked their eye contact. It was evident that Langdon had very few visitors.

"Detective," Langdon said, crossing his arms as he leaned back in the tattered chair, "based on our phone conversation, and what you said you were looking for, I did some checking here in the county tax records. I even checked with the state's archived vital records. Then I looked at all the filed deeded property records for that house. I find it very odd, even somewhat confusing." Langdon frowned, his soft green eyes peering over the wire-rimmed glasses at Finn. "I've never run across anything quite like this in my entire time in County Records."

Langdon gently pulled himself a little closer to his desk, opened a two-inch-thick manila folder, and peered down through the center of the eyeglass lenses balanced at the forward edge of his nose. "Well, according to my research, which I believe is accurate, even though some of the documents are handwritten it looks like that house you spoke of has had a new owner every seventeen years. Not that a house can't have new owners, mind you," Langdon said, gazing up at Finn over his glasses. "But every seventeen years? Not sixteen or eighteen years, but every seventeen years? And here's where it really gets puzzling, at least to me. That house has changed ownership every seventeen years for the past 238 years!"

"What does that mean, Langdon?"

"I don't know, you're the detective. I hope you don't mind, but I took the liberty of searching Oyster Bay's local churches, their birth, marriage, and death records going back to the year 1653. I even checked with an old friend of mine at the *Oyster Bay Tribune*, which is said to be the oldest continuous-circulation newspaper in the country." Langdon paused.

"You searched back to 1653?" Finn said.

"Yes, I did, want to know why, Detective?"

"Sure, of course!"

"Well, I'll tell you," he said in a matter-of-fact tone, pausing before continuing. "I've been here since 1952 doing this work, I've cataloged most, if not all the county's land records, which includes all the buildings and houses, new and old since Nassau became a county, and even when it was part of Queens County. I did it long before computers; in fact, I even cataloged and archived some of the land grants from Kings Charles II and George III. But, Detective, I am not a historian. I just catalog historic records." Langdon continued, as his soft mellow voice deepened, "But I must say, a lot of Nassau County history has passed through these fingers, and I have never come across anything quite like this. I've checked and cross-checked everywhere I could possibly think of with this house. I've spent the entire past week, late into the evenings on most nights, researching this house. There're no records of who built it, or when. But I do have records that indicate the King Charles II was collecting taxes on it back in 1653, when Oyster Bay was first incorporated as a hamlet, the best I can tell."

"Yeah, that doesn't surprise me," Finn sneered, sliding the toothpick to the other corner of his mouth. "What king would want to miss out on any tax money?" Finn added.

"Anyway," Langdon continued. "From 1780, and every seventeen years since, that house has had a new owner. What's even more interesting," Langdon resumed, removing a single page from the file, and holding it up, "are the sudden, unexplained deaths of male children associated with that house. And they've all been listed as unfortunate accidents."

"Unexplained deaths, only male children. In 238 years?" Finn said, sitting upright in the chair.

"Yep, only the male children," Langdon responded. "There's more, Detective. It appears they all died on their seventeenth birthday."

"What?"

"Yep, all on their seventeenth birthday. But would you like to know what is really strange though?"

"Stranger than that?" Finn said with a raised brow.

"Yep, they all died on the twenty-third day of September. Different years, of course, but they all died on the very same day of the very same month."

"Wait!" Finn said, trying to process what Langdon had just told him. "you're saying every seventeen years, the only male child from that residence has become the victim of some unfortunate and unexplainable accident resulting in their deaths?

"Yes, according to these documents, unless of course you believe in coincidences Detective?"

"It's not a coincidence, if there's a pattern." Finn replied.

"Like I said, I've checked, cross-checked, and rechecked all the documentation I could find, and it seems all their deaths occurred by some untimely accident. Perhaps you could check your Homicide Squad records for additional information that could link it with your current investigation."

"Yeah, that's going to be a problem, for a couple of reasons. One, the Homicide Squad doesn't keep records for deaths they don't investigate. If these deaths were all classified as accidents, then the Homicide Squad wouldn't have investigated them, unless, of course, it was an extremely unusual accident that leaned toward a more suspicious incident. Plus, some of these deaths occurred long before there even was a police department, which is probably why most of your information came from old newspapers and church records."

"And the second reason?" Langdon asked.

"Well, that's probably the biggest problem of them both," Finn said, rolling the toothpick from side to side in his mouth. "Homicide hasn't created a case number for this one either. The crime scene techs have it labeled as an accident as well, and the ME's office is dragging their feet."

Langdon slowly pushed his chair away from his desk, like he had just finished eating the largest meal of his life. Folding his arms tightly across his pigeon-thin chest, his black satin bowtie resting squarely under the cascade of rubbery neck skin, he said, "I'm sorry I can't do more for you here, not that I would even know where to look. But from this side of the desk, it seems we've raised more questions than answers. Let's just say I don't envy the task you've taken on, Detective."

"You've been a great help to me, Langdon—now and every time I've asked for your assistance. I appreciate all the time and hard work you have put into this—"

"Unless!" Langdon added suddenly, cutting into Finn midsentence as he removed his thin wire-rimmed eyeglasses pulling an aging off-white handkerchief across his bulging eyes. "There's an old man up in Oyster Bay, lives on a hill, Seely, I think that's his name. I'm not sure if he's still alive. But if he is, he may be able to clear up any questions you have with that house. Or at least point you in the right direction."

"An old man?" Finn added with a hint of skepticism.

"Ebenezer Seely," Langdon suddenly blurred out. "Yes, that's his name, I remember now," Langdon said, his eyes rolling upwards to the right, as he mentally re-checked that name. "I'm not sure anyone up in Oyster Bay will remember him, or even know the name. But he lives in a small English Tudor at the top of Simcoe Street. He's something of an historian, of sorts. You should go see him."

"Langdon, I don't mean to be disrespectful, but how old can he be? I mean, if you're calling him an old man and you're 87," Finn said with a muted chuckle.

Langdon smiled, showing a full set of age-colored teeth. "I'm not sure how old he is, or if he's even still around, Detective. I can only remember he was an old man when I was a kid. I'm not sure he will even talk to you, but he's the only one I can think of that may be able to help you now. I'm sure it's worth a try."

"When you were a kid, he was an old man?" Finn said, thinking this case couldn't get any stranger.

"Yep, he's been living in the same house on top of Simcoe Street for as long as I can remember."

"Maybe I'll just give him a call," Finn said reluctantly.

"Can't." Langdon said. "he doesn't have a phone, never has." Langdon stood from his chair and handed Finn the thick manila folder. "You'll find all the names of all the dead kids associated with that house and how they died in this file, Detective, dating back 238 years." Then he added, "Just one more thing. If you don't mind my asking, I'm very curious as to why you wanted me to look at this particular house to begin with. And why is the Homicide Squad only now interested in the house, given all the unexplained deaths of young men attached to it over the years. I can't recall there ever being anything in the newspapers or local media connecting this house to all these deaths before. So why now, Detective?"

Finn was glad Langdon asked him that question. He felt a sense of relief that he could bounce this unusual case off someone else, especially a guy like Langdon, who wouldn't think he was just spinning his wheels by looking so deep into something that could very well be nothing more than a sad chain of events. Then again, it wasn't like Finn to share anything with anyone if it wasn't absolutely necessary. Finn sat back down in the worn oak armchair, shifted his weight around a little, and gave Langdon the condensed version of events.

He told Langdon how he'd been up in Oyster Bay the week before taking a couple witnesses' statements to close out a past murder-suicide case, and when he was leaving the village around 11:30 p.m. heading back to headquarters. He was southbound on Mill River Road approaching the first blind curve, when he slowed and hit his high beams as he began to negotiate the sharp turn. His headlights caught the glimmer of a piece of chrome from a car that had apparently crashed through the horse fence ending up in the pasture, near a large tree. He continued to provide Langdon with the details of the two dead kids, and that he was working this investigation as an unofficial homicide case, meaning he was working it cold, without the aid of any forensics support or technical assistance from within the department, because the case had been classified as a fatal auto accident.

Plus, Finn related, his suspicion of foul play in the deaths of these kids had so far failed to provide anything physically or scientifically solid, or anything even remotely close to a lead. He hadn't been able to come up with any witnesses or supporting evidence of anything other than what his gut was telling him as a homicide investigator. Finn purposely left out Laura Buckley's odd story of the disappearing eighteenth-century female ghost or the grim details of the autopsies.

"I can see you have your work cut out for you, Detective." Langdon responded. "Now don't forget to go see old man Seely, I'm sure he'd be willing to help you, if he can."

Eleven

ON HIS RETURN WALK to Police Headquarters, Finn's mind rolled around like a runaway marble over the strange details he'd just learned from Langdon. He struggled to make sense of any of it. He wasn't the kind of guy who believed in folklore or sophomoric campfire stories but having copies of Langdon's well-documented history of 20 West Main Street gave him pause.

He hadn't been prepared for the revelation of so many unexplained deaths associated with that house, or the names and cause of death of each victim. What could have happened back in 1780, and every seventeen years since, in this little hamlet that would have created such a bizarre chain of events? It was beyond logic that fourteen unexplained deaths of occupants of one house went unnoticed for so long, by so many. And all occurring on the twenty-third of September, to males on their seventeenth birthday. Where was the rational explanation for all these deaths? There's always an explanation for someone's death if one looks hard enough, he told himself.

"1780," Finn said aloud, his tongue rolling and shifting the gnawed toothpick from one corner of his mouth to the other. "Then where does Susanne White, the sole female victim, fit in?"

The first twenty-four hours of any homicide investigation are the most crucial. This one wasn't any different. Finn spent the rest of his Friday and late into the night, and again, all the following day deep in the department's subterranean records morgue searching through the archived records for anything that would remotely support Langdon's findings. He found nothing, except a faded paper copy of a seventeen-year-old police dispatch form directing the lone Oyster Bay village patrol car to make a death notification to the family at 20 West Main Street. This must have been Karl Stackhouse's initial assignment for his death knock to the family who had lived at the house before the Buckley's, he thought, then he noticed the cause of death: accidental gun shot, Saratoga New York, seventeen-year-old male. There were no other records or documents in the department's 93-year history for police-related issues or calls for assistance at 20 West Main Street, not even a call for a parking condition at the address.

He turned to digging deeper into the victims' inner circles, not waiting for Coddling Collier to sober up and make the deaths a classification of homicide. He was discreet with his inquiries of the victims' friends and their immediate families, not wanting to draw too much attention. He kept his line of questioning generic, always explaining he was just conducting a follow-up to the tragic accident, and always avoiding the word "murder." The only things he'd learned was that Tom Buckley and Susanne White were the most popular seniors in their high school, no one seemed to have had a run-in with either of them over anything, ever. He couldn't find anyone with an unkind work to say about either one of them, which was almost unbelievable. What high school kid never crossed that thin line of adolescent mischief? None he'd ever heard of.

He dumped their cell phones, found nothing. He cross-referenced every cell number, text message, and instant message. He ran every name in both their cell contacts through every database the department had, and all the social media platforms, nothing. He did criminal background checks on everyone. Still nothing. No domestic disputes, no social media threats, no juvenile delinquency reports, no drug dealing, not even the slightest hint of recreational drug use or even a single traffic ticket. He found absolutely nothing pointing to or even suggesting the slightest motive for murder. He'd contacted every local, state, and federal law enforcement agency for similar homicides within the last twenty years, there weren't any. Local street thugs weren't taking credit for the killings, and local snitches knew nothing. These kids were every parent's dream, and their every nightmare. Their deaths were a complete mystery.

Entering the windowless, poorly lit second-floor Homicide Squad room, Finn saw four other detectives busy at their desks. Sundays were no different than any other day when it came to police work. The squad had twenty-eight assigned detectives. Fourteen worked the day shift, and fourteen worked the night shift, rotating every other week, with minimal coverage for overlap. The main squad room was laid out in an oversized rectangle with fifteen identical forest green metal desks, all handmade by prisoners from the New York State Department of Corrections, all with fifteen identical phones, computers, and desk lamps. Fourteen of them were shared desks, shoved front-to-front against each other, creating an island hub of computer and phone activity in the center of an overcrowded room. The walls were haphazardly plastered with colored photos of wanted criminals, along with a few grainy black-and-white images of older wanted posters, all accompanied with fingerprints and pedigree information from their most recent arrest.

One special desk positioned at the entrance door of the squad room was reserved specifically for the overly plump civilian gatekeeper, whom the detectives referred to as the Troll. Her desk was positioned at the door's entrance to control the authorized and unauthorized traffic into and out of the squad room. She closely monitored those who left with what and made everyone sign in or out in Homicide's official thick blotter, for continuity.

Three of the walls that surrounded the center of clustered desks were lined with five-foot-high, five-drawer, olive green World War II metal file cabinets that had been salvaged from a military airplane hangar at Mitchel Field, the same airfield Colonel Lindbergh used to take off from on the first historical transatlantic flight back in May of 1927. The fourth wall was made up of three small offices, one for the commanding officer, one shared by the day sergeant and the night sergeant. The last office was a closet-sized interview room, with a small wooden table and two metal chairs.

Finn had no sooner removed his suit jacket and was hanging it up when the house mouse, Detective Jimmy Doyle, mysteriously appeared seemingly out of the thin air. Detective Doyle was the boss's personal lackey, complements of his oldest daughter, who married the nerdy police officer but wanted her friends to know her husband was a county homicide detective, like the ones you see on TV. He was the yes man's yes man.

"The boss wants to see you, Finn!" Doyle fired out in a rapid, high-pitched nasally tone.

"Yeah, well you tell him I'll be there after I get some coffee," Finn answered, turning his back on Doyle.

"No, Finn. He wants you now. He's pissed!" Doyle demanded.

"I heard you, Doyle. Relax." Finn said nonchalantly, before taking his coffee mug from the bottom right drawer of his desk.

Hughes must have witnessed Doyle's frustrated encounter with Finn through the half-glass wall of his office. Standing in his open office doorway, he yelled "Finn! I want you in my office now, not after you have your coffee. NOW!"

Finn calmly flipped one hand over his shoulder in acknowledgement, while pouring coffee into his mug with the other. Taking his time. He entered the lieutenant's office, grabbing the closest of the two heavily worn oak armchairs that sat on a threadbare maroon carpet in front of his desk. Then, deliberately placing his mug of hot coffee on Hughes's imitation woodgrain neatly arranged desk, saying he cheerfully. "What's up, Lieutenant?"

"You tell me, Finn?" Hughes said with a furrowed brow. "I just intercepted a call from the ME's office, from pathology. Is there anything I should know about?" he added.

"I'm not sure I know what you're talking about, boss?" Finn said, as he took his coffee mug off the desk, leaving a large wet circle and taking a quick sip.

"You know exactly what I'm talking about, Finn!" Hughes bellowed, raising his voice, along with his blood pressure. "I am tired of you going off on your own, picking and choosing whatever case suits your fancy. So now we're investigating auto accidents, are we?"

"What did pathology have to say?" Finn said, sidestepping Hughes question.

"Never mind the ME's office, Finn. You're still on the board with the Gambrelli case, unless you've forgotten, and it's getting stale."

"I haven't forgotten," Finn said, turning his head to glance up at the murder board on the wall, then adding, "You'll have your arrest in a couple days, Lieutenant. I've been waiting for the right time to scoop the husband's squeeze and put her on the box. Plus, I've had a couple undercovers tailing her for the past week. They recovered the murder weapon she dumped over the Loop Parkway Bridge. We also have the husband on video purchasing a *wife-disposal kit* from the local hardware store. It's just a matter of time." Finn took another sip of coffee.

"I don't care about all that. I want an arrest, and I want it now. If the husband, did it, arrest him already."

"Who said the husband did it?" Finn shot back.

"You just did!"

"No, I didn't." Finn laughed, shaking his head incredulously, thinking that the investigative talent Hughes possessed could fit in a fly's ass with room to spare.

"Enough of that bullshit. I want an arrest! Do you hear me, Finn?" Hughes barked, slapping his open palms on the face of the desk. "This is your last warning. You're quickly working your way over to the Highway Patrol, back into the bag, pushing a marked unit back and forth on the Long Island Expressway. Is that what you're looking for?"

Finn ignored his rant. "So, are you going to share the pathology results?"

"I don't have the results," Hughes responded sheepishly, averting his eyes to his cleared desktop. With a childlike pout, he said, "Carrie from the ME's office called. She said she had some results, but she wouldn't give them to me. She wants you to call her back when you get in."

"Great! Hopefully that's my start," Finn said, grabbing his coffee mug as he started to get up.

"Whoa, wait just one minute. I'm not finished with you yet. Sit back down there," Hughes yelled as his posture straightened in the desk chair.

"Now what?"

"Do I need to remind you that I decide which cases get investigated around here, and who does the investigating? Have you forgotten that?"

"Of course not. How could I? You're constantly reminding me. It's just that I've been waiting for the medical examiner to finally make his classification of those two deaths."

"From what I've been told, Finn, that was just an auto accident. There was nothing suspicious, and it's not a murder case. Unless, of course, you know something different?"

"Who said it was just an auto accident?" Finn charged.

"Sergeant Casey from the Crime Scene Unit called to let me you wanted a couple of his boys to process an obvious fatal car accident like it was some kind of double homicide scene. Is that right?"

"Yeah, I asked them to take a look at the scene and process it like any homicide, because it is a homicide!"

"Finn, they make the decision which scenes to process and not to process, especially if there was no clear evidence indicating it was nothing more than an unfortunate accident. I was told the car ran off the road on a sharp turn, crashed through a fence, hit a tree, all because the driver was speeding," Hughes said. "Am I missing something here? Or do you have additional information or evidence to suggest otherwise?"

"I saw the kid's body. He'd been cut up pretty bad, like nothing I've ever seen before in an auto accident."

"And the girl, what about her injuries?"

"She didn't have any injuries. But her body was lying outside the car too."

"Finn, it sounds like an accident, like they were ejected. I'm not going to justify time and money for an investigation into something that has no basis."

"If you'd seen the kid's body or the car, you'd agree with me, Lieutenant."

"OK. What did the ME say about the autopsies? Is he willing to make the call its a homicide?"

"No, not yet. The ME is Coddling Collier, and he's not making any decisions. He's waiting for pathology and toxicology to hold his hand, making that call for him."

"And the car, you had it impounded?"

"Yeah. There's not a scratch on it. Plus, there's not a drop of blood on the interior of that car, which means the kids were killed outside the car, which means they didn't die as a result of any car accident."

"OK, then. How did they die? You have no autopsy report, you have no ME classification. Any weapons at the scene? Have you found any motive for somebody wanting to kill a couple kids? Any witnesses?"

"I'm not sure for certain how they died, and, no, no weapons were found at the scene, and no motive for anyone wanting to kill them, so far. And no witnesses yet either."

"So, you have nothing. No further developments since the twenty-third. That's eight days ago. Is that correct?"

"Yes, that's correct."

"And you're a homicide detective, or supposed to be?"

Finn didn't really need to be asked these questions. If he'd told Hughes what Langdon had discovered in his research of the house at 20 West Main Street, that there were fourteen male deaths attached to the Buckley house dating back 238 years, he knew what Hughes's next question would have been, And how many of those fourteen deaths were reported murders?

"So, who made the death notifications to the kids' families?" Hughes asked.

"I did."

"You did? Hughes said with a surprised tone. "Did you tell them their children were murdered?"

"No."

"What did you tell them?"

"I said they died as a result of a car accident," Finn answered, his shoulders slumped, knowing he'd just hit the canvas, he'd lost the fight.

"Well, there you have it, Finn. No crime scene, just an accident scene. Case closed. You just answered your own questions. Now go close out that Gambrelli case, and stay the hell away from Oyster Bay, do you hear me? I know how you get when you get one of your *ghost* hunches. But, believe me, there will be consequences for you this time if you don't listen to me. Understand?"

"I just need a couple more days, Lieutenant. Just give me two more days?"

"You've just had eight days, and you couldn't turn a simple car accident into a double homicide. How's two more days going to change that, Finn? But I will tell you this: this is the Homicide Squad, not the Fatal Accident Reconstruction Team. We solve murders here, not auto accidents. If you want to investigate auto accidents, I can arrange that for you too. But if I catch you up in Oyster Bay chasing *ghosts* in this auto accident, or even if I hear that you're up in Oyster Bay enjoying a nice beachside lunch, your sorry ass is history in this squad. Do you understand me, Finn?"

"Yeah, I hear you. You won't catch me in Oyster Bay again," Finn said as he slid his dripping coffee mug off the desk, leaving a long, wet trail, before exiting Hughes's office.

"I mean it, Finn! Don't push your luck, or your ass is history here!" Hughes yelled at Finn's back as Finn left the room.

Crossing the squad room to the coffee machine, Finn poured another mug of stale black coffee, then retreated to his desk, out of view of Hughes's office. He dialed the ME's office, and after the second ring a soft, seductive voice said, "Nassau County Medical Examiner's office, Carrie speaking."

"Morning, Carrie. It's Finn."

"Oh, hi, Finn. I have the results here on that metal shard that was removed from the Buckley boy. Do you want me to tell you over the phone or email you the finished pathology report? It's pretty odd though," she said.

"Can you give me the short version on the phone, then email me the official report?"

"Sure. I have it right here. It seems that this specific piece of tri-bladed metal contains the raw elements of a few different compounds that were only used back in the eighteenth century."

"The eighteenth century?"

"Yeah, and only in Europe."

"Europe?"

"But listen to this, Finn: this metal was only used to make military swords and bayonets, mostly bayonets."

"Really! An eighteenth-century military weapon from England?" He thought back to the image of the boy lying dead at the scene.

"That's what the report says. Oh, and there's more. Your particular three-pointed shard of metal appears to be the broken tip of a tri-bladed Brown-Bess socket bayonet carried by British Infantry soldiers. Pathology has identified the maker of this particular bayonet as Thomas Grill from Birmingham, England, a military sword maker between 1776 and 1780. And those long lateral lacerations on the boy's body, they're consistent with a single-bladed long instrument, like a sword. Isn't that odd, Finn?" Carrie added.

"Yeah, it sure is," Finn replied.

"Oh, and get this, Finn. Pathology also examined the skin tissue from the circular abrasions to the boy's wrists. They were created by leather restraints, identified from trace fragments of cowhide embedded in the abrasions. Based on the uniqueness of the tanning method, they say it's from around 1780. Hey, Finn, you know what? This doesn't look like a simple auto accident to me anymore. Do you think this kid could have been killed by someone who collected antique military weapons?"

"I'm not sure, Carrie. Could be. Could you email me that full report?"

"I'll send it over to you right now."

"Thanks, Carrie. Take care."

Finn ended the call with Carrie, then dialed the evidence section of the fleet-maintenance garage. It took three rings before he heard, "Fleet Maintenance, Tony speaking."

"Hey, Tony, it's Finn from Homicide. Did you get a chance to finish with that Toyota Camry yet?"

"Yep, it's all done," he said loudly into the phone. "But you'll have to speak up. It's extremely loud here today."

Finn could hear the deafening metal-on-metal sounds echoing throughout the high-ceilinged repurposed World War II aircraft hangar, now used as the department's maintenance shop, mixing with the sporadic riveting sounds of a pneumatic impact wrench. Tony raised his voice above the racket. "Finn, I went over that car with a fine-toothed comb. I couldn't find a single thing wrong with it."

"Nothing?" Finn questioned.

"Not a thing. All four wheels, the undercarriage, the breaks, the steering—it's all good, nothing worn, nothing damaged or broken. We even put the seat belts through the lock and release test. Everything is in excellent working order."

"What about the crash box?"

"Yep, I pulled it and downloaded the digital data myself. There was absolutely nothing unusual about the driver's operation of the vehicle. He wasn't speeding. The data indicated that the vehicle was traveling in a northerly direction at exactly 23 miles per hour before slowing to a full stop. It suddenly went dead at exactly 12:31 a.m. The airbags didn't deploy, nor did they malfunction. Finn, if you want my professional opinion, this car wasn't involved in any auto accident, with either another car or hitting any fixed object. As a matter of fact, I wouldn't have any problem letting my seventy-five-year-old mother take it out for a quick spin."

"Thanks, Tony! One other thing. What speed was the car traveling as it negotiated the last curve on Mill River Road?" Finn asked.

"Let me see..." Tony paused. Finn could hear papers rustling, now that the banging had stopped. "According to the GPS from the car's crash box, this car never entered that last northbound curve. The last GPS reading was recorded about 400 feet south of that location. But remember, Finn, the car must be running in order to record information. So, if it left the roadway or lost its electrical power, nothing would be recorded," Tony said.

"Like when someone turns the car off?" Finn asked.

"Yes, that's correct."

"But, Tony, could someone disconnect or alter the data that is recorded in that crash box?"

"I guess anything's possible, but you'd have to have a pretty extensive technical background and all the right equipment to do it. I mean, these boxes aren't hermetically sealed or tamper proof."

"Thanks for that, Tony. And thanks for the quick workup."

"Hey, Finn, there was a guy here from the Latent Fingerprint section for some repair on his van, so while he waited, I had him throw some print powder on your car. You're not going to believe this, but the car was clean: absolutely no prints inside or outside the car, not even the driver's fingerprints. The tech said it looked like it had been intentionally wiped clean, by a professional."

"I'm not surprised," Finn replied.

"Oh, and I released the car to the registered owner, a Mr. Thomas Buckley Senior. He said he needed it right away, said he and the misses were moving off Long Island, he said they'd be safer in New York City."

"Moving, huh? Thanks again, Tony," Finn said. He wasn't surprised the Buckley's would be in such a hurry. After all, they were part of a 238-year-old pattern.

Tony's report gave Finn a couple answers. Though they were weak, it was a beginning. It also officially removed the kink in everyone's way of thinking that the car had been involved in an accident. Though it did add a few more pieces to the puzzle, like that last GPS reading. So how did the car end up in that horse pasture, in front of that lone scarlet oak tree?

Finn downed the rest of his coffee and decided to head up to Oyster Bay, to pay Mr. Seely a quick visit on Simcoe Street. He would rather first telephone him, keeping him comfortable, unsuspecting of anything, like he did with Tom and Susanne's two high school friends, who told Finn they had gone to the movies with the victims to celebrate Tom's birthday. Afterward, they all stopped for a late-night snack at the Syosset Diner. They'd all eaten cheeseburgers, French fries, and had soft drinks before they departed the diner at about 11:10 p.m. or so, in separate cars for the twenty-minute ride back to Oyster Bay. Neither could think of any reason why Tom and Susanne would have taken the Mill River Road home, especially when it was quicker and safer to take Pine Hollow Road at that time of day. Their stories seemed truthful, but they weren't consistent with Dr. Collier's autopsy findings for Tom and Susanne's time of death. The autopsies showed the kids had almost empty stomachs. How could they have eaten fatty burgers, which usually take longer to digest, so late in the day, and still have almost empty stomachs?

Collier's time of death wasn't fitting the puzzle pieces either. Certain atmospheric conditions were needed for blood to congeal; time and environmental issues were also mitigating factors. But Finn witnessed firsthand that Tom's blood had started to congeal, to the point of developing that top layer of a drying skim on the pooled blood. Plus, the bodies' lividity revealed that pinkish-red discoloration on the skin from the collective blood vessels settling in the body after death, from the lack of circulation. Granted, Tom's body revealed only the slightest evidence of lividity, but it did show evidence on the lower portions of his back and buttocks, though extraordinarily minor, it did add another undisputable factor for the kid's time of death. Collier said that Tom's body was in the first stage of rigor, which placed his time of death out of the range of their friends' statements, making the time of death a crucial issue for the truth. If Collier hadn't been so buzzed at the scene, he may have been able to take the kid's body temp, which would have been extremely useful. What were the friends hiding? he wondered. Had there been some kind of falling-out, some argument? Did it get ugly enough to escalate to murder? Were two teenagers capable of such a vicious act of violence? Sadly, he knew better: everyone could kill.

The more Finn kicked around the scientific evidence, the more he knew he needed to speak with Tom's high school friends again, only this time face-to-face. He needed to see their reactions when he told them of the autopsy findings, that their story didn't jive with the science. Plus, he thought it was time to show them the gruesome autopsy photos. Maybe that would jar their memory, maybe seeing the aftermath of their handiwork would invoke the truth.

The diner's parking lot's gritty CCTV camera showed Tom and Susanne, along with their friends, exiting the front door of the diner and getting into separate cars at 11:08 p.m. with Tom's Toyota following their friend's car out onto the Jericho Turnpike, then heading east toward Jackson Avenue. Was it possible they somehow had manipulated the parking lot surveillance cameras for a timeline alibi? It wouldn't be the first time something like that had been done. But how they managed it would be another issue.

By now Finn was at a thorough loss, especially since he personally arrived at the scene at 11:45 p.m. The science and witnesses' accounts were contrary to what Finn knew for certain. He had no reason to question the science, but witnesses accounts could be mistaken, or intentionally misleading. He was thinking that an early morning surprise visit from a homicide detective was almost certain to get their young witnesses' juices flowing, more so if you they had something to hide, especially since they were reportedly the last ones to see either victims alive. He'd need to see their faces judge their body language to accurately gauge their demeanor. At this point not only were they the main suspects, but they were his only suspects.

Finn crossed the squad room and stopped at Hughes's open office door, stuck his head halfway in and said, "Hey, boss, I'm heading out on a fresh lead on the Gambrelli case. If you need me, I'll be available on the police radio or my cell."

"OK, great, Finn. I'm glad we had that little chat, but I haven't taken that Highway Patrol transfer off the table yet!" Finn gave Hughes a thumbs-up and a quick smile displaying more of the toothpick tucked in the corner of his mouth, before he headed to his car, at the far end of the parking lot.

Twelve

IT WAS A SUN-FILLED autumn afternoon with a bright blue, cloudless sky. A slight eastern breeze swirled a few fallen leaves across the black asphalt of New York State Route 106 as Finn drove north toward Oyster Bay for a quick drop in at old man Seely's, when he had a quick thought. Since he was heading up that way anyway, he might as well take a short detour along Mill River Road and make an unannounced stop at the Cook estate. He'd been curious to see if the estate's gate cameras had captured the Buckley kid's Toyota passing by and, if so, what time had it passed, and whether it was followed by any other cars.

Nothing could be considered useful information or evidence until it had been corroborated, whether in the form of a statement from an actual witness or an established timeline based on facts. A spontaneous confession from the actual killer or killers was wishful thinking, but he was hopeful to learn something new with an unannounced visit in the morning, and the face-to-face with the victims' friends, which would be the only way to tie together some of these hanging autopsy questions.

Turning his black unmarked Crown Vic, the last in the department's fleet, off Mill River Road, onto the graveled driveway apron of the Cook estate. Finn stopped short of the large wrought-iron gates, noticing an embossed, highly polished brass plaque attached to the decorative metal stanchion on the estate's control keypad. In old English script, it read, *House of Fredrick*. He remembered that back in the day, these large estates didn't have house numbers. The owners preferred to give them names to separate themselves from the commoners. Finn lowered his car window and pushed the weathered black button for "Entrance" fixed on the small keypad. The button was situated right above the rectangular glass biometric pad. A slight echo of electronic static sounded, and a second later he heard a male voice coming from the scratchy speaker. "Yes, can I help you?"

Finn also heard the slow whine of the tubular camera fixed atop the left river-rock column swivel toward him. The lens telescoping outward, presumably to focus on Finn's face. He turned his head back to the keypad and said into the speaker, "Police," as he unclipped his police badge from his belt and held it up for the camera to see. Finn watched the gates open slowly. An aristocratic baritone voice gave short, clear instructions. "Follow the driveway up to the first building on the right, to the gatehouse. Stay in your car; someone will come out to meet you." Then the hollow static sound clicked off, without waiting for a response.

Passing through the opening gates, Finn noticed an impressive-looking family crest affixed to the shiny iron bars; studying the crest, it looked vaguely familiar. He purposely slowed his speed as he followed the winding driveway made of uniform pea-sized bleached white pebbles, which gave off a rolling crunch sound under his slow-moving wheels. Almost a quarter of a mile later, he came upon a small, two-story, white-brick house covered entirely in thick English ivy, from the foundation to the top of the chimney, resembling an old English countryside manor. Finn came to a rolling stop in front of the gatehouse and gazed around the elegant landscape, with its sloping, manicured lawn and meticulously pruned hedges and countless perfectly shaped evergreens trees. An exceptionally large gray limestone fortress of a home stood majestically at the top of rolling inclining grassy knoll, still about another quarter mile away. It resembled a medieval English castle, complete with conical towers at all four corners.

Finn exited his car for a closer look of the magnificent estate, crossing the wide, pebbled driveway for a better view of the main house, when he heard the same male voice from the gate's intercom behind him. "You were told to wait in your car, Detective!" Finn turned around to see a well-dressed man in his mid to late forties walking toward him. He was at least 6-foot-3 and 200 pounds, with a squared, muscular, rugged frame. He was dressed in an expensive dark blue business suit, with expensive looking but very large brown loafers. By the way the guy carried himself, rigidly straight, stiff-legged, with broad shoulders, Finn suspected he was prior military. Maybe even military intelligence, or one of those other clandestine Washington, D.C.–based organizations that no one takes ownership of. His polished bald head accented a large, crooked nose that bore visible signs of past breaks, along with other battle scars on his square-jawed face. Finn's first impression was, he's not a guy who'd go down easy.

"Oh yes, I heard you," Finn replied with an apologetic tone, not really caring what the guy had told him. "I was just getting a better look at that beautiful house up there on the hill." He pointed toward the main house. "You have a beautiful place here; it looks like we could be in the English countryside."

"This is private property, Detective. No one is authorized to wander around the estate."

"Of course. I understand completely," Finn answered. As he studied the stranger for his reactions, sizing him up, Finn extended his hand in a friendly gesture. The guy's bear-paw grip was dry and strong. Finn had never been good at being told what he could do or not do, especially from some stranger.

"What can we do for you today, Detective?"

"I'm investigating an incident that happened late last week, on Saturday night, the twenty-third, in that horse pasture around the corner here on Mill River Road."

"Yes, that pasture is part of Mr. Cook's property. What can I help you with?"

"Mr. Cook's property? Is that who owns this estate?" Finn already knew that from the tax-records database he'd searched earlier.

"Yes, J. Barrington Cook the Fourth. It's been in his family for 238 years."

"Wow, imagine that. And what is your name, sir?" Finn enquired.

"Lawrence Joseph. I manage Mr. Cook's security."

"Great. Just the guy I'm looking for," Finn said. "Then you would have access to those gate cameras out by the road, right?"

"Yes, that would be my responsibility."

"Are they on DVRs?"

"Yes, they are. What are you looking for, Detective?"

"I'd like to view your DVRs for any activity from last Saturday the twenty-third, say, between 11:30 p.m. and 11:45 p.m."

"Sorry, Detective, you can't. But if you'll just wait in your car this time," Joseph stated in a scolding tone, "I'll see if there is anything captured on the gate cameras for that time period."

"Sure, I'll just wait right here in the car," Finn answered. Taking a quick read of Joseph's cocky, suspicious demeanor, or maybe it was just his way of protecting a $30 million dollar estate. Returning to his car, Finn watched Joseph disappear into the gatehouse.

Finn immediately opened and closed his car door with a loud thud. Once Joseph disappeared into the gatehouse, Finn waited a few seconds before he followed Joseph's footsteps through the unlocked door. The interior of the gatehouse wasn't anything he'd imagined. It was more of an elegant vacation cottage, much grander than it appeared from the outside, and impressively furnished. Finn stood in the narrow vestibule, looking into the large open living room, with its coffee-colored tile floors and dark English wainscoting. The walls were lined with eighteenth-century tapestries. A large wood-burning fireplace highlighted the outside wall to his left, along with a matching dark oak staircase leading to a second-floor loft at the end of the 40-foot living room, which had a vaulted ceiling nearly as high.

He hadn't taken but a few short steps past the vestibule and into the open living room when he heard muffled voices coming from behind him, from inside a room past a partly closed door to his right. Wondering if he had activated any sensors—believing he surely had, but he didn't care—he moved closer to the wainscoted wall and the half-open door, recognizing Joseph's commanding voice mixing with another male voice.

Peering through the vertical crack created by the door's hinges into the estate's elaborate security control room, he recognized

Joseph's back, and saw another male, an inch or two shorter, wearing a subdued military style uniform complete with an exposed automatic sidearm with three extra clips of ammo on a black equipment belt. They were bent over in front of one of the eight large plasma-screen monitors that displayed various locations around the estate. He could also make out the telltale bulge of a firearm hidden beneath Joseph's suit coat. Its positioned confirmed what Finn had guessed earlier that Joseph was left-handed. Finn had suspected Joseph was armed when he first saw him walking toward him from the gatehouse, though he couldn't see a gun. The immediate unbuttoning of his coat and the less flowy left flap of the suit told him this guy was preparing himself for the unknown.

Four of the closest monitors contained multiple split-screen interior images of what Finn thought could only be of the main house up on the hill. There were thirty camera views, maybe more. He could also make out a bank of DVRs against the farthest wall, alongside a shelf that held a series of satellite phones resting in their chargers. A loud squelching sound from the estate's patrol radios came through the desktop receiver in front of the monitors. Garbled voices of the estate's roving security were communicating with each other. Finn faintly recognized a female 911 police dispatcher's voice coming from a police scanner somewhere in the background of the control room. Finn had the sneaking suspicion that Joseph and his crew weren't really friends of the police. There was a mechanical joystick sticking up from a small control box sitting next to the security patrol's base station radio transmitter that he suspected was used to manually control all the cameras' microwave PTZ's.

Finn had seen this exact style of high-tech security equipment, though on a much grander scale, a few years earlier when he was with a consortium of homicide detectives selected from around the country to testify before Congress on the real issues behind the rising homicide rate in the country. He'd been personally invited by a Special Agent of the Diplomatic Security Force to tour the U.S. Department of State building, specifically their main control room, which was located on a secret subterranean floor within the Harry S. Truman Federal Building on C Street Northwest. The State Department's global command control center was second to none in security and detection, and massive in size compared to Joseph's backroom security, but oddly similar in their arrangement of high-tech cameras and their overall protection monitoring capabilities.

From what Finn could see, Joseph's control-room operators had the ability to pan, tilt, and zoom any camera within the system from the simple joystick. Functions that would occur automatically if a camera detected an unauthorized breach, alerting and sending a series of signals and commands for specific functions within the system. If it were modeled anywhere near to that of the U.S. State Department's system, it was apt to include illuminating any breached area of the property with high-density LED floodlights when activated by an intruder's body heat or motions along with the immediate identification of the intruder based upon a multiple-sourced face-recognition database.

He wanted to see more, he wanted to be invited for a tour of the estate, especially the control room. But he knew that wasn't going to happen. He'd immediately sensed the adversarial barrier between Joseph and himself, a feeling of who was the good guy and who was the bad guy. Plus, there was that cold feeling that came after he identified himself as police through the gate's intercom. Joseph hadn't even asked him about the nature of the incident he was investigating, and, why hadn't Joseph's security patrol responded to the horse pasture that night?

Finn's attention was engrossed in eyeing the high-tech control room, when he heard Joseph tell the other security guy, "Yes, that's it, that one. I'll just give the nosy cop that one. Print it out."

Finn quickly backed away from the door and stood off to the side of the control room's entrance. When Joseph emerged from the room, he stopped, calmly gazing at Finn. "I see you can't follow instructions too well, Detective."

"Sorry, I just wanted to save you some time and a trip back out to my car. That's all," Finn said.

"Well, this is all we have, Detective. It isn't clear because it's a fast-moving image captured on a stationary infrared night lens. They tend to be very grainy at best," Joseph said with a smirk as he handed Finn the copy of the image containing the date *9-23-2018* with numbers *2330* captured in red at the bottom right-hand corner of the copy, military time for 11:30 p.m.

As Joseph was continuing with his hollow apology, Finn happened to glance over Joseph's shoulder and noticed across the room, above the fireplace, hung a much larger, more detailed coat of arms, identical to the smaller one attached to the entrance gate. This one seemed to hold a very prominent position in the stately eighteenth-century room furnishings. The rampant lion at the left of the family crest was awfully familiar; less so was the rearing horse at the right. But the lion was identical to the one on the crest of the *House of Nassau*, which was the present-day seal of

Nassau County, New York. It was also proudly displayed on the shoulder patch worn by all uniformed personnel within the police department. The same rampant lion symbol was also embossed on every police badge in the county police department.

Below the coat of arms hung a sword, fixed at an odd angle. Narrowing his stare, Finn focused harder, realizing a matching sword should have hung at the opposite angle, in a crossed-sword display. He turned his attention back to the photo printout and said, "You're right. This isn't very clear." Though he could still make out it was the Buckley's' car but didn't let on.

Joseph said, "That's the only image of a car passing the gate that night around that time, Detective. There was an earlier one, but that was at 10:45 p.m. The next one wasn't until about 11:57 p.m. That was an ambulance." Having noticed Finn looking over his shoulder, he turned to see what drew his attention. "It's a handsome-looking coat of arms, isn't it, Detective? It belongs to the *House of Fredrick*."

"House of Fredrick?" Finn replied.

"Yes, Detective. But you may be more familiar with the name King George III."

"Yeah, not really," Finn said as he continued to inspect the grainy image. "I know the name. I'm just not into history, that's all."

"That's too bad. A lot can be learned from history," Joseph said. "Fredrick is the family name of the English monarch of King George III," Joseph volunteered smugly, before adding, "Well, I would love to stay and chat with you more, but if that will be all, I have to get back to work, Detective."

"One other thing, Mr. Joseph: do you have cameras covering the horse pasture?" Finn said as he moved across the room for a closer look at the coat of arms and the one sword.

"Uh no, sorry. We don't."

Finn stopped and turned back to face Joseph. "But isn't the entrance for the horse paddock accessible from the pasture? Wouldn't that be a security vulnerability? I mean, couldn't someone gain entrance onto the estate by sneaking up through the pasture, then passing through the paddock gate?"

"No, Detective, that would be completely impossible. This property is patrolled by armed security 24/7, supplemented with live monitored cameras. We also have military-grade IDS throughout the perimeter." Joseph's mouth curled in a sly smirk.

"IDS?" Finn submitted with a raised brow.

"Intrusion detection system, Detective," Joseph replied. "We have motion and heat sensors established throughout the property, and strategically buried sensors throughout the estate's grounds that are weight and vibration activated, which enhances the military-grade, forward-looking infrared radiation system. Which you may know as a FLIR. Upon activation, it's capable of illuminating any compromised area. It's a passive thermal imaging system as well. So, you see, Detective, no one can penetrate our perimeter."

"That's very impressive!" Finn said in an enthralled tone, like an inquisitive child. "Oh, by the way, Mr. Joseph, who repairs your horse fence when a car crashes through it?" He added turning back to the coat of arms and the missing sword.

"That would be the Oyster Bay Fence Company. They have standing orders to repair all the fences on the grounds. This includes anytime a car should crash through it—which, by the way, Detective, occurs quite often on that dangerous curve. Anything else?"

"Yes. Did you know you have a missing sword, Mr. Joseph?" Finn stated, pointing toward the fireplace as he crossed the room.

"You're very observant, Detective," Joseph said tightly. "The house cleaner must have taken it down to polish it."

"What kind of swords are they?" Finn asked, standing on the large stone hearth, reaching up, running his index finger across one of the sword's double blades to feel the sharpness.

"They're called spadroons, they'd British military thrusting swords made in 1780. Now, if there are no further questions, I must get back to work," Joseph said, turning toward the vestibule door.

"Wow, that's sharp. You could shave with this sword!" Finn said as he stepped off the stone hearth and put his index finger into his mouth to suck at the blood from the razor-sharp cut.

"Please turn your car around right here in the driveway, Detective. I'll have someone from security escort you to the gate." Joseph held the gatehouse door open for Finn.

"Mr. Joseph, where's the horses? It didn't look like there had been any horses in the field the other night."

"All Mr. Cook's horses are currently in Argentina at his ranch. They are only here during certain seasons of the year, and they aren't scheduled to return for another month or so. Is there anything more, Detective?"

"No, no thank you. You've been very helpful, Mr. Joseph."

"I must say, Detective, I find the police so professionally naïve when it comes to physical security." Joseph shook his head in amazement. "You didn't know you have been under constant surveillance from the time you drove into our driveway, even while you listened at the security control room door." He added with a sneer, "You activated the interior IDS when you entered the gatehouse behind me." He shot Finn an insolent grin as he closed the gatehouse door behind him.

Finn had the oddest feeling that Joseph had just challenged him in some way. Finn liked challenges.

Thirteen

A SLIGHT GRIN OF satisfaction crossed Finn's face as he was unceremoniously escorted to the entrance gate by two of Joseph's uniformed security detail, who shadowed him down the winding, white-pebbled driveway on their heavily armed, camouflage, four-wheel ATVs. The wrought-iron gates swung closed. In the rearview mirror, Finn could see the family crest and the shiny brass plaque with *House of Fredrick* emblazoned on it.

Turning left, back onto Mill River Road, he headed toward the village of Oyster Bay, as he thought of another important aspect of detective work, knowing how to read, and treat, a suspected foe, what he considered investigative diplomacy. The unannounced visit to the *House of Fredrick* went relatively well, he thought, especially the revelation of that missing spadroon. Was it the murder weapon? Was Lawrence Joseph prior military? Or had he possibly been part of some secret government contractor's covert operational unit, before turning to the private security sector? But why, he wondered, would a filthy rich guy like J. Barrington Cook the Fourth need someone of Lawrence Joseph's caliber to open and close a big wrought-iron gate? Unless, of course, maybe J. Barrington Cook the Fourth was more than just filthy rich. Maybe he was also filthy dirty?

The thought of him and Joseph sharing an equal zone of adversarial energy was evident, like two warriors meeting for the very first time on the field of battle, exchanging pleasantries before the inevitable contest. Saber rattling without the show of weapons. What Joseph offered up in the form of a grainy infrared camera image gave Finn the strong suspicion that Joseph was holding back on much more. Finn had the impression that the last thing Joseph needed or wanted was some detective poking his nose around in the affairs at the *House of Fredrick*, especially their security system. He needed to find out how this factored into the kid's murder and wondered if the *House of Fredrick* was harboring its own secrets.

Where did J. Barrington Cook's money come from? Had the Cook lineage managed their money so well that after 238 years they were still living larger than anyone else on the North Shore of Long Island? Although he'd been feeling like he was stumbling through this investigation like a blind drunk in a snowstorm, he was slowly beginning to pick the pesty little ticks off the dog. He had two teenagers who'd been killed in a car accident, in a car that hadn't been in an accident, that had passed a wealthy private estate at exactly 11:31 p.m., seemingly without being followed, and a less than friendly estate security manager, who never even bothered to ask him what he was investigating, or from what detective squad he was from. Then there was that missing antique military thrusting sword, a British one at that. But what he didn't have was any witnesses, or motive, or physical evidence, other than maybe a tiny piece of a metal tip from an eighteenth-century British military bayonet. Besides, he wondered, who takes down just one sword to clean two swords? "Try telling that to Hughes," Finn said out loud as he slowed his car near the road's curve and his old crime scene.

Finn had to do a double take. The horse fence had been repaired, the inkberry holly shrubs had been replaced, and the grass along the road's edge was not even in need of a mowing. The crime scene had returned to its former placid landscape. Giving Finn thought to the few passing cars or anyone out walking along the road, who'd have never known what brutal killings occurred in this picturesque horse field just eight days earlier.

Continuing into Oyster Bay for his quick, unannounced drop-in at Ebenezer Seely's house, Finn reluctantly fingered his contact list in his cell phone, until he landed on the one that made him hesitate. He didn't need this reminder of his past. Giving a heavy sigh before pushing the toothpick hard into the corner of his mouth with his tongue then hitting the Call button. After the fourth ring, he was ready to hang up and lie to himself that he tried. He had no intention of leaving a message on the voice mail. He could live with that, what he couldn't live with was the thought of an unturned rock he'd neglected to look under. Finn had his thumb over the red End Call button when a male voice answered.

"Oyster Bay Fence Company. How may I help you?"

Finn took a deep breath, and in a fabricated joyful tone said, "Hey, Tater!"

"Hey, Finn, old boy. Where've you been?"

"How'd you know it was me?"

"Because you're the only one who still calls me Tater," he answered with a slight hint of annoyance.

"Sorry," Finn answered.

"No problem, Finn, I don't really mind. It's all part of our past, and we can't erase it, can we?"

"No, I guess we can't," Finn said.

"Anyway, you know I've been calling you, and I've left a ton of messages for you, both at the Homicide Squad and on your personal cell phone. I've left at least twenty messages for you over the past couple years. Never heard a word back from you. Always calling to say hello, nothing more, just to see how you're doing. I saw you on the news last month, at police headquarters, doing your perp walk for the news cameras. You look good."

"Yeah, I'm doing good. How about you?"

"I'm doing just great. Judy and I had our third child—finally, a boy!" He laughed. "Life is great, Finn. Did you ever get married?"

"No, not yet," Finn answered with a forced chuckle.

"Don't wait too long, buddy. Life was meant to be shared. You'll love it, and you'll never have to be alone again, especially with kids."

"Yeah, I hear ya," Finn said.

"So, to what do I owe this honor of you finally calling me?" Tater said, laughing.

Finn's bunk was next to Tater's on the second floor of Saint Xavier's for better than ten years. Tater was a year younger than Finn, an only child, with no living family or relatives. When Tater was only seven, his father had been killed in a freak military training accident at Fort Benning, when his parachute malfunctioned. About a year later, his mother was killed by a westbound Long Island Railroad express train passing through the Mineola train station. Though some said it wasn't an accident, no witnesses came forward, and Tater was ultimately sent to Saint Xavier's.

It wasn't until much later that Finn realized all the boys at Saint Xavier's were the sons of deceased US military personnel, from all five of the branches. Which left him wondering who he was, where he fit into that scenario, who was his military father, if he was part of that pattern.

He remembered Father Dom assigning Tater a job in the kitchen, peeling potatoes. His sole job was peeling potatoes all day long for all three of the day's meals, with the other boys giving him the apropos name acquired by his kitchen skills. Tater was larger than most kids his age, with squat legs, a full torso, a ball-round face, and a chin that blended evenly into his thick neck. He wore oversized, dark-framed glasses that magnified his beady little eyes. Later, Father Dom got him a job with the Oyster Bay Fence Company while he was in high school. He never left, he even bought the company from the owner after he retired.

"Do you have an occasion to do any fence work up at the Cook estate on Mill River Road?" Finn finally asked.

"Yeah, that's one of my accounts. Why do you ask?"

"I was just wondering, when was the last time you were there?"

"Finn, if you're asking me something about one of my clients, it's because someone's in trouble," Tater said in a doubtful tone.

"Nah, I'm just looking to confirm the replacement of a section of fence up there a few days ago, that's all." Finn didn't like sharing details of active investigations with anyone, sometimes not even fellow cops.

"OK. Whatever you say. But I know you, Finn, like no one else knows you. You don't go around asking questions for nothing. You never have. There's always some reason behind it, and it's usually not good for someone."

Finn was somewhat surprised to learn that Tater had hung on to the fence company. Knowing that it was physically demanding work, Tater had always seemed a little lazy, the kind of guy who liked to take the easy road, anything for a quick buck. And he had a talent for blaming other people if faced with a problem.

"Well, there is something, but I can't tell you everything, not yet anyway," Finn said.

"We'll leave that for another time. At least I know you're still alive and well. But, yes, I replaced a small section of their wooden horse fence closest to the roadway a few days ago. It was a quick repair job, looked like a car had run through it."

"How did you know to make the repair? Were you called, or did you just happen to drive by there?"

"Butch called me, but the estate owner has had a long-standing account with the Oyster Bay Fence Company since before I've owned it. But I always get a phone call for any repairs. Now that you mention it, it was a little odd when Butch called, asking me to come by and fix the section of fence at the curve in the road because a car had crashed through it. He called my cell, and I didn't tell him that I was on Mill River Road when he called; I was giving an estimate at another estate when I got his call. Well, anyway, as I drove along Mill River Road alongside his property, I didn't see any broken fence or even a damaged fence, especially where a car had gone through it. I didn't think much of it at the time, I just figured he meant another section of fence where I couldn't see it. So, on Monday, me and Lucas go up to the estate, and sure enough there's a broken fence section by the curve on Mill River Road, where a car must have gone through it."

"Who's Butch?"

"That's Lawrence Joseph!" Tater said in a surprised tone "Oh, you don't remember him, do you? We were so young. He's an X!"

Finn hadn't heard that term in many years. The boys from Saint Xavier's referred to themselves as X's. Most didn't like the term *alumni*, especially when associated with a boys' home. Besides, most of the people in Oyster Bay always called them the X-boys.

"He's an X?" Finn said.

"Yeah, don't you remember hearing about him? He's much older than us, by ten to fifteen years. Remember some of those stories about the guy named Butch?"

"Ah, vaguely. I do remember some stories about a guy named Butch from Saint Xavier's, but wasn't that name short for Butcher, like in *butchering*, like in killing?"

"Yep, that's him."

"Yeah, I do remember some stories." The more Tater talked; the more Finn remembered his past with Tater at Saint Xavier's. Tater had a bad habit of embellishing events, especially if it put someone in bad light. Remembering it was wise to believe little of what could be seen, and nothing of what Tater said about anyone.

"Yeah, he liked to kill small animals that wandered too close to the hill. That's where he got the name. There's also some legend of him biting the head off a live snake once."

"He likes to kill things?" Finn asked, thinking maybe Butch has moved up the food chain with his bad habits.

"Yep, or so he did, not sure if he still does though."

"How long has he been head of security at the Cook estate?"

"Oh, he's always been up there, doing one thing or another. He started working on the estate part time when he was still at Saint Xavier's, after school. Father Dom got him the job. Then he moved over there when he was eighteen, when he had to leave Saint

Xavier's. But he did disappear for a few years, resurfacing back at the estate a couple years ago."

"How do you know all this, Tater?"

"From Father Dom. He used to stop by the shop here once in a while and we'd talk. We even talked about you; you were always his favorite, Finn." Tater laughed. "Father Dom also used to visit with Butch up at the estate."

"He did?" Finn said, bewildered.

"Yeah, in fact, that's where Father Dom died. He was up visiting with Butch at the estate the day he had his fatal heart attack. You weren't around for some reason."

"Yeah." It was all Finn could say. He hadn't learned of Father Dom's death until a year after he was gone. Another X had gotten himself involved in some financial fraud and was arrested. Finn saw him in court one day, and he asked Finn if he'd heard that Father Dom had passed. The X had said he hadn't made it to the funeral himself, nor was he even sure there was a funeral, and he didn't know where Father Dom had been buried. A true X, Finn thought, knew little but talked a lot. Finn had always meant to learn which cemetery he'd been buried in, but that would take a lot of toothpicks, and he wasn't quite ready for that.

"Hey, Tater, do you know if they ever did an autopsy on Father Dom when he died?" The thought of Father Dom having a sudden fatal heart attack up at the Cook estate, in the presence of a guy like Butch, seemed a little concerning. But then, Finn was skeptical of just about everything and everybody anyway, and probably would have been even if he'd witnessed Father Dom's fatal heart attack himself.

"Nope, we were pretty lucky. Butch knew a doctor who signed the death certificate, so they didn't need to cut him open. In fact, I don't think the police were even called. The Whispering Pines Funeral Home picked up Father Dom's body from the estate and they made all the necessary arrangements."

"Is Father Dom buried in Locust Valley?" Finn asked.

"Uh, no Finn." Tater hesitated. "He was cremated."

"Cremated?"

"Yeah, that's what his family wanted," Tater said, then added, "Butch paid for everything. He really liked Father Dom."

"Yeah, that was big of him," Finn responded. "Tater, which day did Butch call you to repair that fence?" Finn asked, sidestepping Father Dom's death and funeral.

"Oh, let me think a minute." Tater went silent as he thought about Finn's question. "It was Friday! Friday afternoon around three or so. I can check my phone for the exact time and get back to you if you want?"

"No need for that, Tater, as long as you remember that it was Friday. Friday the twenty-second, right?"

"Yep, it was definitely Friday the twenty-second. That I know for sure because I only do estimates on Fridays."

"Thanks, Tater!" Finn said with a friendly appreciation, knowing Tater had just lied to him again.

"Hey, Finn, when we getting together? A couple of the X's that are still on the island keep asking about you. They all want to get together for dinner and some drinks, kick around old times."

The mere thought of kicking around old times with guys from Saint Xavier's sent the pulp stuck in Finn's mouth into a frenzy.

"Ah, yeah Tater. When I finish up with this case, I'll get back to you," he lied.

"Well, don't make it so long this time. I want you to meet the family."

"Absolutely. I can't wait to see them," Finn lied again, and thumbed the red End Call button on his phone.

Finn was generally happy for any of his fellow brothers from Saint Xavier's who somehow managed to break out of that dark, hopeless life of never having any real family, of being stuck in some lonesome Jesuit boys' home, only to later end up in a world full of heartache and evil. Even though he was happy for them, he didn't care to witness their happiness, because then he'd be forced to see his own lack of happiness. He didn't need anyone reminding him of that. He lived with it every day.

Making a rolling stop, Finn approached the end of Mill River Road at Lexington Avenue, then made a right turn passing Orchard Street, where Susanne White had lived with her family. He continued a short distance before making the next left onto Simcoe Street and following it to the top of the hill, to the street's end.

Older single-family, two-story homes lined both sides of Simcoe Street, the second of the four hills of Oyster Bay. Simcoe Street dead-ended at the top of the hill directly in front of the only house that occupied a postage stamp–sized plot of land. As there was barely enough room in the street to turn his car around, Finn decided to park head-in at the curb-less edge of the crumbling asphalt, facing directly into the front of the small, aging, two-story English Tudor.

Before exiting his car, he picked up his cell phone and dialed the Electronics Squad at headquarters. The detective who answered was one of those old-timers with more knowledge and tricks up his sleeve than a three-card monte dealer on the streets of New York City, someone who could get you anything you needed when it came to surveillance or intelligence—if he liked you. Detective Elmer Rhoads was the father of a beautiful teenage daughter who had been abducted a couple years earlier on her way home from school by two sex traffickers who poached innocent young girls right off the busy streets, then sold them to the highest bidder from a long list of buyers.

The sex-trafficking kidnappers had the misfortune of running into Finn before they could flee the state with their newly acquired booty. What had started out as a sunny, pleasant spring afternoon on a residential, tree-lined street in a South Shore community was broken when an observant senior citizen heard a young girl's screams for help and called 911. The responding officers, however, were too late. The abductors had overpowered their victim and were getting away with their catch. Finn happened to be driving nearby and overheard the police radio transmissions of the responding units, so he decided to assist the uniformed officers. Only a few blocks away from the location of the abduction, he noticed a van fitting the description of the suspect's vehicle driving in an erratic manner at a high rate of speed in the opposite direction. Turning his car around he followed the suspect's vehicle at a safe distance until the suspects seemed confident, they were no longer being pursued by the police. He tailed the suspects into the cookie-cutter housing development of the Levittown section of the county, where he observed them park their van in the driveway of their stash house.

Finn continued past the house, parking his car a few houses down the street, and sat on the suspect's stash house for a few minutes, eyeing the two abductors carrying the bound-and-hooded girl into the house through the driveway's side entrance door of the house. Keeping the house in view through his driver's side door mirror, he didn't bother calling for backup, just readied himself.

Removing his service weapon from its holster, he double-checked the ease of the slide, and rechecked the chambered round. He double-checked the clip, satisfied it held its full fifteen-round capacity, before taking another two fully loaded .40 mm spare clips from the glove box of the car, tucking them into his left-side suit jacket pocket. He replaced his soggy toothpick with a fresh one, exited the car, and proceeded to walk calmly down the sidewalk to the side door of the suspect's stash house. After kicking in the side door by the driveway, he quickly disappeared into the interior of the house, calmly announcing, "Police! Don't anyone move!"

Neighbors would later say they heard a short, rapid burst of gunfire, then an eerie quiet, then another series of rapid gunfire. Then it got quiet again, followed by a loud finale of gunfire from inside the house. When the gunfire subsided, witnesses saw Finn emerge from the front door of the house, politely holding the door open with one hand, clutching his weapon in his other hand. As the abducted Rhoads girl and two other girls who had been abducted earlier in the day filed past him, down the walkway to the curb. Horrified residents of the tranquil neighborhood later recounted that Finn led the kidnapped girls nonchalantly down the middle of the tree-lined street to his waiting car, where they calmly got into the car and drove away.

Any other detective would have waited for backup. Not Finn, he immediately drove the traumatized girls to the County Medical Center, after they'd called their families from his phone. While the responding uniformed officers found the bullet-riddled bodies of three dead sex-traffickers scattered in different locations throughout the stash house.

Detective Elmer "Dusty" Rhoads had more connections in the cyber world than almost anyone assigned to the National Security Agency. It was even rumored that he had a few secret access codes for some top-secret military satellites.

"Hey, Dusty, how've you been?"

"Finn, where the hell have you been?" Dusty asked like he was annoyed. "We've missed you at the house. Zoe's coming home next weekend from school, and she specifically asked me to call you and insist that you come for dinner on Sunday!"

"Sure, I'd love to see her again. And I'd love to stay for dinner too," Finn lied. He never understood why people needed to create some lasting bond, just because he did his job. "So, how's Zoe making out, Dusty?"

"Oh, she's hanging in there, Finn. Still has some underlying emotional effects. Guess that will take her some time to put it all behind her, if ever. We don't know how we could have managed without you, Finn. We owe you everything," Dusty said, starting to choke up with emotion.

"You guys don't owe me a thing," Finn said, stopping Dusty short. "But I would like a favor if you don't mind? Could you reach into your bag of surveillance tricks and run a name through your magic databases for me?"

"Sure, anything for you. How can I help?"

"Dusty, I need a comprehensive workup on a guy named Riley Russet: his pedigree, emails, social media accounts. See if he has any communications with gamblers, hookers, drug dealers, or any known seedy characters. Plus, I have two cell phones I need dumped, everything from their SIM cards. All calls, texts, and GPS tracking, starting from the thirteenth of the month, until today. Thinking ten days prior to the discovery of the bodies, until now should be enough time to establish if there were any murderous conclusion between them. I'll also need any calls or texts to be referenced from cell tower locations, specifically on the afternoon of Friday the 22nd. I need the works—everything you got, the whole enchilada."

"That's all?" Dusty laughed.

"Oh yeah, and one other thing: do you think you could somehow get into one of your secret satellites and see if they captured any activity on a private horse pasture up in Oyster Bay, the one on Mill River Road? You can't miss it; it's the only piece of open land with a giant tree stuck right in the middle of it on Mill River Road, next to the first curve, just south of the pond. For the night of Saturday, September 23, between 11:30 p.m. and 11:45 p.m.?"

"What are you looking for, Finn?"

"Anything. Any activity in or around that horse pasture on Mill River Road during that time frame."

"Yeah, I should be able to capture something for you during that time if there's anything to capture. But you do know that any images I get will be military-grade satellite images. You can't use them for prosecution. In other words, they don't exist," Dusty warned.

"I'm well aware of that," Finn acknowledged. "I'm just trying to establish the players in this case for now" he added.

"Anything else?" Dusty asked.

"No, that's it," Finn laughed. "For now, anyway."

"I think I know what you need, Finn. How much time do I have?"

"Well, that's another thing, Dusty. I need it all right away, like yesterday. Sorry for the short notice. I'm going to be doing a couple unannounced witness interviews first thing in the morning, allegedly good friends of my victims. I'm not sure where they fit into this, and I want to be prepared."

"No problem. I'll get right on it."

"Great, thanks. Oh and Dusty, if I don't answer my phone, just leave me a voice mail, or email me the results; don't call the squad with any of the information. And one final thing: don't let anyone else know about this, OK?"

"Got it, and I'm on it. Don't forget next Sunday, say around 3:00 p.m.?"

"Thanks, Dusty. I'll be there." Finn ended the call, then checked his watch. It was 4:30 p.m. He had to make his visit with Ebenezer Seely as quick as possible if he was going to make it to Karl's celebration dinner in Glen Cove.

Replacing his gnawed toothpick, Finn studied the dilapidated house in front of him, reminding himself what Langdon had told him about the old man who lived in the only house at the top of Simcoe Street. Getting out of the car he noticed there was no house number or mailbox. The front yard was nothing more than a mass of dying, waist-high weeds that swayed freely back and forth in the afternoon breeze, just beyond a knee-high rusted iron fence. Two double-hung windows faced the street. It didn't appear they'd been washed in years. The window treatments were a set of thinning, sun-bleached sheer curtains streaked with rust-colored stains from years of heavy condensation on the interior panes of the glass. He wondered if anyone could even live in this house.

With little effort, he pushed open the rusted, decorative gate and followed the half-hidden weeded path up to the faded yellow stucco siding that was cracked and peeling.

Curiosity quickly crossed over into suspicion. If Langdon was correct with his directions, this house appeared abandoned. The shrubs below the dirty windows on both sides of the small wooden front door were dried and dying, or dead. He stood to the side of the door and pulled back on a heavily rusted iron door knocker shaped like a small eagle in flight. As he let it fall forward in a loud thud, the unlocked door moved open a few inches. Cautiously, he removed his service weapon from the holster and waited a couple of seconds before pushing the door completely open with his left foot. "Police!" he yelled into the darken house. Straddling the door's open threshold, the only light streaming into the narrow hallway came from the open door behind him, Finn's eyes darted quickly to the top of an old oak staircase to his right, then back down to the long, lightless, narrow hallway directly in front of him. "Police!" he called out again into the blackened house. His service weapon pushed out in front of him, he crossed the threshold and entered the darkened hall. His toothpick wrestling with a nervous tongue. Three steps in, he heard a brittle voice call out from somewhere down the hall, from the rear of the house, on the first floor.

"Yes, yes, come in, Detective. Back here, please. Just follow the hallway," the voice instructed.

Finn hesitated, lowering his service weapon toward the floor in front of him, wondering why he hadn't brought his flashlight with him. He could tell by the crackle of the voice that it was an older male. The strong odor of wood smoke filled the hallway as he made his way deeper into the house.

"In here, Detective, the first door to your left," the voice instructed.

Silently he slowly moved down the lightless hallway, closer toward the voice. At the first open doorway on the left, he could see the dancing shadows of flickering flames from a fireplace against the hallway wall, opposite the door. He approached the door unhurriedly, with his finger on the trigger of his service weapon. Taking a quick glance inside the open room, his body shielded by the interior wall of the doorjamb. The interior of the room was only a little lighter than the hallway. Finn could make out the backs of two dark-colored, leather-upholstered wingback armchairs in front of a large, well-lit fireplace that covered the outside wall in the windowless room.

"Come in, Detective. I've been expecting you."

"Ebenezer Seely?" Finn asked as he eyed the top of a small, bald head in the chair farthest from him.

"Yes, that's me, Detective. You can put your gun away now. You won't be needing it here, not right now anyway. Come in and sit," he said with a slight chuckle.

Holstering his service weapon beneath his suit coat, he entered the room slowly, scanning its interior. He noticed the only light in the room came from the unsteady glow of the flickering fire. Finn sensed something different about the old man's voice, a slight accent or possibly a lisp, maybe both. He also noticed the old man hadn't moved his head when he spoke, keeping a stiff stare focused on the fire.

Stepping into the quiet room, Finn immediately felt the comforting warmth from the fireplace. Two of the walls were covered with built-in, floor-to-ceiling mahogany bookshelves that were jam-packed with dusty old books in a variety of thicknesses. The wall behind the door held portraits from another time, some painted, others hand sketched, including a couple silhouetted portraits facing each other encased in wooden frames. Above the fireplace hung a long-barreled flintlock rifle, and above the rifle hung a large, dusty, gilded-framed painting, a profile portrait of George Washington in his commander in chief military uniform, kneeling in prayer next to his white horse. Finn slowly made his way deeper into the dimly lit room, eyeing the elderly figure seated in the leather armchair, whose gaze was fixed on the flickering flames of the fire.

Fourteen

THE OLD MAN WAS small framed and starvingly thin, and short, maybe only five feet tall, his toes barely touching the floor. He was dressed in an oversized, long-sleeved puffy white linen shirt, with dark trousers that stopped just below the kneecaps. Sheer off-white stockings continued where his trousers ended, flowing into a pair of uncomfortable-looking boxy black leather shoes with wide silver buckles on the face of them. Finn quietly moved closer to the chair, bending forward for a better look. The man's ashen cheeks were laced with deep, crisscrossed wrinkles. Jowls sagged below the jawline like melted wax. His lips were full, though discolored with a hint of purple, and tightly squeezed together, creating a sunburst of wrinkles around his small mouth. A small portion of his bottom lip hung slightly open at the right corner, forcing him to occasionally slurp back drool. He had a high forehead, and at the top of his dry, flaking scalp were a few runaway strands of long white hair.

Finn moved closer until he had positioned himself directly in front of the old man's chair. The static figure hadn't moved since he'd entered the room. There was just enough light from the fire for Finn to study the old man's glassy, clouded eyes, partly concealed by the drooping skin of his aged eyelids above a small, wrinkled nose. Finn could feel the old man's body heat mixing with shallow breath against his face, as he studied him closer.

Suddenly startled by the abrupt, butter-smooth voice of the motionless figure in the chair. "Satisfied, Detective?"

Flinching backward, Finn stood upright. The fire snapped and popped loudly behind him. Finn felt somewhat embarrassed for invading the old man's personal space.

"Yes, Detective. Your suspicions are correct. I'm blind. But not to worry. Please have a seat." The old man chuckled as he lightly tapped a metal-tipped cane against the floor with satisfaction. The wooden cane rested unseen against his chair, gripped firmly in his right hand by the solid silver decorative eagle's head.

Finn moved cautiously backwards toward the other worn leather armchair facing the fire while continuing to gaze around the dimly lit room. Most, if not all, of the books were incredibly old and covered in thick layers of dust. Some titles on the bindings were faded, while others were completely worn off. He'd thought it had been a long time since the old man had read any of them, for obvious reasons. The room was tight, compact, with only four pieces of furniture: two leather armchairs separated by a long-legged, dark wooden table caked with dust. The smell of wood smoke, old pipe tobacco, and mustiness filled the room. Finn was surprised how antique everything appeared, even old man Seely seemed antique, he thought, as he stole another quick glance at him, before taking a seat in the other leather armchair.

Finn started. "I'm Detective ...." but was quickly cut off mid-sentence by the old man.

"Yes, yes. I know who you are, Detective. Like I said, I've been expecting you."

"You've been expecting me? Did Langdon call you?"

"No, Detective," Seely answered without returning his look.

"So, how could you have been expecting me, Mr. Seely?" Finn asked.

"You're investigating a double murder, aren't you?"

"Yes, that's correct. But how would you know that?" Finn said. With a half turn of his body he peered at the old man again.

"Because I know who the killers are, Detective!" Seely said confidently, still staring blankly at the fire.

"Killers?"

"Yes. Aren't you investigating a series of murders, Detective?"

"A series of murders?" Finn repeated suspiciously as he kept his eyes fixed on old man Seely's face.

"Yes. The toll is up to fourteen, by my count."

"Fourteen?"

The old man countered with certainty, "However, therein lies your problem."

"My problem?" Finn asked.

"Oh yes. I do apologize, Detective. I forgot you are not familiar with the Simcoe malediction."

"Malediction?" Finn laughed halfheartedly. "Are you saying there are fourteen deaths, fourteen by your count, not mine, due to some magic spell?"

"I'm not sure *spell* is the correct word. Maybe *curse* would be better, or even *incantation*. But no, those aren't any good either," Seely said with commitment. "Let's just call it what it is: a malediction."

"Malediction, spell, curse, incantation. What's the difference?"

"There's a huge difference, Detective. A malediction is an utterance of condemnation. It's a declaration of malice toward another person or persons. And it carries with it the absolute infliction of death."

"Isn't that the same as a curse?" Finn said in a questionable tone.

"Ah, but for a malediction to cause its perpetual infliction of evil and death, it must be uttered in vain by someone who has wickedness streaming through their veins, whose actions are premeditated and utterly immoral."

"Sorry, I don't believe in ghost stories," Finn said.

"Ah, but you do believe in facts. Correct, Detective?"

"Of course. But only actual facts!"

"But of course, you do Detective! Then you will be glad to know that a malediction inflicted upon the innocent, uttered by the immoral, can only be prevented by someone who was born on American soil, and who is the last living male in the direct male bloodline of the person who was the original cause for that uttered evil malediction. And that, Detective, is fact!"

Being that sort of investigator who had little tolerance for bullshit, even if it came from some smooth-talking, blind old man who lived on the top of a hill in a run-down dilapidated eighteenth-century house, Finn had a feeling he was being played. He'd never listed to old wives' tales or folklore, nor could he understand those who enjoyed board games that attempted to solve murders for entertainment. He was agitated by what he had let himself walk into, or be led into, by Langdon Foster.

Still, the old man seemed to share some knowledge that fit with Langdon Foster's research of the fourteen unexplained deaths at

20 West Main Street, if any of it was to be believed. Curious, he wanted to know what the old man knew, and how he knew it.

"I'm sorry, I don't have a lot of time, Mr. Seely. I have other places to be," Finn said as he stood from the chair.

"Yes, yes, of course you do," old man Seely said in a confident voice, his clouded gaze never leaving the crackling fire. "But you'll have plenty of time for that, Detective. Karl Stackhouse's celebration dinner must wait. I have things to tell you, things you need to listen to, things you will need to know about these murderers. So please sit back down."

Finn cocked his head and raised a brow at the old man. "How do you know about Karl Stackhouse?"

"I know a great many things, Detective. We have extraordinarily little time. So please listen carefully."

"Wait a minute!" Finn said in his most commanding voice. "You may know who I am, but I don't know who you are."

"I was getting to that, Detective. Please bear with an old man's constitution. First, I'll need some beverage to continue, as my throat tends to get a little dry and scratchy if I speak too long. Especially since I haven't spoken with anyone in a very long time. You'll find a glass carafe, full of the finest rum you've ever had the pleasure to pass over your tongue, along with two silver tankards, on a small table next to the open door. Rum from the island of Barbados, not that blackstrap rum they offer at these local taverns. Could you please pour us each a tankard, so that I may continue?"

Finn was more than a little skeptical by the old man's knowledge of his plans for the evening, especially since he hadn't told anyone about them. He wasn't even sure he was going to the dinner party himself, though he felt duty bound by his pledge to his dying friend. Plus, Finn liked to eat alone; it was his routine, he wasn't comfortable changing his routine, for anyone. And he had another thought: how did the old man know he had had his service weapon drawn when he was navigating the darkened hallway? Maybe he wasn't totally blind.

Following the old man's instructions, Finn crossed behind both chairs to the wall beside the open door. Firelight illuminated a small table against the wall containing a large carafe with two small silver tankards. Upon examining both mugs, he noticed a maker's mark, *Revere,* stamped near the bottom of each one, under the curved handle. Without a word, Finn half-filled each tankard. Normally he didn't make it a habit of drinking while he was working, but he thought he would need it this time.

Finn stood silently in front of the old man's chair and held out the rum-filled tankard. With his left hand, the old man reached up for the handle. In the wavering light of the fire, Finn studied the old man's eyes as he gently pulled the tankard of rum away from his reaching hand. Then, as the old man stretched his left arm farther for the tankard, Finn again pulled it back from his reach.

"It's an odd thing, Detective, when one goes blind." The old man addressed Finn in a mellow whisper. "You no longer have the ability to see light or images, but you can feel them, even hear them. Your other senses become amplified, allowing, for instance, the sensation of movement, even the movement of air, however slight. It's like your mind seeing things without the use of your eyes, permitting sight through the mind's eye, if you can understand that Detective? For example, I could feel the presence of your hand holding the tankard of rum in front of me, then pulling away from my hand, both times, as I reached for it. Besides, you're blocking the warmth of the fire. I hope I have passed your test, Detective! And, yes, those are handmade silver tankards, a personal gift from the Boston silversmith who made them."

Finn felt awkward though unregretful as he placed the tankard's handle in the old man's open left hand, but he needed to know.

"Before we start, I want you to be aware of something. I know everything there is to know about you," the old man said softly as he took a small sip of rum from the silver mug. "I have always known about you, ever since you were a baby. For example, I know you are a highly intelligent, loyal, and self-committed person, that over time you have proven yourself to be a resourceful, successful detective. Above all, I know you're a diehard, combat-proven American patriot. Ah—" Seely hesitated for a second as he licked his rum-coated lips. "There is one other thing you'll be surprised to learn that I know about you, Detective." He took another long, slow draw of rum. "Your real name isn't Finn!" he added, tapping his cane against the floor with enjoyment.

Before Finn realized, he had drunk half his mug of rum while listing to old man Seely tell him things he knew about him, things he'd never even consider himself. How did he know so much? Or was this some kind of test, to see how long he'd listen to some old man he'd just met before giving up? Finn never gave up. Did the old man know that?

"OK!" Finn said finally, sliding the toothpick to the other corner of his mouth. "I'll play your little game since I'm drinking your rum and since we're telling everything about each other. But now it's your turn, who are you?"

"Ah yes, Detective. But wouldn't you like to know more about these fourteen murders first?"

"I would like to know all about you first, then we can get to how you know about these so-called murders, Mr. Seely. Though I am not so sure how you would even know about some deaths going back 238 years, let alone that they were all murders."

"Come, come, Detective. Do you want me to think that even you haven't considered all the facts? Remember what you said: only the facts tell the real story. Answer me this: how would you explain a series of unexplained deaths that have occurred every seventeen years, over the past 238 years. With all the victims being males, who have all resided in the very same house, though at different times throughout those 238 years, all found dead under different circumstances, with no valid explanations to their untimely death, all on their seventeenth birthday. Coincidence? I think not, Detective, and neither do you, or you wouldn't be sitting here."

"Sorry, but I don't have a reliable source going back that far, Mr. Seely. Plus, there's no evidence to suggest that there were even any murders associated with that house."

"So, you're saying that young Thomas Buckley wasn't murdered, Detective?"

"Um no, I'm not saying that at all. That's just one murder that I know of that is associated with that house."

"But you have been told of the other thirteen one's, correct? All seventeen-year-old males that have unexpectedly died on their birthdays, who had lived at 20 West Main Street. Am I right, Detective?"

"To some degree, yes. Unexplained deaths, not murders!" Finn responded, thinking that he had somehow been set up by Langdon Foster to entertain some senile senior citizen, that he should just humor him with his exaggerated hypothesis on 238 years of unexplained deaths, which he believes are murders. He was wondering if Langdon was having a good laugh at his expense.

"OK, I'll bite," Finn said to old man Seely. "Suppose what you're saying is true. How would you explain the murder of the only seventeen-year-old female in those 238 years, who had never even lived at 20 West Main Street?" Finn said.

"Ah, that was purely an unfortunate incident, Detective. Susanne White wasn't meant to die. Something went terribly wrong."

"You know about Susanne, then?" Finn asked.

"Of course, I do! She was just in the wrong place at the right time. She was forced to witness evil at its worst. A frightening encounter, the poor girl. I'm truly sorry!" Seely said.

A silence hung in the room as Finn and the old man paused, absorbing the warmth of the fire and the inner glow of the rum, Finn's mind pondering how the old man could know so much about him and 238 years of unexplained deaths, even Susanne's death.

Maybe he's a lucky guesser? But no one gets that lucky with that many facts, he thought. Still, he needed to learn everything the old man knew. These deaths were sounding more like unsolved mysteries than actual murders, or was it the rum? If they were murders, fourteen of them over a span of 238 years, were they the result of some bizarre ritual murders? Or maybe a serial killer? Two hundred and thirty-eight years, it'd have to be the work of many killers. He shook his head, that's not logical by anyone's way of thinking, even with the rum.

The silence was finally broken by the old man. "So, Detective, do you have any interest in American history?"

"Not really."

"But you are familiar with the conflict of the War of Independence, aren't you?" Seely said as he sneered at Finn?

"Yes, of course I am."

"I'm happy to hear that Detective. As for your lack of interest in history, well, you should take an interest—a deep interest. You will in time. First let me tell you a few especially important details that may help convince you that not only are you and you alone tasked with solving these murders, but only you can put a stop to them from continuing, forever." The old man said as he drained his tankard of rum and held out his empty mug. "Detective, would you be so kind as to refill me, so that we can get on with the pertinent details you'll be needing to solve these murders, then I will tell you who I am."

With a heavy sigh Finn reluctantly stood and took the empty tankard from the old man's extended left hand. He refilled the old man's mug from the carafe and cautiously added just a few drops to his own mug and returned to the front of the old man's chair, extending the mug. Without announcement, the old man reached up, took the handle, and brought the mug straight to his lips for a large gulp.

Fifteen

"OK!" FINN SAID. "I'M ready. So, who are you?" He said taking a mouthful of rum.

"I should have anticipated your impatience, Detective. You have always shown an intolerant side. I guess it's just part of your obsessive-compulsive disorder. Or maybe it's that self-doubt side," he said with a slight snicker as he tapped his cane on the floor again. Adding, "Most good detectives, I've noticed, have some degree of obsessive-compulsive disorder, amongst many other issues." He sighed. "As you know, I'm Ebenezer Seely," he said with a slight hesitation, then adding, "To be more formal, and more accurate Detective, I'm—Dr. Ebenezer Seely."

"What kind of doctor are you?" Finn asked.

"I'm a surgeon."

"A blind surgeon? This keeps getting better!" Finn said, suppressing a disrespectful snicker caused by the buzz he was getting from a mug and a half of rum, on an empty stomach.

"I no longer practice medicine, Detective, haven't for many years," Dr. Seely said before continuing. "I was born in Norwalk Connecticut, only a very, very long time ago, then I moved here to Oyster Bay, and I have never left."

"What's a very, very long time ago, Dr. Seely?"

"When I was twenty-six years old, I married a woman named Phoebe Townsend. She was the youngest daughter of Samuel and Sarah Townsend's eight children. Our marriage was somewhat of a social scandal in Oyster Bay, particularly to the Quakers who knew the Townsends, because I was twenty years younger than my dear Phoebe." He continued, "But that is not the reason we are here today, to discuss my marriage." Finn thought it must have been a sore spot for the old man as he watched his somber expression change.

Seely took another small sip of rum and continued. "Phoebe's father, Samuel Townsend, had originally purchased that house at 20 West Main Street back in 1738, when it was just a modest four-room saltbox. He'd owned all the land north of it, to the water's edge at the harbor. He even owned the land we occupy right now. In fact, we're sitting at the top of what once was his cherished apple orchard, until the brutal and oppressive Queen's Rangers cut down all his prized apple trees and used the wood to build a defensive fort with its unobstructed view of the harbor. Which is why the top of Simcoe Street is also known today as Fort Hill. But I digress, I'm getting ahead of myself. If, when you exit this house, instead of returning to your car, you follow the narrow path to the left of my gate, alongside the last house just south of us, you will find in the rear of that house the forgotten Townsend family cemetery, dating back to the death of the first Oyster Bay Townsend in 1669. Among the many Townsend family headstones scattered in that now abandoned small unkept graveyard, you will find a weathered blue-gray marble obelisk that stands tall in the foreground, rising above all other headstones. That lone marker preserves the memory of young

Sarah Townsend, Phoebe's next older sister. You will also see the year of her birth on that marker, 1760."

"So, you're telling me that you're over 200 years old?" Finn said with a slight snicker.

"Actually, I'll be 236 years old on my next birthday, Detective," Seely said, slurping up a runaway dribble of rum from his hanging lower lip. "But," he continued in a smooth, somber tone, "what you won't find on that obelisk is Sarah's date of death."

"Wait!" Finn laughed. "You're 236 years old and you still celebrate your birthday? Do you really expect me to believe this?"

"It matters not if you believe my age, Detective. This isn't about me, nor is it about you. It's all about stopping a killer. Haven't I at least demonstrated some knowledge of the facts that are unknown to others?"

"I suppose you have," Finn said, totally confused. This case had more twist and turns than a burlap bag full of aggravated snakes. Then Finn added, "Isn't that a little unusual, not to have a date of death listed on someone's headstone."

"Normally, that would be true. However, her body was never found, no one knows when she died, how she died, or if she's even dead," Dr. Seely continued in a solemn tone. "Those were troubling times for most patriots, Detective. Two hundred thirty-eight years ago, when our original thirteen colonies were embroiled in a fight to the death against an oppressive invading force, against a tyrannical English king for their God-given right to freedom, against the mightiest army in the world. That same foreign army not only occupied the colonies but took whatever liberties they enjoyed or needed from the colonial people, whom they considered a lesser class citizen of the crown. They brutally slaughtered soldier and citizen alike. Unknown to many and lost to history is the fact that our victorious outcome of the American Revolution was centered right here in this little hamlet of Oyster Bay, during King George III's cruel and inhuman occupation."

"Were you even born during the Revolution?" Finn asked, doing the math.

"Yes. Toward the very end, and I did witness the aftermath of the British soldiers' savagery, through the eyes and ears of my family," Dr. Seely continued. "They especially treated the nonviolent Quakers harshly, plundering their crops, cattle, and homesteads, and at times violating their women. Forcing many families into total starvation, while countless others simply just disappeared, never to be heard of again."

Dr. Seely's impassioned narrative slowed as he took another sip of rum. "The Townsends were one of those Quaker families. Samuel Townsend was extraordinarily successful in the merchandising and shipping trade. As such, he and his family were the perfect targets for King George's occupying army. Every American schoolkid knows that the English king levied unfair taxes on the hard-working colonists. But what they don't know is the real story, the real suffering behind the Revolution. I'm sure you don't either, Detective. Someone once said, *'One must live a war, before one can accurately describe a war.'* Do you recognize the date of September twenty-third, Detective?" Dr. Seely asked.

"Yes, that's the date Thomas Buckley and Susanne White were murdered."

"Precisely, Detective! It also happens to be 238 years to the exact day that our colonial patriots captured the head of British military intelligence, Major John André. In what could have been the single most important victory for the oppressive British forces here in the colonies. I say could have been, because if it had been a victory for the British, it would have been the unimaginable deciding factor in the outcome of the American Revolution, resulting in there never being a United States of America." Dr. Seely paused to take another sip of rum. "The only other, and perhaps equally important date, for you to know, Detective, is October second, one day away from now. Which is why you and I are gathered here today."

"And why is that Dr. Seely?" Finn asked.

"Because, Detective, that only leaves you one day to stop these murders from continuing."

"Wait! You're telling me that by tomorrow, I'll be able to apprehend a 238-year-old serial killer, one that no one has ever known about or even heard about?" Finn laughed. Maybe all that rum was going to the old doctor's head.

"No, Detective, what I'm saying is that by tomorrow evening, you will have stopped the murder of fifteen young, innocent victims. It will take you longer to identify the real killer. Isn't it your personal investigative theory that if you know the *how* and *why* of a murder, you'll know *who* the killer is?"

"Something like that," Finn answered, wondering again how this old man knew so much about him. Draining the last of the rum from the mug, he watched Dr. Seely finish his.

"You must listen very carefully to me now, Detective! You have victims that have yet to be discovered, yet to be identified. They are not the result of some unknown serial killer. There is an obvious *why* to their murders, or what others call motive. Though they share the same *why*, only you can sort out the *who*, because only you will have learned the answers. Time is not your friend here, Detective. You will be limited until the stroke of midnight, exactly 365 days from tomorrow, October second, to apprehend your killer. But only if you are successful in stopping Simcoe's malediction will you learn the identity of your killer." Dr. Seely added, "Detective, we've come this far. We'd might as well finish it up."

"Your story?" Finn asked.

"No, Detective, the rum!" Dr. Seely added in a humorous wheezed chuckle tapping his cane on the floor.

Finn refilled Seely's tankard, adding only a few drops to his from the carafe that hadn't seemed to empty, and returned to his comfortable leather chair in front of the fire. A flushing kick from the warmth of the rum was beginning to numb his body. Then he realized the flames in the firebox hadn't changed. The crackle and popping of embers remained constant, as did the same three logs that hadn't burned out since he sat down, even though the warmth from the fire maintained its even heat. Finn looked around the room again, noticing there weren't any additional logs, even if they wanted one. And where were the normal fireplace tools that usually stood near a fireplace?

Dr. Seely recounted the patriots' disastrous defeat of their first major battle of the Revolution, on Long Island at Brooklyn Heights in August 1776. The Revolutionaries were easily defeated by 30,000 British troops under the General William Howe, who pushed General Washington's outnumbered, out trained soldiers up through the rugged northern terrain of New York City into the Hudson Valley. The Continental Army's victory at Saratoga a year later rallied the much-needed movement and support for General

Washington's troops with their fight for freedom. Afterward, General Howe was knighted by King George III for his success in the Battle of Long Island, where he remained the British Commander-in-Chief in America until he resigned in February 1778. His second in command, General Henry Clinton, assumed command of the British army in North America.

Dr. Seely continued in detail. "In 1780, General Henry Clinton's strategy for winning the war for the Crown was to gain control of all the Hudson River, which was the only inland water transportation route connecting New York City's deep ocean port with everything north of the city. He could then cross Lake Champlain into Canada, allowing him to control all troop and supply movements from Canada to New York City." Dr. Seely paused for another sip of rum.

"Another major concern of General Clinton's was the gathering of intelligence by General Washington in the New York area, especially on Long Island. Clinton believed Washington was amassing it through a covert spy operation. He feared an attack from General Washington on his weakest flank, from the east across Long Island, combined with multiple strategic attacks from the north and west, which would cut off Clinton's land supplies and allow Washington to lay siege to New York City. General Clinton had his own methods of gathering intelligence, sending and receiving coded correspondence from his officers in the field. He knew General Washington would have his own methods as well, especially since he was an ex-British officer himself."

"Is there some reason you're telling me all this?" Finn asked.

"Do you not think background information is necessary for any murder investigation?"

"I suppose it is," Finn responded, and took another gulp of rum.

"As I was saying," Seely added, with a bite of sarcasm, "Clinton hadn't forgotten that a few years earlier, one September evening, Washington had dispatched a young Continental soldier from Connecticut to cross the devil's belt, what you would now call the Long Island Sound, landing him in Huntington in the pre-dawn hours. On the rocky shores of Long Island's North Shore, for a reconnoitering mission to gather information on Long Island's large population of British loyalists, and to document the position of British troops supplying information for Washington.

"That twenty-one-year-old spy was an unemployed schoolteacher. More importantly, he was a captain in the Continental Army who had volunteered to travel to Long Island, out of uniform, to conduct his intelligence. An amateurish mission that was destined to fail from the start, some say because he was quickly recognized by loyalists who had fled the patriot stronghold of Connecticut. Plus, there was his above-average height and a disfiguring facial scar that once seen, anyone would remember. A burn scar to his face was the result of an overloaded pan of gunpowder that prematurely flashed from a malfunctioning flintlock rifle. More importantly, he was unfortunate to have naïvely been taken into the friendship of a disguised British Army officer, Colonel Robert Rogers, while at Cheeks Tavern in Huntington within days of landing on Long Island. Colonel Rogers had openly deployed a guerrilla style of warfare against the colonial militia and the Continental Army. His troops were comprised of a long list of drunken loyalists, thieves, and outlaws that operated openly, without reprisal from anyone, even from General Howe."

Seely's tone grew melancholy. "Rogers's style of warfare was outside of the dignified boundaries of King's George's gentleman style of combat but was completely sanctioned and funded by General Howe. If pressed, General Howe would openly condemn the brutal atrocities of Colonel Rogers and his renegade Rangers. Secretly, he favored their actions, knowing they instilled fear in the rebels. With fear came control. Control wins wars. All the while hiding behind the veil of decency as the protector of King George's colonial subjects."

Dr. Seely added, "A standing rule of warfare at the time, for both sides, was that any military personnel captured out of uniform and behind the enemy's lines, would be considered a spy. And the penalty for spying was public execution, by hanging. A method of punishment that was reserved solely for the lowest of all violations of integrity and trust; not even prostitutes would be subjected to hanging. Spying was considered the lowest undignified form of any ethical principles of honesty. The deception of one's character was never admitted to, or accepted, and always punished, by hanging. Which was the sentence imposed and carried out for unknowingly confiding his secret mission to British Colonel Rogers, by the young, trusting Continental captain, Nathan Hale. Colonel Rogers had a well-earned reputation for numerous bad habits—drinking, gambling, and plundering, to name a few. He was frequently unavailable for recruiting or missions because of his drinking. Rogers's Rangers became more of a liability than an asset for the British commander in chief, so the Rangers were decommissioned, and Rogers was rounded up and returned to England.

"However," Seely added, "as the war continued, General Henry Clinton assumed the position of commander in chief of the British forces in the colonies. He realized an absolute need for an intelligence unit on Long Island to root out the leaders of Washington's spy ring, so he reestablished the Queen's Rangers, named in honor of King George III's wife, Queen Charlotte. He appointed Colonel John Graves Simcoe as the commander of these new rangers."

"That's a very interesting story, Doc. But I'm not really sure how any of this relates to my investigation."

Sixteen

"WE HAVEN'T MUCH TIME, Detective, or should I say you haven't much time. So please allow me to continue with the relevant information that you'll be needing to successfully complete your investigation."

"Fire away, Doc," Finn stated, while suppressing an uncontrolled yawn with the back of his hand. He figured he'd placate the old doctor a little longer, plus, he liked the warmth of the fire and the butter-smooth rum. Maybe he was even enjoying some of the story. Though he did think the whole visit was somewhat odd, if not totally bizarre and a complete waste of time. Still, he thought, the old doctor was revealing some relevant information toward the unexplained deaths associated with 20 West Main Street, or so it seemed. The thought of how much Seely knew about these unexplained deaths was forefront in his mind as he listened to Seely recount the death details of 238 years. Then thinking, if he knew so much about all these old undocumented killings, maybe he was also part of the problem, unless, of course, he was the killer. Or did he just have a good memory and a knack for telling an interesting story? He figured he'd give the old doctor a few more minutes, or until the rum ran out, to see if he gave up anything useful in his murders.

"Am I boring you, Detective?"

"No, of course not, Doc!" Finn replied, glaring at the doctor and wondering how he knew he'd yawned.

Finn sat motionless in the smoky room as the mesmerizing fire snapped its hot ambers in the firebox, sending loud popping sounds throughout the smoky room.

Dr. Seely resumed his story of Colonel John Graves Simcoe and his Queen's Rangers. "John Graves Simcoe was born in a small village in England, in February of 1752, his parents were Captain John Simcoe, of the Royal Navy, his mother Katherine Stamford. John Graves was the third of four sons. His two older brothers had died young, leaving just him and his younger brother Percy. He was given the middle name of Graves, after his godfather, who was a close friend of his father, also a captain in the Royal Navy." Dr. Seely added, "As young boys John and Percy were subjected to an extremely harsh upbringing, by an overbearing father, who was seldom home. His father demanded nothing but absolute obedience to a rigid set of rules of conduct he'd laid down for young John and Percy. Failure to comply to the inflexible set of rules was met with nothing short of severe physical punishment. Young John was either physically unable to follow these rules or mentally unable to demonstrate their understanding."

Then he added, "In 1759, when John was only seven years old, his father was killed in battle off the coast of Quebec while fighting in the French and Indian War, at forty-nine years old. Leaving behind a wife and two children. By all accounts, young John's developmental years had been spent under violent and distressful conditions from an autocratic and domineering father, a figure of authority, which may well have contributed to his violent and uncontrollable outbursts toward anyone whom he viewed as being inferior. With John and Percy being the remaining children in a fatherless family, John was sent to school in Exeter, England, until he was thirteen. He wasn't considered a good student and managed to skimp by with less-than-desirable grades, and he was also prone to sudden bouts of depression. He was also present when his younger brother, Percy, drowned at a local swimming hole.

"It seems Percy, who was two years younger than John, was developing into a promising young man, much taller than his brother John by his twelfth year. He was an outstanding student, with an eye toward studying law. He'd become well-liked by everyone he met, socializing with many friends, plus he was considered by many to be more desirable to look at than his squat-framed, doubled-chinned, puggy older brother John. It was reported in a local newspaper, that on a hot June day he and brother John had gone swimming down to Sandy Point, a favorite swimming hole for the local children. But, on this particular day it was only John and Percy at the swimming hole. The paper said that John did everything he could to save poor Percy, but nothing he seemed to do could save young Percy's life. The official report was drowning, raising a crooked brow to those who knew the young Percy, because he was known to be an excellent swimmer, better than his brother John, many would later remark.

In 1770, John coerced his mother into parting with a large share of her meager life's savings to purchase him an ensign's commission in the 35th regiment of foot, mostly due to him being physically weak as a male for his age, which was an obvious factor in preventing him in following his father's footsteps into the Royal

Navy, as life at sea may have proven too strenuous. Another issue that plagued Simcoe was his frequent, and violent, headaches that were known only to a select few.

A commission in the King's Army could present unimaginable opportunities for political and social advancement for someone who lacked the motivational drive to achieve it through the more conventional route, like through a higher education in law that would offer a refined path. It was also an ideal place for someone to unleash cruel, inhuman, and sadistic activity against others, in the name of the King."

After a quick sip of rum, Dr. Seely resumed his story. "Simcoe also demonstrated little integrity, coupled with the ever-present lack of military leadership ability. Which didn't go unnoticed by his superiors. The colonel always seemed to teeter on the edge of luck, somehow landing on his feet. He garnered little admiration or respect from any of his senior officers, and only fear from his subordinates. He'd been turned down on numerous occasions to command any formidable regiment into battle, though he did see action on few occasions, though mostly at a distance, from bringing up the rear.

Colonel Simcoe rose through the ranks not by his own merit, but at the expense of others. He was a skilled manipulator with high aspirations of being the sole leader of America's colonies. But first, the British military had to put down the costly rebellion, and he vowed to see it accomplished.

After finally manipulating his position as commander of the Queen's Rangers, either through bribery, great promises, or nagging persistence, General Clinton caved and gave Simcoe command of the Queen's Rangers, 400 strong, 100 being dragoons, with one mission only: to identify and flush out every rebel spy active on Long Island's North Shore.

"Clinton's own intelligence officers were keenly aware of a rebel spy ring working along the North Shore of Long Island from New York City to Setauket. He knew the names of two of its leaders, using the code names of Culper Senior and Culper Junior, but that was all that was known, that was all anyone knew, or that was all that was being shared." Seely paused.

Twisting the upper half of his body in the leathered armchair, Finn faced Seely and said in an uncertain tone. "Are you saying that this street, Simcoe Street, this one right out here in front of your house, is named after a brutal, murderous tyrant, a known enemy of the American people?"

"That's absolutely correct, Detective. But there's much more to tell you, much more you'll be needing to know, and much more that you will experience for yourself," Dr. Seely added with a slurp of his sagging lower lip.

"Next thing you'll be telling me, he's the killer in all of these unexplained deaths." Finn sighed and straightened up in the chair to face the warmth of the fire, disgusted to learn that an American street was named after an American enemy.

"Oh no, Detective. He's not your killer. But he is the *why* of the murders associated with 20 West Main Street, which you will come to see."

"And how will I come to see that, Doctor?"

"By taking a short trip, Detective."

"To Simcoe's grave?"

"Oh no, Simcoe isn't buried here in the United States."

"You mean he's still alive too?" Finn asked with a slight smirk.

"He will be for you, Detective."

Seventeen

"So, HOW DOES THIS all come around to me, if you don't mind me asking?" Finn said, somewhat surprised that he was even following along with the old doctor's theory on how to solve a murder.

"Not at all. But let me pose another question. Who is the most notorious traitor in the annals of American history, that one person whose name has become synonymous with a single act of cowardly behavior? That one person who sold out this great country, for a few pounds' sterling, for a position in the enemy's occupying army, taking up arms against his own countrymen, against his own blood. What name does that bring to mind, Detective?"

Finn fell silent, not contemplating his answer, but wondering why every time he'd asked the old man a question, it seemed like the old man responded with a question of his own. That was a classic perpetrator response to keep an interviewing cop off balance while allowing for more time to reason out a lie. Why would the old man need to distract me? he thought; it didn't make any sense, then again not much of this case was making any sense anyway.

"OK, I'll play your silly guessing game. But first you must answer me this: why is it that every time I ask you a question, you answer it with a question of your own? When it was I who sought you out for answers?"

"Ah yes, that would seem so, wouldn't it?" Seely said, his lips parted with a slivered smile, then added further. "Because it was you who sought answers from me, coming to my door, might that be a good reason to believe what I'm telling you is the truth, Detective? And haven't my questions provided you with all the necessary answers you have been seeking?"

"I'm not really sure they have," Finn stated, thinking maybe in some oddball way Seely had given him something, since he was only there looking for the *why* of his murder, and seemingly he had just given him that, or at least how to find it. "But never mind," Finn suddenly said. "My guess, that would be Benedict Arnold!" Finn added, finally answering the doctor's question.

"Ah yes, Benedict Arnold, that would be the one, that infamous military traitor who brings us together today, Detective. Which leads me to another question: have you ever wondered why Father Dom always referred to you as the Final One?"

"Father Dom! You know about Father Dom?" Finn asked.

"Yes, yes, of course I do. Like I said, I know a great many things," Dr. Seely answered in a dismissive tone with a slight lisp on the word *things*. "Do you know why he called you the Final One, or should I say Finn-ally One?" Dr. Seely said, giving another throaty chuckle.

Finn believed the rum was having a greater effect on him than on the old man. Or maybe the doctor was just accustomed to drinking all afternoon. "Of course. I've always wondered that, and a good many more things about myself," Finn answered in a shallow tone as he stared at Dr. Seely. "What does this whole thing have to do with me?" Finn asked again.

"It has everything to do with you, Detective, and nothing to do with anyone else. Do you remember Father Dom telling you that you had been chosen for a special task in life, a task that no one else could perform? That you're the final one?"

"Yeah, he said it all the time."

"Well, the time for that special task has finally arrived for you, Detective. I'll tell you why. First, let me start with your name, you can surely thank Father Dom for that one. Anyway, like I said earlier, Finn is not your name, or at least it's not your given name; that would be Henry Mansfield, Detective Henry Mansfield to be more exact. Also, with the knowledge that you have no children, it effectively makes you the last living biological descendent, in the direct blood line of that infamous American traitor, born on American soil."

"I'm not sure how you know my name, but you're right: it is Henry Mansfield. But if I were in the direct bloodline of that traitor as you seem to think I am, shouldn't my last name be Arnold?"

"Ah, in most cases you would be absolutely correct, however not in this case. Unbeknownst to many, Benedict Arnold had two wives: his first wife, Margaret, was from Norwalk, Connecticut, not far from where I grew up. She was the beautiful daughter of the local sheriff. They had three sons before she unexpectedly died at thirty-five years old while Arnold was away fighting with the colonial militia against the King's army up in Saratoga, and where he was wounded, I might add. His second wife, also named Margaret, however she preferred to be called Peggy—well, she was from Philadelphia, the daughter of a well-to-do and prominent British loyalist. She also happened to be twenty years younger than Arnold." The doctor gave another little chuckle, then continued. "Together they bore seven children. A son and a daughter died shortly after birth. They had another daughter, and four sons, who followed their treasonous father into the British Army, as did two of his sons from Margaret, his first wife. His youngest son though, Henry, from his first wife, did not become a soldier."

"But he was an Arnold, right?" Finn said.

"Yes, that is correct. However, because of your father's..." Dr. Seely abruptly stopped. "Sorry, it must be the rum." Then he added, with a slight growl to his tone, "I mean that traitor, with his infamous behavior, his devious, treasonous conduct toward our revolutionary cause for freedom, betraying his fellow countrymen, his cowardly attempt to surrender the most crucial of all vital military positions in the colonies, General Washington's Fortification on the Hudson River...Sorry, I can't help getting emotional." Dr. Seely paused for a couple seconds, drew in a short breath, composed himself, then continued. "When Henry was only a couple months old, Hannah, Arnold's own sister, absconded with young Henry, giving him his mother's last name Mansfield. Fleeing Connecticut they settled in New York City, where he could live a life of safety and anonymity. Arnold's other two children from his first wife fled to England with their treasonous father, abandoning all ties with America. His other male children with his second wife were all born on foreign soil. Which leaves you, Detective, the surviving male in the direct bloodline of your biological descendant the infamous traitor, and the last Arnold born on American soil."

"Do you know how absolutely crazy that sounds, Dr. Seely? But let's just say for argument's sake that you're on to something here. What does this have to do with me and these unexplained deaths?"

"Ah yes, I was getting to that. Remember when I told you about the Simcoe malediction earlier, that there was a huge difference between a curse and a malediction? That a malediction is an absolute utterance of condemnation, a declaration of malice toward another person or persons, that it carries with it the hostile infliction of death?"

"Yeah, yeah, yeah, I remember all that," Finn answered impatiently.

"Well, what I didn't get to tell you before was that for a malediction to have its perpetual infliction of death, the malediction must be uttered in vain by someone who has a forethought to be immorally evil against another. In Simcoe's malediction that *other* was a true American patriot, someone who had access to Simcoe's private conversations with Major André. Someone who witnessed their clandestine plans for Arnold's betrayal. Someone from right here in Oyster Bay, someone who had lived at 20 West Main Street. The rites of Simcoe's malediction can only be celebrated or enacted upon with the death of that *other*. And only then can the malediction be completely exorcised by someone being the last in a pure bloodline of a biological descendant of the person who had been the actual incentive for such malediction. Since Benedict Arnold was the catalyst, or the actual incentive and reason for Simcoe's malediction, that leaves only you. Though you may be known by another name, you cannot hide the fact that the direct blood of an infamous American traitor runs deep through your veins, Detective. So, you see, you are the only one who can stop Simcoe's malediction and prevent it from ever occurring. You have been tasked with a great responsibility, Detective, for many lives and futures will depend on your success. Maybe even restore some dignity to your infamous ancestor's name, though I doubt it." Seely finished off in a loathing inflection.

"Whoa, that's some tall tale, Doc!" Finn stated with a dubious tone. Gulping down the last few drops of his rum, he then added, "Yeah, that's really deep. But thanks for that amazing story, your great-tasting rum, and all that investigative advice. But I think I'll just stick to the old-fashioned method of police work right here in the present," Finn said, as he stood up from the comfort of the soft leather armchair and warmth of the fire, placing his empty silver tankard on the small table that separated him and Dr. Seely, before slowly moving toward the open doorway.

"I know you, Detective. You choose not to believe what you cannot see," said Dr. Seely, then adding in a tone of skepticism, "If I chose that same path as well, I would not believe in you, Detective!"

Finn stopped briefly as he reached the threshold of the dark, smoky room. Turning his head back over his shoulder toward Dr. Seely, who continued his unbroken stare at the fire. "It's called survival, Doc; I should have walked out of here a long time ago." Finn stopped again as he passed through the threshold, but before turning down the darkened hallway, to pose one final question. "Oh, I almost forgot, Doc. You ever heard of a woman named Sally who once lived at 20 West Main Street?"

"Why, yes. Of course, I have, I know her well," Dr. Seely responded jubilantly. "And so will you, Detective!" Dr. Seely added as he unmistakably turned his head toward Finn, finishing with a noticeable eye wink and a mischievous smile before adding, "Enjoy your travels, Detective!" tapping his cane to the floor with a final, satisfying dry chuckle.

Exiting the front door of the run-down Tudor, Finn felt a surreal uneasiness. Retracing his steps along the unworn path to the iron gate, he slowed to steal a quick glance at his watch. Stopping to study the face of the watch closer, he then tapped the crystal a couple times with a fingernail in disbelief of the time displayed. Maybe the battery had died? He glared closer but noticed the second hand continued to move with the precession of an expensive timepiece, as it should, while his mind questioned what his eyes were telling him. According to his watch, it was 4:35 p.m., meaning he'd only been in Dr. Seely's house for exactly five minutes. Shaking his head in disbelief, he knew he'd been in there for at least three hours, with as many mugs of rum. He could still feel the effects of the rum buzz, a slight light-headedness, like he'd felt all the while he'd been inside the house. Or was it something totally different? "Nah, couldn't be, must be the rum," he said aloud, pushing open the rusted gate with his knee.

Deciding to walk off the rum buzz, he followed the narrow foot path that ran from Dr. Seely's dilapidated house parallel along the south side of the last house at the top of Simcoe Street, to an old, unattended family cemetery hidden from public view, except for the few bordering houses' backyards that surrounded the hallowed ground in an unwitting protective shield, seemingly guarding it from the encroachment of time and change.

He shouldered the cemetery's tall, narrow, rusted metal gate partway open with a full-bodied push, then he squeezed through with little room to spare. He gazed around the small family patch of worn and faded headstones, some toppled over from age and neglect, most all with unreadable faded inscriptions. Then his eyes were drawn toward the largest of all the markers, the bluish-gray marble obelisk just beyond the entrance. He pushed through the thick, knee-high uncut grass to get closer, to read its inscription. Only five short steps into the forgotten cemetery, he felt a gentle but mysteriously cool current of air brush against the left side of his face. Then just as suddenly he felt a compassionate nudge against his left arm, followed by an invisible presence nestling closer, like someone joining him.

He studied the cemetery again, seeing nothing. He took another couple of cautious steps toward the obelisk, stopping again when he walked directly into an ethereal cloud of a pleasurable fragrance that hung in the air between him and his intended marker. Still, he saw no one, while continuing to smell the pleasing fragrance of lavender. That same enchanting fragrance he now remembered smelling after feeling that spray of cool air against his back when he was up on Mill River Road in the early-morning hours at his crime scene. He remembered that Laura Buckley had mentioned that Sally, the woman in her house, always appeared with the aroma of lavender. Finn drew in a short breath and gazed quickly around again, before focusing on the front of the obelisk. A chiseled dedication mid-way up on the face of the towering monument---the upper top left of the inscription cornered with a winged angel, the upper right cornered with a winged eagle. Though it was weathered, he had little trouble reading its inscription.

SARAH TOWNSEND IIIVV
BORN Oyster Bay-1740
DIED-

The brave shall never Perish for they live in the hearts of all free men, from an indebted nation in humble gratitude to a silent but selfless true American patriot.

What had this to do with his murder investigation? And why had Dr. Seely even mention Sarah Townsend? What did she have to do with anything, except that she once lived at 20 West Main Street? Could a *"True American Patriot"* also be a *true hidden killer*? Was she part of his *why*?

He noticed the epitaph had a date for Sarah's birth but not her death, just like the doctor had mentioned, but what was the significance of the roman numerals after her name? And why was she a *True American Patriot*, how had she earned that distinction? Why was the nation indebted to her? And why had she been silent? Turning back toward the gate, Finn felt a soft, amorous press against his left check, like he'd been kissed. He hesitated, savoring the sensuous, comforting sensation, again inhaling the intoxicating scent of fresh lavender.

Eighteen

DRIVING THE FIFTEEN MINUTES to the Stackhouse home in Glen Cove for Karl Junior's celebration dinner, Finn reflected on the odd encounters he had had with some of the strangest people over the years. Some had horrendous stories to support their oddball conduct, but not one of them was as odd as his visit with Dr. Seely. The old man's appearance, his house, his mannerisms, his lack of movement, except for the couple times he banged his cane on the floor. Then when Finn was leaving, he moved his head. All that aside, what really bothered Finn was not Seely's odd story. It was other things, certain facts Seely knew, things no one else would have or could have ever known. How did he know about all those unexplained deaths tied to 20 West Main Street? Father Dom? The Buckley kid, or Susanne? How did he know about Karl Stackhouse? And how did he know so much about him?

Pulling up in front of the Stackhouse home, he glanced at his watch, thinking he would have arrived early. But by the number of cars parked in the driveway and all along either side of the street, he was surely one of the last to arrive. He must have been in the cemetery longer than he thought.

At the front door he was met with the festive sound of laughter and music coming from inside the house. After giving the door a few loud knocks, he was greeted by Denise Stackhouse, Karl's widow. "Oh, Finn, you've made it!" Denise announced, throwing her arms around Finn, pulling him close. "I can't believe it. You've finally made one of our family gatherings. We've been hoping you would. Karl wanted to wait, he didn't want to start, hoping you'd make it." She gave him a tender kiss to the cheek. "Come in, come in. Karl!" Denise called out. "Looks who's here. He's going to be so excited to see you, Finn."

"It's nice to see you, Denise. I'm sorry it's been so long, I've been pretty busy at the office," Finn lied. "I'm glad I could make it, though; I wouldn't want to miss Karl's announcement for anything," he added graciously. Unsure of what gift to bring, he'd settled on the popular, but always appreciated, gift card.

"Hey, Finn!" Karl Junior excitedly cheered as he greeted Finn inside the doorway near the crowded living room. Grabbing Finn's right hand while pulling him in for a tight man hug. "I'm so glad you could make it. It means so much to me. You know why, right, Finn?"

"Yes, of course I do! It means the same to me, Karl." Finn scanned the room, looking for Karl's wife. "Where's Eileen?"

"She's here somewhere," Karl said, looking around the room.

Eileen emerged from the kitchen carrying two long-stemmed glasses of champagne. She handed one to Karl and the other to Finn. "It's time, Karl," she whispered. "Hello, Finn. We've missed you." She moved in closer, giving him a sisterly hug and a welcoming peck on the cheek. "Dinner is getting cold," she added with a smile as she stepped into the living room.

Karl tapped the side of his champagne glass a few times with a pen he had removed from his shirt pocket. "We can start now—Finn's here! Please, will everyone join Eileen and me for a few seconds?" Scanning the living room he asked, "Does everyone have a glass of champagne?" Karl and Eileen stood next to each other, their backs to the glow of the fireplace, as their family and friends filled the room.

Seeing everyone in the room holding congratulatory glasses of champagne to toast the announcement, Karl said, "We have two announcements tonight! Please hold off on the toasts until you've heard them both." Karl curled his arm around Eileen's waist, drawing her close.

"The first good news we have to report: it's finally official, I've been promoted to sergeant!" Karl smiled as he leaned over to kiss Eileen while the room erupted with cheers and whistles of excitement. Denise crossed the living room carrying a bundle of mixed bright blue and orange helium-filled balloons, the police department's colors. She released them to more cheers and clapping.

A month earlier, in a rare phone conversation for the family invite, Denise had excitedly informed Finn that Eileen was trying to get pregnant, they were undergoing expensive fertility treatments with one of the most successful fertility doctors in the world, conveniently located right there in New York City. She said Karl's promotion was nothing short of a miracle because of the expense of the treatments, saying the fertility doctor had almost guaranteed Eileen she would be giving birth by the end of September of next year. "Isn't that so exciting?" He'd remembered her saying.

Karl waited for the room to calm before adding, "The second bit of great news Eileen and I would like to share with everyone tonight is, we've purchased our first home. We can now move out of Mom's basement." He said, sending a loving smile to his mother. "We just received word that our offer has been accepted by the sellers. We can even move into the house this coming weekend if we want, while we wait for the mortgage. The sellers have left everything to the real estate agent, because they're returning to live in New York City."

"And it's totally furnished!" Eileen said, giving Karl a loving kiss.

Stepping forward, Denise said, "Please raise your glasses in a toast to Karl's promotion and his and Eileen's new home in Oyster Bay."

Glasses were raised in celebration. Someone in the rear of the room yelled out, "Denise, where is the house in Oyster Bay?"

"Oh, it's a beautifully maintained eighteenth-century house, the oldest historic private home in all of Oyster Bay. It's right in the middle of the village at 20 West Main Street." She smiled proudly at Karl and Eileen.

With half the glass of his chilled bubbly still swashing firmly around in Finn's mouth, that last bit of celebratory information caused his throat to close up tighter than a frog's ass on a rainy day, as he involuntary blew some of the effervescent liquid out through his nose, then choked and coughed out the remaining champagne, along with the soft pulp of a dislodged toothpick, on to the waxed, decorative, solid wood hallway floor, near the entrance to the living room. While those around him jumped and scrambled for safer ground, acting like he'd miraculously parted the red sea.

Later, still reeling from Karl's surprising news, Finn drove eastbound toward Oyster Bay, wondering how he could prevent young Karl and Eileen from ever moving into that house, after learning of the stories of Langdon Foster and Dr. Seely. If this had been anyone else's life, he might not have concerned himself with it. But these were people he cared about.

Still, he didn't think it was his place to tell anyone how to live their life let alone what house to buy, especially a young married couple just starting out in life. The longer Finn let that thought marble bang around in his head, the more he realized that the Stackhouse's were as close to any real family he'd ever had, even if it was from a distance. He owed it to Karl Senior as a friend, and the promise he had made to him as he lay dying, that he would look after his family.

He was thinking maybe he could discourage Karl and Eileen if he just told them about the deaths of Tom Buckley and Susanne White. Or maybe he could tell them that he knew exactly why the Buckleys had suddenly decided to sell their lovely home at such an irresistibly low price, completely furnished. Or he could tell them he knew why the people who lived there before the Buckleys did the exact same thing, as did the twelve previous families, going back 238 years. But he knew he couldn't tell them any of that. He had no corroborating evidence. Hell, he didn't even have a homicide case number. He had plenty of speculation, with nothing conclusive. The best he had was a reported fatal car accident involving two seventeen-year-olds from Oyster Bay, one who had coincidently lived at the same house they were buying. He knew he couldn't tell them about Laura Buckley's strange story of some spirit named Sally, who she had mysteriously shared her house with her for the last seventeen years. And he surely wasn't going to tell them or anyone else about his bizarre visit with a 236-year-old blind surgeon named Ebenezer Seely, and his crazy story of Simcoe's malediction.

That dilemma occupied his thoughts as he continued east in the starless night along old Oyster Bay Road toward the village. The road soon became Mill Hill Road as it continued to the top of Mill Hill, the fourth of the four hills that shared the spectacular views of Oyster Bay's beautiful little harbor.

The hill's summit gave a distant view of the lights in the quaint village, though to Finn's eyes they appeared more like lights of a small rural airport runway than a historic village. Finally, he made up his mind: the only way to prevent the Stackhouse newlyweds or any other unsuspecting couple from moving into that house was to eliminate the house permanently. He wasn't proud of his decision, but there was no other way. Knowing Karl and Eileen would be moving some of their personal belongings into the house any day now, he had to act fast, strike while the iron was hot, while he still had the nerve. He didn't want to keep thinking about it or he wouldn't do it. There'd be plenty of time later to be pissed at himself or reflect on his regrets, but now he could see no other way. If he it, and did it right, he'd be happy with the results: and there'd be no more unexplained deaths related to that house.

He crawled to a stop at the bottom of Mill Hill where three roads connected: Shore Road to his left, Lake Avenue to his right, and West Main Street ahead. Finn continued straight, crossing over the small bridge on the north end of the Mill Pond as the road turned into West Main Street, directly into the heart of the sleepy little village. Slowing the car, he approached the traffic light at South Street. Passing the darkened and deserted saltbox home that had been built sometime before 1738, on his left. He eyed all the unlit storefronts on West Main Street for any external surveillance cameras as he waited for the traffic light to change. Making a slow right turn, he noticed there were only two cars parked in front of the local watering hole on the east side of South Street, across from where the street intersected with West Main. Finding no external cameras directed toward 20 West Main Street, he continued south to the one and only gas station two miles away. He parked his Crown Vic on the sidewalk, off the road, out of clear view of the station's surveillance camera, if there was one, and walked the remaining 200 feet to the station.

The sole station attendant was busy bringing in his signs, oil racks, and other outside displays in preparation for closing. Finn checked his watch: it was 8:55 p.m.

Stopping at the open door at the entrance of the station Finn asked the attendant, "Do you have a gas can?"

"We're closed," the pimple-faced, stick thin kid responded, without even a quick glance toward Finn.

"Yeah, I ran out of gas," Finn said, following the kid back into the lightless station.

"Sorry, mister, we're closed. Can't you see the light are off?"

"I only need a gallon of gas," Finn said.

"I can't help you, mister. The register is closed out for the day, plus I turned off the pumps."

"How about turning the pumps back on, so I can get a quick gallon of gas. Here's twenty bucks; you keep the change," Finn said, holding out the twenty-dollar bill.

The kid quickly snatched the twenty, adding. "I'll need another five for the deposit on the can."

Finn took a small roll of cash from his pocket, peeled a single bill off the top, placed it on the counter, and said, "Thanks."

"There's an empty can by the door. I'll turn the pumps back on but make it quick. You can return the can tomorrow, and I'll give you your deposit back then." The kid was in such a rush, Finn didn't think he ever looked at his face.

With the can filled, he walked back to his car and placed it in the trunk. Making a quick U-turn, he drove back into the slumbering village. Slowing on South Street, at the edge of where most of the village retail stores began, he looked again to make sure the streets were deserted before making the left onto Orchard Street. Parking his car between two large box trucks that were parked on the north side of the deserted street, he turned off his lights and engine, and listened to his police radio waiting for the one and only police cruiser assigned to the village to be given an assignment from headquarters.

While he waited, he checked his cell phone. Dusty had left him a voice message. "Hey, Finn, I've got something on that name you wanted me to check out. Riley Russet, he's the subscriber of the first phone number. His phone pinged off the only cell tower in Oyster Bay on Friday the twenty-second, for most of that day. So, it is pretty safe to say he didn't leave the village of Oyster Bay at all on that Friday afternoon, or at least his phone didn't. But he does text and call the other number you gave me quite a lot. That number belongs to a Lawrence Joseph. I emailed you all the SIM card info from both phones, with all the cross communications and all the pertinent social networks and the email addresses associated with both. Plus, I sent you the satellite images of that horse farm, for the times that you asked. But I have to say, if you were looking for something specific, you're going to be surprised by all the activity in that field for that time of the night, for a supposedly vacant field." Dusty chuckled. "Anyway, if you need anything else, just call me. Otherwise, we'll see you next Sunday. Stay safe, my friend!"

Finn immediately fingered his cell phone's email icon, anxious to see what Dusty's secret military surveillance satellite images had captured. He opened the jpeg attachment and saw three grainy black-and-white surveillance images of the horse pasture dated 23-09-2018. Although it was challenging to view the details on the small screen, he did notice they were all military time-stamped in numerical order, starting at 2330 hours, or 11:30 p.m. in civilian time. The next was at 2335 hours, with the last at 2340 hours. Dusty's satellite images finally confirmed Finn's suspicions about Tom's car: showing the kid hadn't driven through the fence as it appeared at the crime scene. The whole thing had been staged, just like his body at the base of that oak.

Minutes later, Finn's police radio squawked awake. He listened as the lone Oyster Bay police cruiser was assigned to assist an adjoining car with an occupied burglary investigation in Syosset. Knowing that the cruiser would be out of service for quite a while, he quickly emptied his pockets, took his wallet, loose change, cell phone, and service weapon still in the holster, and placed them into the glove box. Keeping only his folding universal master door key with its five-inch blade. Quietly he exited the car without slamming the door, then locked the door with the key, avoiding a loud chirp from the fob. Glancing around the darkened, deserted street, he was happy he didn't see a soul in sight. It was time, nice and quiet. Except for a distant barking dog, he heard nothing, perfect conditions for torching an old house, he thought, while his teeth gnawed aggressively at the toothpick for what he was about to do.

He quietly removed the full gas can and one road flare from the car's trunk before placing the keys on top of the right rear tire. After quietly closing the trunk, he moved quickly but silently, with nothing rattling in his pockets, cutting between the first and second houses on the north side of the street, which by his calculations would put him directly across from number 20 on the next street over, West Main Street.

A couple minutes later he was standing in the darkened shadows alongside a closed storefront, next to the vacant parking lot opposite number 20, Finn stared at the front of the abandoned Buckley house, then waiting to make sure no one was on the sidewalk, out walking their dog.

With an unobstructed view across South Street to his right, he could see through the large window of the well-lit tavern. A bartender with two patrons, presumably the owners of the two cars parked out in front of the bar.

When he thought the coast was clear, he casually crossed West Main Street clutching the gas can tightly to his left leg, noticing the black number 20 posted on the mailbox to the right of the front door. A light but warm steady drizzle began to fall before he reached the curb, and he welcomed it. It quickly gave the blacktop street a slippery, high-gloss sheen that easily reflected the changing traffic lights' glare, hopefully forcing any passing motorists to focus on the wet road conditions, rather than the actions of an amateur arsonist.

Quietly unlatching the white picket fence gate, he entered the yard, disappearing into the shadows alongside the high shrubbery on the west side of the Buckley house, where he paused. Seeing no interior lights, he continued along the side of the house until he reached the rear door. Keeping his darting eyes and ears open for any movements, unusual sounds, or interior lights. He waited a few more seconds surrounded by the darkness at the back door, until he was satisfied the coast was clear. He was grateful for these older homes, with their antiquated door locks. With a couple quick sliding movements of the blade of his folding pocketknife between the door's lock and the jamb, he was standing in the kitchen.

He purposely didn't bring his flashlight, thinking it would be better to wait for his eyes to adjust to the lightless house, rather than run the risk of someone seeing its illumination in a vacant house. Listening for movements and sounds, he proceeded cautiously to search every room throughout the first floor for occupants. Taking the stairs near the front of the house, behind the living room wall, he continued his search throughout every room on the second floor. Then he returned to the first floor, rechecking every room. When he was confident the house was completely vacant, he went back through the house again, every room, just to make sure. On his third time through the house, he splashed a sloppy rail of gasoline down the center of every floor in every room, on both floors, ending at the front door.

Opening the front door, he backed out onto the porch. Leaving the entrance door wide open, he quickly eye-scanned both sides of West Main Street, then threw the empty gas can back into the house, hearing it bang and bounce down the darkened hallway with an echoing hollow tin sound. Standing under the overhang of the small front porch, out of the rain, he removed the twelve inch round road flare sticking from his right hip suit pocket, and pulling the thick round cardboard topping off one end. Using its built-in striker, he struck a quick glancing blow against the flare's igniter at the top of the flare. Within seconds it was completely engulfed with a fiery flame, spewing potassium perchlorate with its noxious sulfur smell onto the wooden deck of the small porch. With the determination of a professional arsonist, he threw the flare deep into the lightless hallway of the vacant house.

Finn's obsessive thoroughness to detail was engrained, the hallmark of his compulsive subconscious. Whether he was solving a complicated murder, or torching a vacant house, he was meticulous to a fault. So, he waited until he was sure he had used the right amount of gasoline to ensure the house would burn completely and quickly to the ground. A job so thorough he figured that not even the efforts of two fire departments could save it, or so he hoped. Thinking if what he'd been told by both Langdon Foster and Dr. Seely had even the slightest chance of a ringing truth, the connecting pattern of 238 years of unexplained deaths to this house, well that was going to end, right here, right now, tonight.

He took a half step backwards to watch as the frenzied flames sucked oxygen from all around him at the open front door, feeding its wild fury. Pushing a trail of curling flames down the center hallway, the flaming trails turning into each room throughout the first floor before sneaking upwards to the second floor. Seeing the fiery glow reflecting off the interior panes of the living room window, he slowly backed off the front porch onto the worn brick walkway, as the heat intensified.

Not pleased with his behavior, he stood in the shadows of the flickering inferno, in a light but steady rain, yet he was confident he'd saved Karl and Eileen, and countless others, a future of heartbreak and misery. He justified his criminal actions with the sole thought that one bad deed was necessary for a greater good.

Placing his hands into his pants pockets he optimistically watched the house quickly be overcome by the spreading flames, almost like it'd been made of paper. Suddenly, he realized something was terribly wrong. Swiftly removing his left hand from his pants pocket and running the palm of his left hand higher to his belt, in panic he peered down through the dark night to where his police badge should have been. Instantly searching his memory, he couldn't remember putting it in the glove box of the car with his other things. Then he remembered he'd forgotten; he'd screwed up. He hadn't removed his badge from his belt and put it with his gun in the glove box, with the rest of his things.

Frantically he scoured the ground around him, in all the shadows, his eyes fixed on the wet bricked pathway. Then looking back toward the burning porch, rescanning the grass on either side of the walkway in the fire light, back to the brick pathway again, desperately searching the dark and wet ground as he unconsciously gnawed at the toothpick.

The clip holding his badge to his belt must have been jolted loose when he was swinging the gas can, he thought, or when he struck the road flare. He couldn't believe it had come loose; that was the first time, ever. Moving closer to the front porch, he felt the intense heat of the burning house. Repeatedly sweeping the wet ground with darting eyes, back and forth, nothing. Until something reflected in the blaze caught his attention: a shimmering speck of gold.

Staring at it for a brief second in disbelief. But there it was, just about a foot from the front door, only it was inside the burning house. He didn't have time to think about it; the fire was raging out of control, soon someone would be calling the fire department, then the police. He couldn't have his police badge found at the scene of an arson, especially in a house that was suspect in the unexplained deaths of fourteen kids.

Why didn't I just keep it simple? He questioned himself. Why didn't I just throw a couple Molotov cocktails through a front window like anyone else would have done and call it a day? He'd never be able to explain why he was committing an arson, torching some eighteenth-century vacant house, leaving him with only one choice, to retrieve his badge. Nervously he glanced up and down the street, seeing no one, and grateful for the rain.

Pulling his suit jacket up over his head, he knew he had only one shot at retrieving his badge. Standing up straight, shoulders back, chin pointed out, he tilted his head back and sucked in giant gulps of wet night air, filling his lungs until he thought they would burst. Judging by what he had to do, by the speed which he needed to do it in, he figured he wouldn't need to take another breath of air until he had his badge safely in his hand, plus he didn't want to run the fatal risk of sucking any hot gaseous air into his lungs.

Bending at his waist, with his left hand holding the rain-soaked suit jacket tightly over his head, his lips firmly sealed, he made a mad dash toward the burning front door. Stopping short at what was left of the wooden door frame. He was quick, but the fire was quicker. It felt like the flames were alive, reaching out for him, trying to pull him closer to the blaze. He could barely see his badge through the heavy smoke, just inside the doorway, lying there on the floor, a foot away.

Crouching low, he made a desperate reach for his badge through the thick smoke and flames. The heat was too intense, he had to pull his empty hand away from the flames. The heavy smoke mixed with thick black soot swirled all around him, everything seemed to be slowing; he struggled just to move his arm. He figured he had one more chance left in him before he would need to take a breath of air.

On his second attempt, he crouched low again, only this time he turned his covered head away from the intense heat and hot flames. In a quick but blinding movement he forced his sleeved arm down across the floor at the threshold where the front door used to be. Groping frantically through the flames for his badge, he was quickly overcome by the intense heat of the fast-moving fire, his movements weighted, sluggish. Exhausted and confused, he pulled his empty, singed hand out of the flames with the only thought of wanting air. Mentally he continued to fight, he needed his badge, but he desperately needed oxygen more. He tried to back away, off the burning porch, but his legs had turned to stones, something was stopping him, holding him. He wanted to pull his suit jacket off his head, he wanted to fight, to free himself, but the heat and roar of the fire told him not to.

The extreme heat and lack of oxygen had quickly sapped all his strength. His arms became too heavy, falling limp to his sides. He thought if he could take one short breath of air, just one little quick one, it would be all he needed, at least that would give him some strength so he could retreat into the fresh night air away from the intense heat and flames, into the cool of the falling rain just a few short steps away. But as soon as Finn parted his lips for that little sip of desperately needed oxygen, the hot gasses from the burning inferno, the one he'd started himself only a few short moments before, rushed into his mouth, along with soot, smoke, and superheated air that immediately replaced what little oxygen remained in his lungs. The last thing Finn saw was his gnawed toothpick falling to the deck of the burning wooden porch, landing next to his paralyzed feet, before the lights went out.

Nineteen

IT HAD BEEN EIGHT excruciating days since the young, handsome head of British Intelligence Major John André had been detained on the rebel's side of the invisible military line separating King George III's British forces and General Washington's Continental forces north of New York City. Cloaked in unidentifiable civilian clothing, save for his proud, knee-high black British officer's boots, his rudimentary disguise was quickly revealed when he mistook his three captors to be loyalist to the crown.

The days since were long and arduous for the talented manipulator Lieutenant Colonel Simcoe, after he learned of the untimely discovery of Major André along with his ultimate incarceration at the hands of the rebel General Washington's Continental troops. Seven long days of torturous, blinding headaches that left Simcoe's mind weak, disorientated, and filled with suppressed rage.

He desperately wanted to reach out to General Henry Clinton for any updates on André's capture. Simcoe wondered what was being negotiated for his release. More importantly, what occupied his every thought was, could his scheme be salvaged? Could the British somehow still manage to take control of the Hudson River and be victorious? Deep down he knew the answers to those questions, as well as he knew that any personal inquiries into André's plight would only draw unnecessary attention to him and his cowardly plot that not only may have sacrificed the popular major's well-being, but also jeopardized the King's efforts for victory in this revolution.

An alcohol-soaked memory allowed him to glance back to the few short months before, when André had managed to finally visit him at his Oyster Bay winter lodgings, at the Townsends' residence. Something they had secretly planned from the very moment they met at the soiree, one of General Clinton's many galas he regularly hosted at Kennedy House, which also served as the British Army's Headquarters on the Bowling Green in York City.

Reflecting on their first encounter, when he'd finally been invited to attend one of General Clinton's popular and splashy events. Ones he'd only heard about, after-party gossip by the few honored attendees of the festive soirees. Simcoe's blind envy of other British officers, many of lower rankings, along with the Hessian mercenaries who had been invited again and again, only added another layer of secret rage to a bitterness that already lay somewhere between hatred and malice. The reason for Simcoe's first invitation wasn't lost to him: he knew he was invited solely as the current commander of the Queen's Rangers out on Long Island, not because he was well-liked or even respected. He'd been given command of the Queen's Rangers because of his brutal methods of interrogation. General Clinton was desperate. He needed to expose Washington's secret Culper spy ring, which was operating with impunity right under their nose.

However, General Clinton incorrectly thought his new intelligence officer Major John André could prompt Simcoe in some way to be more fruitful, less barbaric to the citizens of Long Island in his search for members of the elusive rebel spy ring. It was the only reason Simcoe and André's paths could have ever crossed. What General Clinton did not count on was that Simcoe was a master manipulator and worked solely in his own self-interest.

On their first meeting, there was an instantaneous flash of unbridled lust. The gullible Major André was instantly smitten. Soon after their personal introduction by their gracious host, Simcoe and André paid little attention to the other hundred or so party attendees. Set adrift, they quickly cloistered themselves in a dimly lit corner of a front room in the opulent British mansion, away from prying eyes.

Simcoe fondly reflected on hearing many wineglasses clinked in festive celebration as the string orchestra played one of Bach's sonatas and the guests performed minuets, to the delight of the newly bewitched duo.

Simcoe was clad in his somewhat confining forest green tailcoat, with black facings matching the wide sleeve cuffs, and hefty ornamental silver shoulder epaulettes resting atop his full shoulders. He wore a gossamer ruffled white silk blouse that nearly choked his meaty neck, along with snug-fitting white linen trousers that restrained the loose rolls of skin on his undisciplined legs. The pants stopped at the knee, just below highly polished black boots denoting the full-dress uniform of the Commander of the Queen's Rangers. Major André wore a slimmer, more sharply fitted traditional full-dress uniform: the Royal British Officers' scarlet tailcoat with white facings and matching sleeve cuffs, gold epaulettes, and gold-threaded, ornate designs on either side of the facings. He also wore a white silk blouse with chest ruffles. His white linen trousers descended to handsomely polished knee-high boots. Both men wore powdered white perukes. They were captivated by an exchange of their mutual interest in poetry.

Over the next few months, André made infrequent, clandestine visits to Simcoe at his winter lodgings at the Townsend homestead in Oyster Bay. Where they always started their greetings with exchanges of British military accomplishments won and lost against Washington's Continental forces, and the rebel militia. They also engaged in debated strategies based on the fresh military secrets that André possessed. André was unknowingly, but systematically, being played and pumped for all his secret military knowledge during each visit. They finished each visit with a heated tryst, followed by a recital of their favorite poetry.

During one such rendezvous André confided to Simcoe that he had been receiving secret intelligence reports from one of George Washington's disgruntled, but most-trusted generals. "I trust that you will be pleased to know that I have finally and successfully turned one of Washington's rebel generals to side with the Crown," André boasted.

"One of Washington's generals?"

"Yes, his most trusted general!"

"Can someone of that rank be truly trusted by the Crown?" Simcoe said.

"Of course he can," André said as he glanced around Simcoe's small sleeping quarters located on the first floor of the Townsends' small but elegantly furnished family residence, a home Simcoe had commandeered for his own winter billeting. The room that sat just below and in front of the wooden stairway that led to the second floor, near enough to the unusually large, brick, four-hearted fireplace located in the center hall of the house, just past the front entrance doorway, providing the needed heat for the entire residence.

"But can we speak openly here, in this room, in the home of a Quaker?" André questioned.

"You're safer here with your precious secrets than in Clinton's own headquarters," Simcoe whispered softly into André's ear before nibbling it tenderly. Pulling the major closer. Then adding in a murmur, "The only ones about are servants and women. Your secrets and our conversations are completely secure here. So, tell me the name of this most trusted of Washington's rebel generals, who has finally come to his senses and decided to reveal vital information. Do I know him?"

"Of course, you do. He was General Burgoyne's greatest adversary at the Battle of Saratoga."

"Horatio Gates?" Simcoe said jumping up in surprise, pulling the thin wool blanket off André's exposed body, while turning to face André, who lay on his side, peering up at Simcoe.

"No, not General Gates! He has never raised his sword on any field of battle."

"You can't mean Arnold?" Simcoe questioned.

"I do indeed. None other than Washington's most admired general," André said, pulling the blanket back over his chilled body.

"Can he be trusted?"

"Yes, I'm sure of it. He came to me, or I should say his new wife, Peggy, came to me months ago with details of some of Washington's valued troop movements in New Jersey. The information was most accurate and rewarding."

"How is it you have come to know her so well that she sought you out with such vital rebel information?" Simcoe asked with a jealous tone.

"I know her from Philadelphia, where I served before. She's the daughter of one of the King's prominent supporters there. She has only recently married the twice-wounded General Arnold, though she has quickly turned his rebel's perception for our benefit."

"I see," Simcoe stated as he refocused his eyes aloft while his entangled mind conjured the unique possibilities.

There was silence while Simcoe pondered this new revelation of a rebel General providing critical information for King George III, yet it was a tantalizing moment for Simcoe, his imagination quickly grasping the enormity of the once-in-a-lifetime opportunity as he calculated the newly discovered information. Simcoe knew that the army that controlled the Hudson River between New York City and Canada would achieve victory in the revolution.

Major André was nothing more than a means for Simcoe, a stepping-stone to something he could never obtain on his own. Someone who held a highly regarded position inside British headquarters, someone who could do things for him, valuable things. The buoyant and agreeable André was in age a year older than Simcoe, though not as mature in cunning.

The middle child of Huguenot parents, André had a pleasing personality that was a joy to all those who knew him. He enjoyed nothing more than the humanities: drawing, painting, singing, and writing verse. Completely naïve to the carnivorous sorts of someone like Simcoe, even thoroughly ignorant to his military position as the new head of the British military intelligence. A supposedly safe military position provided by the British Commander in Chief General Sir Henry Clinton that was meant to insulate the peace-loving major from becoming a casualty of the rebel war. Besides, Clinton immensely enjoyed the private musical and theatrical performances created and conducted by the talented Major André, who was secretly referred to amongst the other British officers in and around British headquarters as Major Ma'am.

André was somewhat naïve and unpretentious to the reality of his recently acquired rebel asset that had so suddenly fallen into his possession. Lacking any military enthusiasm only prevented him from completely recognizing the critical information that this rebel general controlled or could possess as he proudly announced to Simcoe, in a singsong tale, of "guess what I know." Simcoe immediately recognized the potential value of this rebel general. It was the opportunity Simcoe had always dreamed of, the one thing he needed to achieve a coveted position among the ranks of England's aristocrats. Something he knew he was incapable of achieving on his own, without the slightest risk of failure, injury, or merit, while still attaining the highest accolades from King George III. Simcoe had never been dismayed by his own lack of courage. What he lacked in character, moral honor, or integrity, he more than made up in scheming, manipulation, and unchecked brutality.

A devilish smirk formed across his pudgy face. Licking his thick lips, he slowly drew in a measured breath. The *Lord* John

Graves Simcoe, he imagined as he gently exhaled, then perhaps a prestigious seat in parliament, he fancied.

Twenty

SIMCOE BROKE THE SILENCE, shifting his body closer to the exposed back of Major André. He murmured in a hushed breath, "As I lay here, I have come by a most astonishing plan. A plan so magnificently foolproof that you would be seen in a most grand and favorable eye of our esteemed General Clinton. I have no doubt what you possess could be of such an enormous significance in this conflict that it would call for a full and glorious victory for England, and capturing the notice of our Lordship, King George III, from whom I believe you will be most favorably rewarded."

"You have envisioned a plan for me? What could I possibly possess that I could capture the attention of His Majesty?" André rolled over to face Simcoe with uplifted eyes, quirking a questioned smile.

"Nothing short of the greatest military plan yet to be hatched in this rebel conflict," Simcoe teased, then adding, "The simplest of plans, providing a quick and total victory for the Crown, putting an end to these costly rebel hostilities. You possess the unrecognized means for such if as you say, you have recently acquired the total cooperation from that rebel general."

"A simple plan, for which I have already the means?" André questioned.

"Yes! An untapped potential that you have not yet recognized," Simcoe said smoothly, before adding. "You have yet to realize a most powerful element within your complete control."

"And what would that be?" André smirked.

"That would be none other than your General Benedict Arnold himself!" Simcoe stated. "After you have arranged another of your secret rendezvous with your newly acquired asset, you must offer him incentives from the Crown. Then demand he immediately request through General Washington himself, and no one else, to command the key rebel fortification held at the bend of the Hudson River north of New York City. If Washington continues to hold this rebel general in admiration, he will not deny his request. After Arnold has taken command of the fortification and stocked it with the most needed of supplies—food, blankets, powder, rifles, and cannon—he merely turns the fort over to you."

"Most interesting," André replied. "But what incentives could I offer?"

"Offer him everything the rebel commanders have denied him: the rank of brigadier general in the King's army, plus 20,000 pounds sterling. And something the rebels could never give him or his new family: an audience with King George III."

"How could I make such an offer? I do not have the authority," André said, skeptical.

"You won't need the authority. The king will gladly grant an audience to the new Brigadier General Arnold on his own once he learns of Arnold's selfless and heroic aid to General Clinton and the Crown. I do not need to remind you that once the Crown commands all of the Hudson River, the Crown commands its own victory." Simcoe pulled André closer. "I only suggest that you be earnest and act quickly, before your General Arnold has a change of heart."

"I will arrange contact as soon as I take leave of your comfort. But I must advise General Clinton of our plan," André responded, excited.

"Perhaps you should wait on informing the General that I have assisted with such plans. There will be plenty of time to inform him after we have achieved our goal." Simcoe thought he might need to distance himself from the plan in case anything went wrong. "Allow him to think for the moment that it is your plan only. It may be difficult to explain our collaboration," Simcoe said, combing his thick fingers through André's silky brown hair.

"If you think that is the wisest thing to do, I will be silent for now. But I will not remain silent when we have achieved victory. I will rejoice in triumph for all to hear, then all will know of your keen military mind and undying loyalty to our king," André said, turning his face to Simcoe with a twinkle of emotion and a gleam of naïve pride as he gazed into Colonel Simcoe's devious eyes.

Simcoe's contriving mind was way ahead of André's. He knew there would be a better time to inform General Clinton that it was his plan and his alone, but that could only occur after the fort was safely in the hands of the British, and only after he had relieved the traitor general of all his knowledge of Washington's most guarded secrets, the identity of his Culper spies, by whatever means necessary.

Once he'd identified all the spies and their leaders and extracted their methods of intelligence gathering, he would need to learn how they moved freely, passing along their information to their rebel commander. He'd stop at nothing until he had exposed and destroyed everyone associated with that Culper spy ring, no matter whom they were, they'd all hang, like the deceiving dogs they were. Only then would he inform General Clinton that it was he who was the master controller, the great architect of the surrender of the rebel fortification on the Hudson River.

André broke Simcoe's train of thought as he quickly sprang to a sitting position in the narrow bed. Jerking his head about and holding his right index finger up to pursed lips, he said, "Shhh, shhh, listen." André whispered, pointing toward the wood-planked ceiling of the second floor, "We are not alone!"

"Aye, we are not!" Simcoe exclaimed loudly, and lowered himself back down on the bed, unconcerned. "Servants and women are the only ones about. Do you fear either of them?"

"No, of course not," answered André, in a tone that still held concern. "I must return to headquarters." He quickly rose from the bed and began to dress. "I will return when I have learned more of our plan for the rebel general."

"I'll have your horse brought around from the stable," Simcoe offered.

Dressed, they quietly exited the ground-floor bedroom when André, out of the corner of a nervous eye, caught a sudden glimpse of Sarah, the second oldest of the Townsend daughters, standing motionless at the foot of the wooden stairway to the second floor. She was holding a single, unlit candelabra in her right hand and glaring at the two British officers as they exited the bedroom and moved toward the front door. André was momentarily taken by complete surprise at her phantasmal appearance capturing her deep blue eyes. Pausing momentarily to study her, he wondered if her glare was of indifference, judgment, or suspicion. He wondered if she was aware of their hidden relationship or if she overheard their covert plan. Either could bring the punishment of death. André turned slightly to his right and forced a guilty sneer as he gave a slow dip of his head to acknowledge her presence. He didn't wait to see Sarah return the gesture with a strained smile or her compulsory curtsy as he donned his black military tricorn hat and followed Simcoe to the front door. They both failed to notice Ellis, one of Samuel Townsend's Negro servants, standing in the shadows against the floor clock, near the entrance to the kitchen.

Simcoe squinted tightly from the bright southern glare of the summer afternoon sun as he and André emerged beneath the small overhang outside the front door of the Townsends' house. As they waited for André's horse to be brought around from the stable by a uniformed sentry, Simcoe said, "Remember, Major. Mention this to no one. Instruct the rebel general to do likewise. I can promise you results of this plan will exceed your imagination."

"I will, Colonel! When I return, I shall have the complete details of your masterful plan in place." Simcoe clutched the leather bridle of André's spirited charcoal gelding while the major mounted the steed for the six-hour trip back to headquarters. "Make haste, Major, so you can make the last of the night's ferries!"

"Aye Colonel," André said, giving Simcoe a customary salute then guiding his horse toward the South Road, before heading west towards the East River ferry.

Colonel Simcoe had become so desperate to learn the fate of his captured Major André that he couldn't wait for such critical news to funnel its way down through the fractured infrastructure of the British military chain of command. He had to know as soon as possible. He would need time to react, based on any sensitive intelligence he learned from headquarters. He had to prepare himself for General Clinton's reaction upon André's release. If General Clinton learned that it was he who had created the plan, he surely would have him immediately drummed out of the military in total disgrace and transported back to England, if not shot. He needed information, and he needed it fast. Only then could he formulate a plan. His mind raced with confusion.

Simcoe's headaches had become constant, at times unbearable. He struggled to concentrate. The only thing he could safely come up with, without knowing all General Clinton's closely guarded details for Andrés's release was hopefully it'd be a gentleman's release. Knowing the rebels, they would probably want a prisoner exchange. If he could at least arrange to be part of the official escort for André's release from Tappan, he would be able to head off any debriefing between the captive and General Clinton. If he could do that, then maybe he could get André alone, and remind André to inform the General that the Arnold plan was all his idea, that it was his idea to meet with the rebel General unescorted in the woods near Teller's Point on the Hudson for the surrender of Fort Arnold. Why wouldn't General Clinton believe André, he thought, after all he was the British General's commander of military intelligence, England's head spy in the colonies.

This whole Benedict Arnold mess was unnerving for Simcoe. It was also extremely depressing. His personal triumph and glory shattered, what once seemed inevitable was now lost. No audience with the King. Gone also was any hope of a quick and glorious end to this rebel conflict, and his envisioned reward from the King in appreciation for his brilliant military strategy. The thought of being "king" of America was lost forever.

Pouring himself another frothy mug of warm, bitter blackstrap rum, the dejected Simcoe fell back into the high-backed, tapestry-covered chair facing the large double-hung window in the front parlor of the Townsend house. Staring out at the narrow dirt wagon path in front of the house, eagerly awaiting word, any word, from Lieutenant McPherson, who he'd dispatched in the early hours the day before. Simcoe had given the lieutenant strict instructions to gather, as quickly as possible, all the information regarding André's release from anyone inside British headquarters, without drawing undue attention to himself.

Questions raged through his tormented mind. How could this happen to me? I've lost everything, so fast. There must be some way to understand what has happened, to correct this devastating failure! Why had André decided to board the hundred-foot sixteen-cannon *HMS Vulture*, sail it so far up the Hudson into Haverstraw Bay, into enemy territory? That wasn't the plan. The plan was to stop the *Vulture* farther south, well before the enemy line. Did he not think that a hundred-foot warship would attract the attention of rebels that far up the river? Why hadn't he taken an escort when he landed? Why hadn't his troops on the *Vulture* protected him? And why hadn't he secured Arnold's map of the fort someplace other than in his boot? Did he think he could hide his British military identity?

Simcoe downed bottle after bottle of the bitter-tasting rum. The more he mulled over it, the angrier he became, and the more he focused on revenge. He knew he couldn't blame anyone else; he was the only one responsible for the failed plan. He should never have let the inexperienced André negotiate something so vitally important to the war. More importantly, he should never have let him negotiate something so vitally important to his future. He should have used someone else.

Twenty One

SIMCOE POURED THE REMAINING blackstrap rum into his pewter mug before tossing the empty bottle to the floor. Where it landed with a hollow thud, rolling to the corner of the room, coming to rest alongside the other empties. He couldn't come to grips with the thing that bothered him the most. In his inebriated condition, he could only contemplate his own dismal future. Dwelling on what was once the only sure thing that would have guaranteed him one of the five degrees of nobility back in England, and what he thought was his rightful passage "king" of the new American colonies.

Drunkenly lifting an overflowing mug to his rum-soaked lips, Simcoe again fixed on the failed Arnold mission. Wondering how it was that Arnold, a lone rebel traitor dressed in an American Continental Army General's uniform, managed to board his enemy's warship, filled with more than fifty handpicked, highly trained British foot soldiers, unchallenged? Presumably, while it was being pounded from both sides on the fast-flowing Hudson River with rebel cannon fire, during the darkest hours of the night. Then managing to sail south, putting the warship a safe distance from the attacking rebels, to the British-held island of New York City.

All the while, André, disguised in civilian clothing, who was deliberately and tactically evading the rebels behind enemy lines, who seemingly happened upon an innocent encounter with three rebels afoot, somewhere in the middle of a dense forest, under the cover of a moonless sky. Get captured with the most valued and strategically vital fortification plans of all known rebel locations, Fort Arnold. Simcoe's deranged mind refused to admit anything other. Was it subversion that had robbed him of his glory? Aside from some divine intervention, providing he was God fearing, which he was not. Simcoe thought there could be but one simple explanation for what had happened. After taking another mouthful of the bitter-tasting rum, swallowing hard, he swiped at his dripping lips with the back of his hand as his thoughts played out the failed plan.

Why were André's plans and instructions not written in a ciphered code? he wondered. Hell, he was the head spy for General Clinton for god's sake, did he not think of this? Then were not Arnold's final instructions to André that night an intentional method of delivering André into the waiting hands of three of the First Massachusetts Militia? Members of the same small militia unit that reported directly to General Arnold himself at his Fort Arnold, men from the same unit used by Arnold as his final escort to the safety of the *HMS Vulture*, securing his future?

Maybe Washington knew all along what Arnold was up too. Maybe he hadn't given up secrets to the King's men. Maybe the only thing that was given up for certain was Major André, complete with written instructions and a detailed map of the rebel's fortification, all the physical evidence needed to seal his fate as an undisputed British spy. Was Arnold really a traitor, or a clever opportunist?

Taking the last gulp of rum from the pewter mug, he swallowed hard, staggered to his unbalanced feet, glancing around the room with blurred vision, searching for another bottle of the confiscated rebels' foul-tasting rum. When from outside he heard his sentries loudly proclaim "Rider approaching, rider approaching!"

Simcoe crossed the parlor to the front door, where he momentarily paused, trying to stand tall and straight, pushing out his chin, pulling his shoulders back, and sucking in his protruding stomach. After giving a deep, wet cough to clear his throat, he tugged down the front hem of his uniformed waistcoat and brushed an open palm across the front of his rum-soiled, wrinkled trousers. He grabbed his tall black leather hat, with its crescent moon insignia symbolizing the goddess of the hunt and placed it on his numbed head. He drew in a large breath of rum-free air before opening the door, where he was momentarily blinded by the glare of the bright afternoon light.

The pounding of fast-approaching hooves could be heard long before either rider or animal could be seen. Simcoe stepped out onto the wooden porch, beneath its slight overhang, and eyed the two uniformed sentries stationed on either side at the front of the porch. Lieutenant McPherson on his mount quickly came into view, making a hard left turn, his horse galloped to a sudden stop in front of the Townsend house, kicking up a cloud of dried trail dust. He hastily dismounted.

McPherson with a Brown Bess musket slung across his back, hurriedly approached Colonel Simcoe on the porch. Extending a snappy salute as Ellis took control of McPherson's mount. Ellis had long ago been placed in charge of caring for all the horses and carriages owned by the Townsends, though now burdened with many more of Lieutenant Colonel Simcoe's confiscated horses including the upkeep of the Townsend stable. Ellis clutched the bridle with one hand while swiping at the thick froth of sweat gathered beneath and around the hard-ridden horse's neck with his other hand before he led the horse back towards the stable at the rear of the house. Overhearing Colonel Simcoe ask the rider, "What news do you bring me from headquarters of Major André's release?"

"I'm afraid I bring no relief to your fears, Colonel," Lieutenant McPherson stated, exhausted.

"Come inside, Lieutenant. We'll discuss your news while I enjoy some rum," Simcoe stated as he turned and led the Lieutenant into the house, closing the door behind them. Quickly remembering he was out of the rebels' rum. Simcoe opened the door and barked at his sentries, "Get me more rum. I don't care how you secure it, just get me more rum, and plenty of it. Get it now, or you shall never enjoy another taste of rum again yourselves." Slamming the door closed.

"What have you learned?" Simcoe asked the lieutenant. "I want to know everything, and the names of everyone you spoke with at headquarters."

"May I sit, Colonel? It's been a long, hard ride from New York."

"No! You may not sit. You will tell me what you've learned and make it quick."

On nervous and unsteady legs, McPherson began, "I spoke with only one person at headquarters, Colonel, so as not to draw undue attention to my inquiries, as you had ordered. That was with General Clinton's aide-de-camp. He said the General had been in communication with the rebel army's commander, who acknowledged they were holding Major André as a prisoner of war."

"A prisoner of war?"

"Yes, but not as a soldier, but as a spy."

"He used the word *spy*?"

"Yes, Colonel."

"What has General Clinton prepared for Major André's release. What are the rebel's terms?"

"There are no terms, Colonel! Major André is scheduled to be executed tomorrow. The rebels are preparing to hang him."

"To hang him! Tomorrow?"

"Yes, sir. The second day of October, before noon."

"There were no rebel terms for the release of Major André?" Simcoe insisted.

"There was but one demand, sir. General Clinton refused it."

"What was that demand?"

"The rebel commander demanded a prisoner exchange, saying he would gladly release Major André, but only for the return of General Arnold, nothing less."

"General Clinton refused that demand, knowing the head of his intelligence service was to be hanged?" Simcoe asked in a surprised tone.

"Yes, sir, he did. Then the rebel commander reminded General Clinton that the British had hanged a young militia captain named Nathan Hale a few years back on New York Island as a spy."

"Was my name mentioned at any time during your discussions?"

"Yes, sir. The General's aide-de-camp cautioned that you should not venture anywhere near headquarters or even to the island of New York, unless you have been summoned by Sir General Clinton. The General holds you accountable for Major André's sorrowful fate. He believes it was you who orchestrated the plan, or you have somehow sacrificed the major's safety, knowing he had little or no experience to negotiate such an elaborate undertaking."

"Me?" shouted Simcoe.

"Yes, sir. That's the message. I was ordered to bring back to you, Colonel."

"We'll see about that!" Simcoe stated, angrily kicking at the empty rum bottles on the floor in the corner. Then adding, "How can he believe that it is I who is responsible for André's capture? I had nothing to do with Major André's plans. I knew nothing of him working with that rebel general. He only mentioned it to me a couple days before his unfortunate capture, right here in this room, where we had taken tea. There must have been a rebel spy nearby who overheard our conversation." Simcoe peered suspiciously out of the window, looking left and right as if there were a spy lurking nearby. "We must flush out and identify those rebel spies at all costs, Lieutenant. Do you hear me?" Simcoe faced McPherson. "It is up to us to find that spy, the one who has exposed our poor Major André. Do you understand me, Lieutenant?"

"Yes, of course, sir. I understand. What have you in mind, Colonel?"

"I want every available man we have; I want them to round up every suspected rebel in Oyster Bay and have them taken to the oak. I want them all interrogated. I want this spy identified. I want him to pay for his deceitful act. I want him captured before noon tomorrow. Do you understand me, Lieutenant? If the rebel commander plans on hanging our Major André, we'll show him that we can hang one of his own cowardly spies as well."

"I understand, sir."

"Then why are you still standing there? What are you waiting for, Lieutenant?"

"I have only one question, Colonel."

"Yes, what is it?"

"I beg your humble pardon, Colonel, but we have already taken all of the suspected rebels in Oyster Bay to the oak, on prior interrogations, under your direct orders. That leaves only those who are loyal to the King. They have all taken a pledge of loyalty."

"I don't care—I want those spies apprehended, Lieutenant! Do you understand me? If you cannot fulfill this task, I will find another who can, do you understand me?"

"Yes, Colonel. Shall we gather up the women and children as well, sir? And what about the Negro servants?"

"Don't be stupid, Lieutenant. Women are of no concern or threat to the Crown. They lack the intelligence to spy. As for the Negro servants, they care not who oversees them. The children? Any male who has reached seventeen years of age shall be taken by force to the oak for interrogation. If that fails to get us answers, in identifying these cowardly spies in this town, then I want every man, whether loyalist or not, taken to the oak for interrogation. I want them all bound to the oak one by one, while the others in waiting witness the work of the dragoon's sabers. Then I want them slowly finished off with as many thrusts of our foot soldiers' bayonets as may be needed."

"What if they have no information to surrender, Colonel?" Lieutenant McPherson asked reluctantly, avoiding eye contact with the enraged Simcoe.

"It matters not to me, Lieutenant!" Simcoe ranted. "They have brought this upon themselves. And the troops could use the practice." Simcoe gave a full-throated laugh. "Then I want all their uncooperative bodies stacked high along the south road, right here in the middle of this godforsaken village, then set afire for all to see what happens to those who do not cooperate with the Crown. Now be off with you, Lieutenant," Simcoe stated, pointing toward the door.

Twenty Two

CURLED IN A PROTECTIVE fetal position Finn lay unnoticed, or so he thought, in the dark stillness, on the small wooden front porch of 20 West Main Street. He had no idea how long he'd lain there, motionless. Trying to control his labored breathing, listening for sounds, any sounds, the police, the fire department, or anything that would tell him he wasn't alone. Concentrating on broadening his listening boundary, his mind grappled to clear away the cloud of confusion. He was slowly waking, his lungs feeling minor relief from the tightened squeeze inside his chest. After a couple quick muffled coughs, he slowly drew in a small amount of air, his head still buried below his rain-soaked suit jacket.

Perfectly still, his arms folded, pulled tightly against his chest, he wanted to open his eyes, to poke his head out from under the cover of his. Cautious not to move too quickly unless he heard something, thinking maybe he'd been injured from falling house debris during the fire? Though he didn't feel any pain, still he couldn't really feel his legs. Yet he had the crazy sensation that something was somehow different. It was eerily quiet, he heard no raging fire, no popping, no snapping of embers, or crackling of flames, though he knew it should be raging out of control, right next to him, but he felt no heat. Taking a couple quick sniffs to the air, he was surprised he couldn't smell soot or smoke. Briefly, his mind harbored a passing thought, what if he were dead?

He released that thought, because he could still hear himself breathing, and thinking. He was about to lift his head from under his suit jacket for a quick peek around when he felt a sliding motion, the creaking sound of wood, someone had stepped onto the little wooden front porch. Someone was grabbing his right shoulder with a determined grip, pulling him upward onto his feet. In a close whisper, he heard, "Hurry, we must go. You cannot stay here; it is too dangerous for you. We must hurry!"

Wondering if he'd been unconscious, possibly because he had inhaled so much smoke and soot. Or possibly because something from the fire had fallen on him, which was why he felt so dizzy and disoriented. His legs refused to cooperate; they were weak, unsteady. He pulled his suit jacket off his head.

The view he saw through puzzled vision, as his eyes straining to focus, came as a complete shock. The house was no longer on fire. In fact, it was still intact, nothing was out of place, the front door was even closed, with not the slightest trace of fire, nothing even singed.

The night air had taken on a cool, damp chill. His tired eyes labored for clarity as he examined both of his arms, then his legs. He looked back at the house, to the porch. He was in total disbelief. He'd started the fire himself; he watched it burn.

He suddenly remembered the reason why he was on the porch. He'd gone back to look for his missing police badge. Glancing down to his belt, the badge was still missing. Yet his coat sleeve didn't smell of smoke. "What's happening?" He murmured softly. His body unexpectedly tightened from an abrupt squeeze of a strong hand gripping his right shoulder from behind. Defensively he responded with a jolting stance as he turned to face his attacker. "We must hurry. You cannot stay here," came the same deep voice as before. Finn's eyes focused on the tall muscular one-eyed black man staring back at him, insisting in a mellow baritone voice, "Come! We must hurry! The sentries will be returning. Colonel Simcoe must not find you here. Stay low and follow me. But hurry!" the voice commanded as he coaxed the weakened and disoriented Finn off the small front porch around to the west side of the house, stopping briefly in the night's darkness, to listen for alarming sounds.

"Who are you?" Finn finally asked when they paused in crouched positions inside the shadows of the house.

"Shhh, shhh. We must be silent," the man cautioned. "I'm Ellis," he answered without facing Finn, focusing his glare toward the blackened empty night at the front of the house.

"Ellis, what are we doing?" Finn whispered back.

"I'm taking you to safety."

"Why do I need safety, Ellis?"

"We must get you back to the stable before anyone sees you. If Colonel Simcoe or his Rangers find you here, they will kill you for sure. They'll hang you."

"Colonel Simcoe? Are you for real, Ellis?"

"Of course," Ellis replied softly with a questionable tone, taking a second to study himself as if to make sure he was real and wondering why he was even asked that.

Finn suddenly remembered Dr. Seely's outlandish story of time travel. Could it be the old man wasn't as crazy or drunk as he seemed? His mind revisiting parts of that conversation he had with the old doctor. Recounting Seely's mellowed voice and his bizarre coaching.

* * *

"There are certain energy spots, or what men of science commonly refer to as metric energy fields, invisible gravitational fields of super-powerful energy that move quantum particles of compact matter at the speed of light, creating a funneled effect within a confined rotation. If one could possibly view this phenomenon, it is believed it would look something like the condensed matter of our Milky Way, rapidly passing through an invisible tube."

Finn remembered breaking into Seely's explanation mid-sentence. "And you're telling me this because, why? Because you're tired of explaining some ludicrous theory of some unexplained deaths?"

"No, Detective, I'm telling you so you can have a basic understanding of what you will be experiencing as you travel."

"Travel?"

"Yes, on your epic journey to stop Simcoe's malediction. Please pay attention, it is most vital," Seely said while slurping back a string of dripping rum from his lower lip then adding, "Many believe these events are isolated to places beyond earth's atmosphere, however, research has proven of their existence here on the earth's surface." Seely momentarily paused, readjusted his sitting position, then added, "They're undetectable with any known scientific instruments, however they are very real, and very powerful. I'm personally aware they exist, as do a few others. Atmospheric academics and geophysicists referred to them as vortexes or vortices. They believe these mysterious locations are merely flaws in the planet's surface. While some of these locations can be very large, many others are quite small, no larger than the lid of a wooden barrel. All are extremely powerful, with an immeasurable amount of gravitational pull. To those who know of their exact locations, they are considered sacred.

Finn recalled Seely saying, "To the vast majority of the earth's inhabitants these powerful invisible energy fields are unknown, and for the most part they are missed, never recognizing a telltale millisecond blip to one of the more commonly used handheld electronic devices, which would indicate they are near one of these invisible energy vortexes. Most will only register as a momentary weak signal, causing a minor interruption, at worse a dropped call. Other times, causing a device to display no bars at all. Which is most always attributed to a cell tower's location being too far away, and not the area of an invisible energy field. Or, when an invisible energy force field briefly disrupts someone's GPS signal, indicated by a robotic female voice for the need to reconfigure. Though more commonly, perhaps more noticeable, but just as quickly dismissed is when one of these invisible gravitational metric force fields is unknowingly bordered it will register as static on one's car radio, causing the listener fruitless attempts to correct it by readjusting the tuning knob for the lost signal. Ultimately all devices will resume full operational functions, as well as the car's radio, but only after it has completely passed by or over the threshold of the invisible anomaly."

"You know, for a 236-year-old surgeon, you seem to know an awful lot of modern technology," Finn added in a skeptical tone.

"As I've said, Detective, I know a great many things. I'm only explaining it to you in a manner your modern mind can comprehend. I'd rather simply refer to them as history holes."

Dr. Seely continued, "However, some of these mystery spots can be much more powerful than others. Having the ability to draw mass amounts of metric energy from the earth's atmosphere, while also having the ability to project mass amounts of metric energy into the atmosphere. Creating an extremely large invisible loop that self-generates a constant, high-speed rotation of minute particles of matter directly into the fourth-dimensional flow of motion, bending the fabric of time and space." Seely paused, before adding, "And as you well know, Detective, the human body is nothing more than a walking clump of matter." Making his point, Seely continuing, "Which allows all particles of matter to travel back and forth between time and space, creating a portal for travel."

"A time-travel portal? Are you kidding me, you're talking about time travel, Doc? Really? I think it's time we cut you off and put that rum away," Finn said, shaking his head with a comic laugh.

"That is exactly what I am saying, Detective. I'm telling you how this method of time travel functions, so you can understand how it pertains to you on your travels. So you'll be able to recognize one of these portals in 1780, allowing you to return to the present once you have successfully stopped the *why* of your murder investigation."

"Wait! You think I'm traveling back to 1780 to conduct a murder investigation?" Finn chuckled as he shook his head in senseless amazement.

"Oh no, not to conduct your investigation, Detective. Only to find and stop the *why* of your murders."

"If that's the case, why don't I just travel seventeen years into the future and catch the killer when he tries to kill the next kid living in that house? Seventeen years is a lot shorter than 238 years; don't you think?" Finn suggested sarcastically.

"Because you can't travel into the future to correct the past, Detective! But you already know that isn't logical!"

"Not logical?" Finn cut in. "Isn't that what you've done, Dr. Seely, sitting here 236years in the future?"

"Of course not!"

"Then how do you explain sitting here now?" Finn said in an accusatory tone.

Dr. Seely gave a slight shrug of his thin shoulders then added in a toned-down mellow voice, "I haven't traveled to the future to meet with you, Detective. I've been here waiting for you!"

"Waiting for me?"

"But of course, I have," Seely said flatly, before continuing, "These history holes, as I call them, travel in a loop to the past. Anything you'll ever want to know about the future, you will learn from peering into the past."

"If that's true—I mean, if you can only travel one way—how would I get back home to the present?" Finn said, thinking he just put the kibosh on the good doctor's history-hole theory.

"Haven't you been listening, Detective?" Dr. Seely said, thumping his cane on the floor. "It's a loop! Once you have entered that funneled energy field, you can only exit at a date in time predetermined by an incident from the past. To return to the present, after you've reentered that energized loop, you can only exit at the time you had previously entered, which would be in present time." Then adding with a little chuckle, "Minus a minute or two for travel."

"A time predetermined by what?" Finn asked.

"By murder!"

"Wait!" Finn turned to face Seely. "you're saying, and I'm only going along with you here to keep you amused, out of respect. But if I should somehow enter one of your gravitational energy loops, or history holes, as you like to call them. That that loop of invisible energy will carry me back in time to the exact date a murder took place?"

"Absolutely correct! Or from where a murder proposition had been orchestrated in that exact location."

"So, then your history hole of invisible energy will loop me right back here, to the present time?" Finn asked.

"Yes, yes, that's exactly what I am saying. I'm glad you finally understand," Dr. Seely said excitedly, banging his cane on the floor in triumph.

"OK, so how would one find a history hole?"

"Ah, that's the best part, Detective. It finds you!" Seely said, banging his cane on the floor and breaking out in muffled laughter like he had just revisited a private joke.

* * *

"Ellis? Do you know what today is?"

"It's Sunday."

"No, I mean, do you know what the date is?"

"Yes, it's October first."

"What year?"

"What year?" Ellis questioned.

"Yes, Ellis, what year?" Finn asked hurriedly.

"It's 1780, of course, don't you know?"

"1780?" Finn questioned suspiciously in a soft whispered tone. This can't be really happening, it's not logical to be back in 1780, or even physically possible, he considered. Taking a second look at Ellis with his eighteenth-century clothing and concerning awe on his face, Finn realized he needed to find shelter. "Ellis, we better get to your stable."

Finn hoped to buy himself some time to think of someplace out of harm's way, in a place no British Colonel would ever casually venture. Someplace socially beneath them. The stable seemed like the best bet. Finn followed as Ellis guided him around the darkened side of the Townsends' house to a second outbuilding near the privy, at the rear of the residence. Some of it looked surprising familiar, even in the dark, though newer.

Ellis glanced in both directions before he quietly opened the sturdy wooden door leading into the pitch-black stable. Finn followed. Once inside, Ellis lit a thick white candle contained inside a metal-framed lantern that hung from one of the wooden posts that supported the second-floor hayloft. Instantly, large green, buzzing horseflies swarmed the white glow of the glassed flamed candle. The smell of fresh-cut hay was overpowered by the smell of fresher horse manure. Finn eyed the dimly lit interior of the stable through the candlelight, seeing six open stalls, three to each side of the stable, below a half loft. He walked the center of the stable peering into each horse filled stall cautiously covering the complete length of the stable's dirt floor searching for hidden surprises.

"Colonel Simcoe and his green coats are searching for foreigners all over Oyster Bay. They are looking for spies," Ellis warned.

"Spies! Green coats?"

"Yes, sir, the Queen's Rangers. And you are a foreigner, sir. They will think you are a spy."

"How do you know I'm not from here?"

"You are wearing different clothing. And if Colonel Simcoe is hunting you as a spy, you are a friend to me."

"I guess I could be considered a spy of sorts. Just not for this war, Ellis," Finn said as he gazed at his improbable surroundings.

"Not this war?"

"It's hard for me to explain right now. I am not even sure why I am here. I think I'm supposed to be solving a series of murders, or, I should say, 238 years of unexplained deaths, what some people think are murders. And I have no idea where to start. I'm supposedly here to find the *why* of this whole mess," Finn said, his eyes rescanning the interior of the stable.

"Murders?" Ellis questioned with a concerned one-eyed stare.

"Perhaps that word murder wasn't warranted, though I'm still not convinced there is a series of unexplained deaths, yet. But if this is 1780, which it appears it is, I have a lot to reconsider.

"Where do you hail from, sir?"

"Here, I'm from right here in Oyster Bay."

"I have never seen you in the village before, sir," Ellis said.

"Well, I don't actually live here, but I do work here in Oyster Bay. My name is Finn, not sir. Please call me Finn," Finn added, casting a friendly smile.

"But you wear the clothes of a foreigner, and you speak different."

"These are clothes from another time, I think. And yeah, I guess I do speak a little different than you. I'm still from Oyster Bay."

"I will get you some fresh clothing from these times," Ellis said, sending Finn a large, toothy smile. "And something to eat, first thing in the morning. Then we will find a way to hide you from Colonel Simcoe. You can sleep up in the hayloft; you will be safe there for tonight, Finn." Ellis pointed toward the hayloft's ladder. "No one will know you're here, but you must remain quiet."

"I think you're taking a big risk helping me, Ellis. Maybe you should keep a safe distance from me, so Simcoe and his men won't catch you and punish you."

"I'm very much safe from our Colonel Simcoe," Ellis said. "He thinks I am a slave of Mr. Townsend; Colonel Simcoe would never suspect a slave of being anything but a slave." He smiled mischievously. "Besides, the Colonel believes I'm unable to speak."

Ellis reached up and removed the lantern from the wooden support and held it up to his face. "See, Finn, I have a broken face. When I was young, I was kicked by a skittish colt. I must have crossed too close to his flank, he struck this side of my face. I can no longer see from the broken eye, and my face falls low on this side. Everyone thinks I cannot speak, except Miss Sally, and, of course, Master Townsend. So, you see, I have no fears of Colonel Simcoe. He never talks to me."

"It's called palsy," Finn said.

"Palsy?"

"The damage to your facial nerves causes your face muscles to droop. It's either from the horse's initial kick, or from the inability of your facial nerves to repair themselves," Finn said.

Ellis just shook his head, then said, "I must blow out the candle now, Finn. Can't have anyone seeing light in the stable at this hour. You can go up to the loft now. Cover your entire body with hay. It'll keep you warm, no one will see you if they come into the stable, and it will keep the horseflies from biting you."

"I understand, Ellis," Finn replied as he slowly ascended the ladder. Suddenly realizing just how tired he really was. Still a little groggy, his balance not yet steady, he even felt mentally slower, forced to consciously think of what he was going do or say next. It must be the result of traveling through that history hole the old doctor had warned him about, and the physical transition back to 1780, he thought.

Lying on the floor of the loft, in a bed of the brambly, sweet-smelling fodder, he pulled tufts of hay from the surrounding stacks as he piled layers of it over his body. Who would believe what has happened to me? he thought. He couldn't believe it himself, as his body and mind succumbed to the comforting warmth of the layers of hay and his eyes closed from the weight of thought.

Twenty Three

FINN WAS AWAKENED FROM a restless night of unstable sleep by the sounds of someone moving about below him, and hearing a soft, sweet, low-toned singing voice that instantly felt soothing to his weakened body. A comforting tone just above a whisper, calming and pleasant. It was morning; he knew that from the golden sunlight seeping through the cracks in the second-story barn boards next to him. Lifting his head over the loft's edge, he saw a wall of washing sunlight brightening the stable floor below, probably from the larger, open double doors at the rear of the stable, facing the northeast he thought. The warming early light and country-fresh air penetrated deep into the stable. The six horses in their stalls below had been mostly quiet during the night, except for an occasional whinny or the irregular vibrating movements felt through the loft's floor caused by the animals rubbing against the walls of their stalls. Finn lay motionless in the hayloft, waiting for the person to leave the stable, though he enjoyed the soft, mellow tone, thinking it helped his banged-up mind, plus, it helped to know where the singer was as they moved about the stable.

Surprisingly, he felt relatively refreshed. Calmly listened to the surrounding sounds of a chilled, but sun-filled autumn day. There was some lingering fuzziness, with a little dizziness. Even so, he couldn't completely convince himself it was October 2, 1780.

The sharp caws of a couple low-flying crows in the skies outside the stable momentarily broke the calm. Then, an unfamiliar scratching sound resonated from somewhere below him in the stable, possibly from someone grooming a horse with a curry comb, he thought. Then he detected another sound, though much fainter. Listening harder, an outside sound that immediately stopped his mind from rolling over his predicament like a loose marble, forcing his concentration to zone in on this new sound coming from someplace outside the stable, off in the distance. Rustling sounds, though muffled, seemingly a long way off. He focused harder. Nothing; the sounds were gone. Maybe I'm hearing things, he thought. Maybe it was mind fog. One thing he knew for sure: he was now wide awake and hungry.

He thought back to the last time he'd had anything to eat, vaguely remembered having a couple little hors d'oeuvres at the Stackhouse's dinner party the night before. Now wishing he'd hung around for dinner, even though the news of Karl and Eileen buying this house had easily taken away his appetite.

It was probably Ellis down below in one of the stalls, feeding and grooming the horses, he thought. Knowing he'd have to be careful, lest anyone else see him. He slowly pushed off the pile of loose hay and quietly moved towards the edge of the loft. From his position he couldn't see anyone; the person must be in one of the rear stalls. He'd have to climb down for a better view. After selecting a short stalk of yellowish-green hay from the loft floor, popping it into his mouth, and moving it into the creased corner of his closed lips with his tongue—he'd somehow lost his supply of toothpicks from his shirt pocket, this would have to do. There: he heard it again, that distant rustling sound. He was sure of it this time, it grabbed at him, forcing his attention. It was that same abrasive sound he heard just a few minutes before, only this time a little louder, closer. He knew immediately what the sound was, though he wasn't familiar with the 1780 version, he knew enough of that sound that it could be dangerous.

To a trained ear, there was no mistaking the synced tramping footfalls from hundreds of marching feet and swinging arms, plus the clanking and banging of equipment as they moved in a quickened formation. Once you've heard it, you'd never forget it, regardless of which century you were in. It was the unmistakable sound of rapidly moving soldiers, marching with the determination of an urgent mission. The loud unison rhythm told him of their unstoppable energy. He could even make out a faint voice barking commands, though he couldn't make out what they were saying, or what language, along with the strike of a lone drummer. They were moving quickly, somewhere not too distant from the stable.

Finn quietly made his way down the loft ladder to the dirt floor of the stable. The delightful crooning which he now knew was coming from the last stall on the loft side of the stable in the far rear by the double doors, continued. Rather than calling out for Ellis, Finn thought it safer to approach on foot, in case he needed a quick return to the loft, the movement of the marching soldiers grew louder.

Finn crept quietly alongside the open half wall of the three stalls directly under the hayloft toward the open double doors. Moving closer, he saw the snappy movements of a shapely figure with a curry brush in hand, taking short strokes to the left rear flank of the stabled horse. Drawing him closer was the soft sounds of a calming purr coming from the shadowed figure. His mind was telling him that the sweet sound of that alluring murmur wasn't coming from a muscle-bound, one-eyed stable worker. Moving cautiously closer to the open stall, he began to see the full movements of the groomer who had now moved deeper into the rear shadows of the stall, almost behind the horse, their back toward him. Not sure it was Ellis, but thinking he'd recognized the figure wearing Ellis's dark wool coat from the previous night, though much shorter, more graceful. A dark-colored cloth covered the figure's head. Finn stood silently at the front of the stall, near the horse's head. The animal's large brown eyes suspiciously followed his movements.

In a risky move, but with a softened tone, slightly above a murmur, Finn called out, "Hey, Ellis." The words had scarcely left his lips when he realized he'd made a huge mistake. The darkened figure suddenly stopped, turned to face him. Even in the lightless shadows of the darkened stall, Finn quickly realized it wasn't Ellis, seeing the small, delicate features of a woman dressed in a man's work clothes. He immediately regretted drawing undue attention to himself even as his eyes met the captivating gaze of the petite stranger, an intense inner feeling held their eyes locked in a crystalizing moment of emotion, if for only a fraction of a second.

Finn turned to flee when the figure called out, "Wait! Don't go! Wait!" Catching up to him at the open double doors of the stable she grabbed Finn by his loose coat sleeve, pulling him back inside. "It is too dangerous for you to go out there," she cautioned.

Finn's fleeing body whirled to an unsteady off-balance stop from the momentum of being pulled back into the open doors of the stable. He was further caught off guard with a look at the woman's beautiful facial features. Her porcelain complexion glowed in the rays of the bright sunlight could not be denied. Defined cheekbones, a delicate nose, mesmerizing blue eyes, perfectly sculpted lips, with gloriously bright white even teeth, behind a gentle, warm smile. She was dazzling.

Sensing something familiar about her, he locked his gaze into her large blue eyes, while she maintained a soft grasp of his coat sleeve with one hand, her eyes were deep with worry, she spoke. "My name is Sally."

Before he could respond, he was hit with a waft of a pleasing aroma. A magical fragrance that seemed to overpower his senses, drawing him into its powerful bouquet. He immediately recognized the scent he'd smelled twice before, once at the road's edge of his crime scene, then again at the Townsend family cemetery. It was the same scent described to him by Laura Buckley, the aromatic fragrance of lavender.

"I'm Finn," he managed.

"Yes, I know," she replied.

"You know?" he questioned suspiciously, with a raised brow.

"Ellis told me you were sleeping in the loft. He told me how he found you by our front door last night. Do not fear, only Ellis and I know of your presence."

"It seems I may have endangered everyone," Finn said.

"No, not everyone." Sally frowned. "Only yourself if Colonel Simcoe or his Rangers learn of your presence. Ellis will bring you different clothing and something to eat. You are about the same size as my brother Robert. He will bring you some of his clothes."

"What will Robert say?"

"Robert will not know. He's living on New York Island. He no longer comes to Oyster Bay, as the British have commandeered our family home. I visit him weekly, bringing him current news from home."

"That's very kind of you, but I don't plan on staying around here long."

"Ellis told me you needed a place to hide, that Colonel Simcoe may be looking for you. You're welcome to use our stable, but you must stay out of sight. Colonel Simcoe and his Rangers are searching all of Oyster Bay now for spies. If they find you, they will surely kill you."

"I'm not a spy."

"Ellis has informed me of that as well," Sally said with a furrowed brow. "Where are you from?"

"Here, I'm from right here in Oyster Bay. I know this will sound odd to you because it's odd for me. I am a police detective. I am here looking for answers, or should I say a motive, I've been led to believe that I'd find it here, where exactly, I am not sure. I only know I have until sundown on the second of October to find it."

"But today's October second!" Sally said with a puzzled gaze.

"I know. Which means I have extraordinarily little time, with even less to go on."

"Why must you find this motive by sundown?"

"I'm not sure of that either. I've been told that it had to be by this time."

"Who has told you this?"

"That's another long story," Finn said with a little wheeling of his head.

"This isn't a good time to be here, Finn. Simcoe's Rangers will be here soon."

"I have no choice. It's the reason I'm here. I must stop the killer of fourteen seventeen-year-old males, from here in Oyster Bay."

"Seventeen-year-old men? From here in Oyster Bay? Finn, we do not have fourteen men of that age in Oyster Bay. I don't think we have ever had fourteen men of that age in Oyster Bay. This is an exceedingly small hamlet. We had but a few hundred residents before this conflict started; we are less than half of that now. Most are women and old men with very few children. Almost all are non-fighting Quakers. All men of that age or older have fled to Connecticut or have been drafted into the service to fight for King George III. How will you know this killer?"

Shrugging his shoulders, he said, "This I don't know, it's strange for me to accept. It's even harder for me to explain any of this to you if I even knew where to start. I don't know the name of this person I'm looking for, nor do I know what he looks like. I just know I have a limited time to find him." Then Finn added, "I think your Colonel Simcoe may have some knowledge of these murders."

"Colonel Simcoe!" Sally repeated. "He's an extremely dangerous man, if he is the person with knowledge of whom you are seeking. You are but one man. He has almost 400 provincial Rangers scattered throughout Long Island, between here and Setauket. How could you find this person in one day, even if Colonel Simcoe knows who he is? What is a police detective?"

Before Finn could answer, Ellis appeared in the doorway of the stable, holding a folded bundle of clothing. "Here, Finn. Put these on. They should help you fit in." Ellis handed the bundle to Finn, then turned to Sally. "They're looking for you in the house, Miss

Sally. They told me if I see you in the stable to send you back to the house. Colonel Simcoe is incredibly angry again today, Miss Sally."

"Is he drunk?"

"Yes, he's very drunk and in a mean spirit. I heard him tell Lieutenant McPherson to go and get the tax collector, have him make a list of all men left in Oyster Bay, then have the Rangers round them up and drag them down to the oak so he can find out where these Culper spies are hiding."

"But those are all old men, Ellis!"

"Yes, that's what the lieutenant told the colonel, but Colonel Simcoe said that would make it easier to get the information he needed."

"This guy Simcoe—why hasn't anyone stopped him?" Finn asked.

"He has the whole British army behind him. It would be certain death for anyone to try. Haven't you heard of him?" Sally asked.

"Only in passing,"

"Finn, do you know how to ride a horse?" Sally asked, peering at his business suit.

"It's been a while."

"Ellis, saddle Otis for me, and Ophelia for Finn, while I get out of these stable clothes before my father or anyone else sees me. I'll go back into the house and see what the problem is. Is Phoebe in the house, Ellis?"

"Yes, Miss Sally, she is. She's the one asked me to fetch you."

Finn could hear the footfalls of the marching soldiers growing louder, closer, as he climbed the ladder to the loft, the bundle of clothes cradled under one arm, to change. Sally grabbed her house dress draped over an unused feed trough, before disappearing into one of the horse stalls to change. She couldn't take the chance of having Colonel Simcoe seeing her wearing a man's breeches, that would be too dangerous, too suspicious for her to be in men's clothing, even if only to groom her beloved Otis.

In the loft, Finn disrobed, balling up his wrinkled charcoal business suit and ditching it beneath a thick layer of hay along with his wingtips before unraveling the bundle of clothing Ellis had given him. His first thoughts were of how uncomfortable the clothes felt, how outdated they looked. Then again, the latter was relative.

First, he put on the white baggy linen shirt and the roomy tan cotton breeches, then pulled the sheer white knee stockings up over his feet and legs, until they met his breeches at his knees. He forced his feet into a pair of undersized, tight-fitting black leather shoes with a large dull metal buckle attached to the front, knowing the stiff cloglike shoes were going to give him some major blisters if he stayed in them too long, wondering if maybe he could get away with wearing his wingtips instead but quickly dismissing that idea. He finished off his new ensemble with a darker tan three-quarter-length, light wool frock coat, with two usable pockets.

After giving himself a quick once-over in his new clothing, Finn said aloud, "Now I look like a larger version of old man Seely!" He slowly descended the ladder just in time to see Sally exit the horse stall in a light-colored, low-neckline, long-sleeved cotton sack-back dress. Through the curtain-style opening in the front, he could see that it had a dark underskirt. A plain, hand-crocheted piece of lace hugged her graceful neck before meeting her dress line that snugged her voluptuous breasts tightly against her body. Her free-flowing light brown hair had curled ends resting neatly on her thin shoulders, above an hourglass figure that before had been hidden by loose-fitting stable clothes.

Finn stared, slack jawed.

Her striking beauty held Finn's attention captive while he stood at the bottom of the loft ladder in a boyish stare. Sally quickly approached him, reaching out to take his right hand in her bird-soft palm. "Wait for me here, Finn. I'll be right back. Ellis will get our horses ready. We must leave the stable before the soldiers come searching."

"What happens if they find someone?"

"They will take him to the oak."

"The oak?"

"Yes, the scarlet oak tree at the Rangers' bivouac, where they torture their prisoners."

Her tender touch sent a tingling sensation throughout his entire body. His heart thumped from a warmth he'd never experienced before. Hearing little of what Sally was saying, his attention focused on the movements of her alluring moist lips.

He'd immediately sensed their shared objectives—hers to nurture and protect in the name of liberty, while his a devoted quest to catch those with an evil heart. Shared passions though seemingly not equally aligned were still very powerful influences in affairs of the heart. His heart felt an instant tug toward the beautiful Sally Townsend.

Before Sally disappeared through the side door of the stable, she paused momentarily at the inside threshold, casting a glancing eye over her left shoulder, flashing her stunning eyes with her long, elegant eyelashes that shielded a downward gaze, sending a broad smile back to Finn.

Twenty Four

ELLIS CROSSED THE HARD-PACKED earth floor of the stable and handed Finn a cloth bag containing biscuits, meat, and two apples. "I have brought you food. Now I must go saddle the horses. There is drink for you in the small crock next to the door." He pointed to a thin, dark brown ceramic bottle sitting on a wooden tack box below several neatly hung leather bridles and bits, just inside the small stable doorway.

Starving, Finn quickly opened the cloth bag and pulled out an odd-shaped light brown lump. He took a small, cautious bite. It was both odorless and tasteless. He took out a square piece of something that was even darker, harder, and strangely shrunken, and held it up to his nose. "Bacon!" he said softly. "I'd know that smell anywhere." He quickly ate both cubes of bacon and two of the three biscuits; the third he stuffed into one of his pockets, along with the uneaten apples, for another time.

He picked up the ceramic bottle, pulled out the cloth-wrapped wooden stopper, and took a long draw into his biscuit-dried mouth. He had barely pulled the bottle away when his mouth discharged the foul, bitter liquid onto the dirt floor. With a couple urgent coughs to purge the rest, he said, "What is this?"

Ellis was leading a saddled horse out of his stall. "It is ale."

"For breakfast?"

"Do you not like it? I can get you rum if you like."

"No, that's OK. I'm good, thanks," Finn said placing the stopper back into the bottle setting it back on the tack box.

The steady sound of the approaching soldiers grew louder. Ellis finished saddling the horses, then joined Finn, who waited in the shadows of the stable for Sally to return. "You must hurry, Finn. The soldiers are almost here. They will start searching every building in the village."

Finn took advantage of his time waiting for Sally to return to do what he did best: ask questions and learn as much as he could in the short amount of time he had.

"Why are they so determined to find spies?" Finn asked.

"Colonel Simcoe thinks a spy has overheard his plans with Major André. That is the reason why the major was captured."

"The British major who was captured and hanged by George Washington's men?" Finn said, glad he'd paid some attention to Seely's history lessons. He'd even remembered some of the Benedict Arnold story from Sister Margaret Mary's fourth-grade history class at Saint Mary's, though now he wished he'd paid a little more attention, for now he was living some of it. With a disturbing thought that he may even have some traitor blood in him.

"Yes, that's him. But he hasn't been hung yet. They're hanging him later today," Ellis said, giving Finn a one-eyed suspicious glare.

"Today, where?"

"No one knows for sure. Someplace north of New York City in rebel-held territory, maybe Tappan. General Washington told General Clinton if he doesn't turn over Benedict Arnold by midday, they're going to hang Major André as a spy, just like the British did to that poor schoolteacher from Connecticut a few years back."

"Simcoe thinks André was captured because a spy here in Oyster Bay had information about the major's planning with General Arnold?"

"Yes."

"Where does Simcoe think this spy got this information?"

"Right here from Master Townsend's house. Colonel Simcoe makes this house Rangers' headquarters in the winter. Sometimes Major André comes out from New York City to visit him."

"So, he thinks some spy overheard him and Major André discussing a plan for General Arnold to surrender West Point—sorry, I mean his fort on the Hudson River then join the British army?"

"Yes. That's what he thinks," Ellis responded with a suspicious glare.

"What do you think, Ellis? Is one of General Washington's spies here in Oyster Bay?"

"Could be, Finn. Maybe they meet by the Negro cemetery," Ellis said stone-faced, as he tested Finn.

"The Negro cemetery?"

"Up in Pine Hollow."

"Do you know who the spy is, Ellis?" Finn asked.

"I cannot say, even if I was threatened with certain death."

"Well, I'm not going to threaten your life, Ellis. Unless, of course, you know who my killer is and won't tell me," Finn said in a nonthreatening tone, giving Ellis a joking smile.

"I don't know who your killer is, but I'll help you find him, if you want me to," Ellis answered with a trusting inflection.

"Ellis, does Miss Sally know who the spy is?"

"I cannot say, Finn.

"That's all-right Ellis," Finn said, wishing he could take that question back.

"Miss Sally is a courageous woman. She is very strong-willed. She won't tell you either, even if you threaten her life."

"I won't be asking her, and I'd never threaten her, Ellis. That's not what I'm here for."

"Miss Sally is like my sister. I'd do anything for her, and I won't let anyone hurt her either, Finn."

"Oh no Ellis, I would never hurt her!"

"Yes, I know you won't," Ellis said, in a matter-of-fact tone, as his brown eye grew larger, staring Finn down.

"You have nothing to worry about from me, Ellis."

"Yes, but I don't know you. You say you are from here, but I have never seen you before."

"You're correct in not trusting me, Ellis. Trust no one, especially when there is a war going on. You stick with the people you know unless you learn different."

"Yes, I will."

"Ellis, when did you meet Miss Sally?"

"I never met her, me and Miss Sally have always known each other. We grew up together. She's one reason I stay here and work in the stable for her father Master Samuel Townsend."

"You're not a slave?"

"No, lots of people think I am. Master Townsend gave me my free papers, but I don't tell no one. He pays me for my work here in the stable, nobody knows. Miss Sally taught me and my Elizabeth how to read and write. We're part of Master Townsend's family."

Finn's recollection of what the old doctor had told him was slowly returning, the cloudy edges of his mind were beginning to clear. Although he still didn't understand exactly why his investigation led him here, at this point it was more important to draw connecting lines to things that he knew he could connect, hoping it would lead him in the right direction, rather than starting over and hoping for a different outcome. He'd first need to understand the reason he was standing in Samuel Townsend's stable on the morning of October 2, 1780, and its significance to 238 years of unexplained deaths. He'd always preferred the black and white of things; now there was too much gray in the mix.

Finn and Ellis's attention was quickly drawn toward the front of the stable, at the sound of the small door opening and closing. Sally hurriedly approaching them. She had changed again, and was now wearing a sky-blue, tight-fitting jacket with elbow-length sleeves over a white linen bodice. On her bottom half she wore a dark blue riding petticoat and black calf-high riding boots. Her light brown hair had been pulled up high on the back of her head in a tight knot secured with a red velvet ribbon. Her appearance was intoxicating. "I see you have changed your clothes again."

"Yes, this is my riding habit. I told Father I was taking Otis for some exercise," Sally answered with an averted shy gaze.

"You look amazing!" Finn added, taking a step closer to her.

Ellis gave a couple quick, dry coughs into a folded fist to break the silent passion that seemed to physically control the two, then said, "Soldiers are here. You must leave. They will be searching the stable soon."

That seemed to be the only thing that could have broken Finn and Sally's mutual adoration. That and maybe the sound of a cannon being fired inside the stable.

"Phoebe told me that some of the soldiers have already rounded up old men in the village. They're taking them to the oak. The rest of the soldiers will be searching all the buildings in the village, looking for any of the Culper spies," Sally said.

"Culper spies?" Finn asked.

"Yes, Colonel Simcoe is looking for Samuel Culper Senior and Samuel Culper Junior, code names for two of General Washington's spies!"

"How do you know this, Sally?"

"Colonel Simcoe makes no secret of who he is looking for. He knows General Washington has spies here on Long Island. He just doesn't know how many, where they are, or what their real names are."

He'd recognized the name Samuel Culper from old Doc Seely's story, which he took as a good sign that the mind fog was finally lifting.

"Why is he in such a big hurry to identify these spies?"

"He thinks that if he can capture the head of Washington's spy ring, he can exchange him for his precious Major André, saving him from being hanged. That's why he is turning Oyster Bay upside down."

"What if he doesn't find them?"

"I'm afraid a lot of people from Oyster Bay will die," Sally said solemnly.

"Can we stop him?" Finn asked.

"We are only a few against many."

"Can we get others in the village to help?"

"That is hopeless, I am afraid. Most of the villagers are loyalist, the remaining few are afraid of what Simcoe will do to them or their families if they fail. They've seen his brutal side. Many have witnessed their neighbors' sudden disappearance."

"What about your family, are they safe?"

"Yes, I hope so. There is only my mother, father, my brother David, little sister Phoebe, and me here in Oyster Bay. My brother William is in New York City helping my other brother, Robert, with his business. My oldest brother, Samuel, is at sea on his merchant ship. He will not be back for months. Colonel Simcoe has no reason to suspect any of us are part of the Culper's."

"Can you be sure of that?"

"No. With this madman, no one can be sure of anything," Sally said, then asked, "Have you thought of anything that can help you?"

Finn knew people like Simcoe, who hid behind the cloak of war to carry out their evil. He wanted to help, he'd do anything to help, but he wondered if that was even possible, since he was under time pressure to find the *why* of his killer?

"Yes, I've been lucky in remembering a couple things. I remember him telling me something about the Culper spies and Colonel Simcoe's malediction."

"Who has told you this?" Sally suddenly demanded. Turning and defensively facing Finn she demanded, "Who has told you about the Culper's?" Her stance was firm, her face displaying a furrowed brow and tightened lips, her large blue eyes glaring at Finn.

"Dr. Ebenezer Seely. He told me yesterday right here at his house in Oyster Bay. Do you know him?" Finn answered quickly.

"I do not know any Dr. Ebenezer Seely, not in Oyster Bay or any other place," Sally said.

"He told me he was married to your sister Phoebe."

"Finn, my sister Phoebe is not yet sixteen years old."

"Oh yeah, that's right, it's hard to understand, but I think they will be married, only many years from now, Sally."

"And how would you know this?" Sally asked with a suspicious tone.

"I know it doesn't make any sense, and there isn't time to explain it all now. You'll just have to trust me."

"Trust you? When you know very little of what and who you are looking for? Besides, what is this Simcoe malediction?" Sally asked in a doubtful tone.

"I haven't figured that out yet either, I believe it has something to do with my murders, I just don't know how, not right now anyway. You said that Simcoe is rounding up all the men in the village and taking them to the oak?

"Yes."

"Then I'll go to the oak and see what I can learn."

"You can't go to the oak. That's where Simcoe's men are bivouacked. They'll capture you for sure there."

Finn could tell Sally was a dedicated patriot as he considered her eyes. Searching for her trust, he noticed a softening in her large blue eyes, a glimmer of concern was revealed. Sensing she had emotionally dropped her protective guard and wondering if she was believing him, a stranger, from another time. Or maybe she was just giving him a personal grant of limited trust, a little something before she could be totally certain, when she said, "I'll take you; we'll go together."

Finn said, "Where is the oak?"

"It's just south of Mill Pond, by the narrow river."

"Of course it is!" Finn said. "I know exactly where it is!" His mind flashed to his crime scene.

"How do you know where it is?"

"Things are starting to come together for me, Sally. I'll explain it all later."

"To avoid Colonel Simcoe's men, we'll ride down to the harbor and follow the shoreline until we come to the mill. Then we'll head south along the east side of the pond, until we get to the base of the hill. Then we'll ride up the hill and watch the Rangers' encampment from the side of the hill," Sally said.

"That's a good idea," Finn said in agreement. Then he asked, "Why is my horse's name Ophelia?"

"Ophelia is our youngest mare. She's a gentle, caring creature. But be mindful, she is strong-willed with lots of endurance, and not to be crossed. She doesn't show her true spirit until it's absolutely necessary. She'll be a perfect fit for you, Finn," Sally explained in an amorous tone. "My father said she's a lot like me! Plus, Otis is my horse. He won't let anyone else ride him."

She gave Finn a coy smile before she gently threw her head back, showing her perfectly even white teeth as she cupped Otis's reins over his neck.

Twenty Five

IN A SWIFT, GRACEFUL movement, Sally mounted her horse. Then watched Finn as he hesitantly studied his animal, with its high riding stirrups of an English saddle. Ophelia also turned her head to watch him with curiosity. He was about to make his move up on Ophelia when Ellis approached him with a small piece of red ribbon, the same shade and style that Sally had around the knot of her hair. Ellis neatly threaded the ribbon through a top buttonhole of Finn's frock coat. Tying a small knot he said, "You'll need this red ribbon if you're approached by one of Simcoe's Rangers, they'll think you're loyal to the King."

Finally managing to get himself into the saddle without drawing too much laughter from Sally and just a slight snicker from Ellis. Finn began situating himself with the stirrups and reins, when Ellis handed him a small, single-shot smoothbore Toby-style Queen Anne flintlock pocket pistol, saying. "Take this in case you find yourself needing one, I've kept it hidden. You have no further shot or powder; there is only one shot, and please keep a worried eye on Miss Sally. There are many of them but only two of you!"

"Thanks, Ellis, I will," Finn said.

Examining the antique firearm, hoping he'd never have a need for it, knowing how historically inaccurate a smoothbore gun was, more so if it had a short barrel, dropping it into the empty pocket of his frock coat.

Sally ducked as she passed under the header of the double stable doors and into the bright sunlight of the open barnyard, glancing back to see Finn do the same. They rode side by side for a short distance before turning right to follow a narrow wagon track for a short distance. They turned again onto South Road as they trotted out of the village toward the harbor. After a while, they slowed at the water's edge, pulling their horses back to a leisurely stride. Finn gazed in wonderment at the magnificent view of the pristine harbor, its crystal-clear waters glistening like curves of precious stones under the cloudless turquoise sky, scaring off flocks of screeching gulls from the spotless beach as they rode west along the shoreline. He understood the difference of time, how untouched by human beings it was compared to how it appeared the last time he was in the very same spot, only a week before, witnessing the chaotic scene of the recreational boat owners struggling to launch their trailered boats. Finn wasn't surprised at seeing what the destruction of time had caused to the original habitat of this tiny village, knowing the growing population and technology had created irreversible damage to the charming, picturesque village.

He'd also become horrifically familiar with how cruel humans could be to other humans, even without a war. Silently thinking, if there was the slightest bit of truth to any of Dr. Seely's tale of what this barbaric British Colonel's role played with his ruthless hunt for Washington's Culper spies and how a few secretive, dedicated, committed patriots had factored into the outcome of the American Revolution, it would be an enormous revelation to all of America. It was beginning to look like there was going to be a lot more to add to old Dr. Seely's story of spies and murder once he figured out what Simcoe's malediction was, then how to stop it.

By 11:00 a.m., Finn and Sally had made it to the hill that overlooked Finn's crime scene, now the Queen's Rangers' encampment. On their way, they had to backtrack around the pond after Finn spotted some soldiers with wagons on a trail south of the grist mill, between them and the pond. They hid on the bay side, behind the grist mills giant water wheel, as Sally whispered a caution: "These Rangers go out every day with their wagons to steal cattle and livestock from the farmers in the area. They take all the hay and grain they can carry for their horses." She added, "They're heading toward the village. But let's play it safe and go around the other side of the pond."

Waiting in silence, they watched the Rangers pass, before they started around the west side of the pond to a narrow tree-thick covered path on the west side of the pond that passed by the Quakers' council rock, at the base of Mill Hill.

Finn took the lead, at the south end of the pond they crossed over a heavily rutted coach track, which Finn figured was the future Mill River Road. They climbed to the top of the hill, known to the locals as Capital Heights in Finn's time, the third of Oyster Bay's four hills. He had the basic topography of the Oyster Bay area fixed to memory, but this new view of the area with its 1780s scenery, was foreign to him, forcing a recalculation of what he knew of the local roads, pond, even his crime scene from what he could see from the top of the hill. 1780 Oyster Bay was eye opening, no stores in the village, no real roads to speak of, only a few fixed tracks of dirt trails, just wide enough for maybe one narrow wagon, or two horses riding abreast, or for two columns of the King's marching Rangers. The vegetation was impenetrable along either side of every trail. Trees were small and thin near the bay, larger and thicker near and around Mill Pond and on top of the hill, and along the river.

He could barely make out the landscape configuration of the vacant horse pasture, his crime scene was almost unrecognizable. If he hadn't known that Mill River once flowed by this pasture from the stories he'd been told by old Joe, he might not have ever guessed this was the same piece of property. There was no paved road, no charming horse fence, no serene blue spruces. Missing was the sweet smell of fresh-cut grass, replaced by the pungent smell of wood smoke and the foul odor of human excrement. There was no mistaking the one thing that time did share, that was the lone standing scarlet oak in the middle of the field. Though much smaller, it was still large enough for the Rangers to lash a local villager to its trunk or hang someone from one of its lower branches.

After tying their horses to a scrub pine at the top of the hill, they quietly maneuvered down the west side of the steep hill until they reached a spot midway where they had a clear view of the activities in the valley encampment below. They tucked themselves in between the sloping incline of the hillside against a large boulder that lay half-buried from view covered by a low canopy of fanning pine branches that draped the front of the boulder.

He gazed in amazement at a couple hundred small, white cloth tents in staggered, uneven rows across the cramped horse field, with as many small fires tended by Simcoe's Rangers in various degrees of dress—some in complete uniform, others with no waist jacket or hat. Triangular stacks of muskets lay ready in front of each tent. Another group of approaching dragoons came into view, marching a haggard group of old men from the village, Simcoe's spy suspects, daisy-chained together, crossing them over the narrow bridge into the encampment to face the lone oak tree.

A frenzy of Ranger activity filled the British encampment, a free-for-all of the most undisciplined military behavior displayed by any group of soldiers Finn had ever witnessed, anywhere. "There must be 200 of them, they aren't all Rangers, are they?" Finn whispered to Sally, without taking his eyes off the encampment.

"No, I don't think so. I do see some Hessians toward the back, by the far tree line, may be about twenty of them."

"I've never seen soldiers behave like this," Finn stated.

"These men aren't the King's soldiers, they're provisional. Most are criminals who have pledged an allegiance to the King, so they could be released from the sugar house prison. Simcoe could never command General Clinton's real soldiers," Sally said, her tone dripped with loathing.

They're a merry bunch of killers, Finn thought to himself as he rolled a soggy piece of straw around in his mouth, watching the boisterous and rambunctious soldiers singing, laughing, some even fist-fighting. It was like watching a drunken costume party. They staggered about, some falling, others just knocking into one another. They must have been drinking for days, he thought.

His eye immediately singled out one overly aggressive, pudgy Ranger who seemed to be in charge. Finn watched the Ranger viciously and wantonly whip the bare backs of the naked prisoners with a cat o' nine tails as they passed over the bridge and into the clearing. Demanding they reveal the identity of the spy Samuel Culper Junior, and where he lived in Oyster Bay. Finn didn't need to be told, but he whispered to Sally anyway, "Who's the fat guy with the whip?"

Sally turned to face Finn with a saddened look. "That's Colonel Simcoe!"

"Yeah, I thought so," Finn replied, glaring in disgust toward the disheveled, heavy-set commandeer, who continued to whip the naked prisoners.

Finn's attention was quickly averted by a single mounted dragoon at the edge of the encampment farthest from the river who could be seen with his right hand extended high over his head gripping a curved saber that glittered in the mid-day sun, facing down an aged villager who had been lashed to the oak, bound by his wrists around the tree. Without warning, the dragoon feverishly kicked his boot heels into the flanks of his disciplined mount. The horse reared high on its hind legs before obediently lurching forward, galloping toward the lashed prisoner. The mounted dragoon hooped and hollered, swirling a sun glittering saber overhead. In seconds, the quickened steed passed the left side of the tree as the aged prisoner cried out in excruciating pain. His bone-thin, bare chest displaying a widened gash from the slicing blade by the saber welding invader. Finn watched with the eye-blinking speed as the results of the razor-sharp strike from the Dragoon's saber hesitated slightly before a gushing flow of the prisoner's blood began to spout from the wound. The slicing saber so quick and sharp it took the lashed prisoner's conscious mind time to register the wound. "That's barbaric!" Finn whispered.

"Yes, it is!" Sally responded. "That's a Potter saber. I can tell by the curved blade."

"Potter saber?"

"Yes, James Potter, he's a Tory cutler from New York Island. He makes them especially for Simcoe's Rangers. They are rumored to be the finest single edged sabers made in America."

Finn watched as the dragoon circled behind the oak, preparing to come around for another charge at the lashed prisoner, while some of his drunken comrades whistled and yelped with encouragement.

Sally had become silent, her head bowed low with muted sobbing. Finn reached out and put his arm around her shoulder, pulling her closer. She burrowed her face in the side of his chest. He immediately felt the warmth of her breath as her sobs rose and fell from what they were witnessing. There was an unspoken but mutual intensity as he wrapped his other consoling arm round her shoulder and pulled her even closer to his chest. She clasped her arms tightly around his waist. The tempo of her heart beating against his chest was soothing to Finn. He buried his face into her soft, silky hair, cradling her shaking body. Her hair smelled of fresh autumn air, her skin of sweet lavender.

"I cannot watch their pain, their suffering. They are friends, all of them," Sally whispered. "They aren't spies! That's the Reverend Bridwell from the Episcopal church whom they have just slaughtered." Finn held her in his arms until the torturous screams of the reverend were slowly drowned out by raucous Rangers.

"These men have nothing to give this killer. They know nothing. The Culper spies are a secret network; no one knows their real identity. Even General Washington does not know of their identity. It's the only way of protecting them, their families, and their friends," Sally said.

Finn watched as two yelping and hollering foot soldiers made a final charge through matted weeds, over the horse-rutted soil, before thrusting their musket-mounted bayonets deep into the chest of the dying reverend. They probably needed some close quarter killing practice, he thought.

Then, in a surreal revelation, Finn saw it. His first real solid lead since he started his murder investigation. Like viewing an old snapshot from some long-forgotten place, deep within his subconscious mind, snapping at the image like a hungry fish to a dangling worm at feeding time. For the very first time he knew for an absolute certainty of how young Tom Buckley had been murdered. Everything fit, it was all right there in front of him. Bound to the tree by his wrists, the long, deep V-shaped lacerations from the single-bladed saber cut diagonally down and across his torso. The smaller, shallower lacerations on his legs and the insides of the bound arms. The blood spatter high on the tree. The slow, torturous death, it was all right there, even Reverend Bridwell's pooling blood was being absorbed into the base of the tree. This was how Tom Buckley had been murdered. In a move of self-satisfaction in this discovery Finn removed the saliva-soaked piece of straw from his mouth and threw it toward the encampment, watching it land on a jagged edge of the boulder, not two feet away.

Now, he had the *how* young Tom Buckley had died. He just needed to find the *why*, as he stared at the poor Reverend's body slumped at the base of the tree once they'd cut his bound hands free from around the tree truck, like he'd found Tom Buckley. Finn now knew for an absolute certainty how Tom Buckley had died, though he didn't know for certain when he had died. Had young Tom and Susanne been forced to travel back in time, to their deaths? But why?

After witnessing the Rangers lash another elder villager to the tree, Finn angrily muttered, "I have to stop this guy! But first, we'd better get you back." He wiped away the few remaining teardrops from under her red eyes with the palm of his hand. He felt an irresistible drawn from her alluring deep blue eyes, slowly lowered his head to meet hers, his lips finding hers. The petal-softness of her lips sent an instant wave of euphoria throughout his body. Her lips parted as she met his tender passion, drawing her warm tongue against his. Their hands feverishly searching for each other. Their breath's quickening, hearts racing, they silently embraced, falling back against the uphill side of their private lookout, until their moment of ecstasy was abruptly shattered by the sounds of a hard-riding Queen's Ranger calling out below.

"Colonel! Colonel!" the Ranger yelled out as he galloped hard into the encampment. Finn and Sally quickly sat up, their attention drawn to the Ranger as he hurriedly dismounted and rushed to speak with Colonel Simcoe, who was standing near the oak tree, directing other Rangers how to stack the dead bodies on a wagon. Excitement grew quickly amongst the mingling Rangers, presumably from the news delivered by the fast-galloping rider. Finn and Sally watched in confused silence as thirty Rangers mounted their horses, drew their sabers, and dutifully followed the mounted Simcoe across the wooden bridge, over the narrow Mill River, and off toward the village.

"What do you think that was all about?" Sally asked.

"I'm not sure. But it can't be good for someone."

Finn knew he wasn't going to learn anything more from watching Simcoe's Ranger encampment, Simcoe was clearly in a hurry to get to someplace else and Finn didn't have a good feeling about the Rangers' hasty departure. His cop instinct again.

Now it was down to the *why*, he had no idea where he was going to find that, or what he needed, or even how to get it. Simcoe, he figured. Time was of the essence, if what Dr. Seely had told him about finding it by sundown was true, he had little time. Finn checked his watch. It was almost 2:00 p.m. He had only a few hours remaining until sundown.

"What is that on your wrist?" Sally asked.

Finn lifted his arm so she could see as he pulled back the sleeve of his frock coat. "It's a wristwatch, a clock you wear on your wrist."

"Do ladies wear them where you come from?"

"Yes, only a little smaller and much more expensive," he said, smiling, then added, "I come from here, Sally, Oyster Bay, remember." He laughed.

Sally returned the smile with a gleaming eye, then added, "So you say!"

After mounting their horses for the ride back to the Townsend stable, Finn took both of Ellis's apples from his pocket and handed one to Sally. The other he rubbed lightly against his frock coat before taking a small bite. "Sally!" Finn said, slowly chewing the bite of apple. "Earlier, when I asked you if your family would be safe with Simcoe hunting all over Oyster Bay for his Culper spies, you said they would be. You even named your brothers and sisters for me. Did you miss someone?"

Sally thought for a moment. "Oh yes, Audrey. She's the oldest of the girls, but she's married. Her husband is a ship's captain. They are safely away from Colonel Simcoe."

"Audrey?" Finn said. "I was thinking of your sister Sarah."

Sally's bright blue eyes widened in bewilderment, giving Finn a puzzled brow. She seemed to suddenly realize something before she broke out in uncontrollable laughter, her petite body shaking with amusement. Grabbing her stomach with one hand while wiping her tear-filled eyes with the other.

"What? What did I say that was so funny?" Finn asked, with a sunny smile.

Sally's laughter slowed to a joyful whimper as she struggled to gain control of her breathing. She finally said, "Sarah! You asked me about my sister Sarah."

"And you find that funny?"

"Yes, I do."

"Why is that?"

"Because I am Sarah!"

"You're Sarah?"

"Yes. Sally is just an informal name for Sarah, silly. You made my face hurt from laughing so hard."

Finn fell silent, suddenly understanding the sadness of traveling back in time, learning Sally was really Sarah, and how he'd just visited her headstone in the Townsend family cemetery less than twenty-four hours before. Pieces of this bizarre puzzle were starting to fit together for him, some pieces fitting together sadder than others.

"Are you unhappy to learn that I'm Sarah? Or maybe you were thinking of another girl you had an interest in?" Sally asked, flashing a coy look with her eyes downturned and her long eyelashes fluttering for his answer.

Finn paused for a couple seconds to respond to her question. "No, of course not, Sally. I had just heard the name Sarah Townsend somewhere. I thought that you had another sister. That's all. Believe me, you are the only one I've ever had any interest in! I'm just concerned about a few things, that's all, I'm sorry if it shows." For the first time in his life, Finn's heart was overflowing. "Sally, do you mind if I ask you something else?"

"Of course not. You can ask me anything."

"Earlier, when we watched the Reverend Birdwell being slaughtered by Simcoe's dragoon, you mentioned they didn't know anything about the Culper spy ring, that they were secret about who knew their identity, you said even General Washington doesn't know the identity of all the Culper spies. How do you know all that?"

"I guess that's one of those things that's hard for me to explain as well, right now anyway." Then she added, "I'll tell you later, after you tell me who your killer is."

"That's a deal," he said, giving her a warm smile.

There wasn't any reason to press for details, he didn't need any. She said her name was Sarah, that was pretty much all he needed. He'd already visited her grave site at the family cemetery and read the memorial dedication on her obelisk, and knew she was a committed patriot in the battle for freedom and liberty. Though she must have been someone real special he thought, deserving a grand obelisk like she had. Like she'd said, "That's one of those things that's hard to explain." He was intrigued, he wanted to hear her whole story, but it could wait.

They rode silently as they followed a seldom-used trail around the east side of the pond past the grist mill, where they headed north through the woods to the west side of Oyster Bay's harbor. There they followed the high-tide line east along the beach, until they reached the South Road, Taking the hard-packed dirt track back into the village. Turning west at the first narrow trail, what Finn silently thought was the 1780 version of the current Audrey Avenue of the village. When it occurred to him that it was probably named after Sally's sister for some reason.

His brain marble was loosely rolling around, causing some serious doubts about what he had witnessed at the Rangers' encampment. Why had Simcoe and his saber-waving dragoons ridden off at such a determined pace? The thought was concerning, he pushed Ophelia closer behind Otis as they made a southern turn down the path trotting back towards Sally's family stable. He was about to call out to Sally to suggest he take the lead as they approached the barnyard, when they were suddenly halted by three of Simcoe's musket-toting Rangers, who'd jumped from the brushes to block their path just before they entered the opening at the barnyard. They were immediately surrounded by another twenty Rangers with bayoneted muskets, seemingly from nowhere, closing a circled formation. Their horse's bridles were snatched, preventing any attempt at an escape. Sally tried to contain her shock at the surprising movements of their captors but was quickly met by Colonel Simcoe appearing from within the shadows of the open stable doors. Finn wondered if they had found his clothes in their building-to-building search for spies.

Sally spoke first. "What is the meaning of this, Colonel?"

His face twisted; nostrils flared. "You deceitful wench. I have finally captured and unmasked one of Washington's Culper spies!" Stepping out of the stable into the sunlight of the open barnyard, he barked, "Seize them!"

Twenty Six

Finn cried out, "Leave her out of this, Colonel! It's me you're after, not her!" as he tried to stop Simcoe's men from physically dragging Sally down from her horse, while other Rangers jerked Finn from his saddle, landing him face first on the packed barnyard dirt. A heavy dragoon's boot pressed hard against the back of his neck.

"We have discovered your concealment, Culper. A clever disguise!" Simcoe said.

"Let her go, Colonel! She knows nothing," Finn begged, rolling his gaze upward to make eye contact with Simcoe.

"Silence that spy! But do not kill him, not yet. We'll need him to disclose everything about his fellow spies."

Attempting to turn his head, to avoid the striking blow of the incoming Dragoon's rifle butt to the side of his head, he failed, the blow connected with his right ear and jawline, pushing his face harder into the packed dirt with driving pain. Two Rangers grabbed his elbows, twisting his limp body onto his unstable feet and holding him upright while another Ranger struck him in the chest with his rifle butt, causing him to gasp loudly as the wind was forced from his lungs. His knees crumbled, sending him backward to the ground, wildly sucking at the air. Pulled again to his feet, he took another rifle strike to the left side of his face, closing his eye and instantly opening a large gash in the brow ridge. Finn heard Sally's echoing screams.

"Let her go, Colonel! She knows nothing," Finn pleaded, trying to stand upright, while maintaining eye contact with Simcoe with his one good eye. A fresh flow of warm blood streamed down his face, leaving a bitter metallic taste in his mouth.

"Tie their hands!" Simcoe ordered, throwing Finn's confiscated clothing and wingtips to the ground at their feet. Their wrists were quickly bound with thin strips of leather cutting deep into the skin as they were tightened.

"You have discovered me, Colonel. I confess. I am Culper Junior. You must let Sally go; she has nothing to do with the Culper spies," Finn said slightly above a labored murmur, painfully short of breath.

"I know who you are, Samuel Culper! I do not need your confession now. In time you'll have plenty to confess to, including the identity of everyone in your despicable spy ring, along with their real names, their code numbers, and who they report to. Most importantly, you'll tell me the identity of that clever wench on New York Island with the code number three-five-five, the one who must be held accountable for Major André's detection." Simcoe smirked then added, "We have even discovered your spy-code book inside the Townsend house, Culper. We will know if you try to deceive us." Simcoe displayed a thin, worn brown leather-bound journal, held closed with a narrow strip of frayed leather. Handing the code book to his Lieutenant McPherson, Simcoe said, "Secure this in your haversack until we're ready for his interrogation." Finn cautiously watched as McPherson placed the leather-bound code book into a side-hanging leather tote resting at his waist line, hung from a wide leather strap that crossed his chest to the far shoulder.

"I'll tell you everything. Just let her go. You don't need her. I'll tell you everything you want to know, Colonel, everything."

"Of course you will, Culper, in due time." Simcoe grinned. "But your pretty little wench here, well, she'll be strung up today for aiding and harboring an enemy of the King, a Culper spy!"

"Colonel, she has nothing to do with any of this. You want me!" Finn continued to struggle with the two Rangers who restrained his arms. He'd brought all this down on her. He had to save her.

"Silence him!" Simcoe ordered.

Finn could not immediately distinguish the old pain from the incoming rifle butt to the back of his head from the previous strike, except that the new blow propelled him forward on unsteady feet and into the unsuspecting body of Lieutenant McPherson, who had just stepped across in front of Finn. His falling body weight momentarily clung against McPherson's left side as two Rangers pummeled Finn with their rifle butts. McPherson tried desperately to disconnect Finn's falling body from his own. Sliding free to the ground, released from McPherson's entanglement, though not before he managed to secure the leather-bound code book from McPherson's haversack, quickly tucking the small code book into the front of his pants at the waist behind his frock coat, then dropping, seemingly unconscious, to the ground.

"You are a deceitful wench, aiding these Culper's. It took me a while, but I've finally uncovered who you really are, and how you learned of Major André's plans with General Arnold. Do you recognize the name James Barrington Cook?" Simcoe barked in Sally's face.

"Yes, of course I know that traitor. He's your friend. He's the Tory pig you gave Jacob Blair's farm to after you killed him and his family." Sally spat at Simcoe's boots.

"Ah yes, so you do know him. Then again, you seem to know quite a lot of what goes on around here, don't you, Sally Townsend?" Simcoe grabbed her face under the chin, twisting with one hand while pulling back on the tight bun of her hair with the other, forcing her head backwards in pain. "All that ends today for you, you miserable bitch." Scowling, he threw her backwards to the ground. "You don't know what you have caused me," Simcoe sneered, kicking his boot tip into the small of her back. "You see, I would have learned all about you supplying aid to these rebels a lot sooner, but Mr. Cook has only just returned from New York Island on a most important errand, where he has learned from headquarters that Major André was hanged this morning by your rebel friends. That is news I was not prepared to learn. Nor was I prepared to learn that there was a Culper spy living right here under my roof."

"Your roof? It's not your roof, Simcoe. It's not your king's roof either. It is ours! It belongs to my father, Samuel Townsend! Just because you have forced yourself upon our home and etched dubious markings into our window glass with your bayonets does not make it yours."

"You have a sharp tongue, you dishonorable wench!" Simcoe added as he painfully twisted the knot of her hair, pulling her back to her feet. Then he calmly added, "You see, Sally, when Major André and I came up with the plan to have General Arnold surrender the rebel fortification on the Hudson River, to capture your rebel leader at the same time, it was I who told Major André to use the fictitious name of John Anderson if he needed to hide his identity. It was I who drafted that authorization letter for John Anderson to pass freely behind enemy lines, requiring only Arnold's signature. So, you see, Sally, there were only six people who even knew that John Anderson would be passing through enemy territory on the night of the twenty-third of September: me, Major André, General Arnold, you, Culper Junior, and of course that lady spy code named 355 who betrayed our Major André. It was Mr. Cook who delivered the John Anderson authorization letter along with that secret letter from General Washington to General Arnold, asking for a private escort as he passed through Fort Arnold on the twenty-third on his return from Connecticut, where he met in secret with the French. Informing General Arnold to reveal his travel plans to no one—it was written in Washington's own hand. It was Arnold's supporting confirmation to Major André, a written testament of his pending betrayal that was first shared with me. It was meant to be retrieved only by Major André later that day and returned to Arnold at their secret rendezvous with General Arnold on the twenty-third."

"By your count, if I included myself, wouldn't that be actually seven people who knew of the letters?" Sally mocked.

"You are a wise wench, aren't you, Townsend." Simcoe struck her hard across the face, opening a thin cut at the left corner of her mouth. "Mr. Cook cannot read! And he has just informed me that after he had deposited those letters on a kitchen shelf in your family's kitchen as I had instructed, but, before taking his leave by the back door, he noticed you lurking in the shadows of the hallway, near the kitchen. And now I find you here aiding Culper Junior, so it was you who gave those documents to Culper allowing him to pass that information to Washington's spy code named 355. How you removed the wax seals from those documents will be an interesting revelation, sure to be answered by your fellow spy Mr. Culper here," Simcoe said, kicking at Finn's unconscious body. "What do you say to that, you deceitful little bitch?" Simcoe snarled, jerking Sally's head backward.

"I say your valentine poem made me want to vomit, Simcoe," Sally said, forcing her head away from Simcoe's grip.

"Get Ellis! I want him to hitch this bitch's horse to that open wagon. I want her beloved horse to pull the wagon out from under her as she swings from the oak. Get her mother, her father, and everyone in her family down there to watch, now! I want them to see her hang. Better yet, get everyone in this village down to the oak. I want everyone to witness this bitch swing, and to know why. If they refuse, force them. After we hang her, kill her horse for camp meat!" He turned to Lieutenant McPherson and grunted. "Lieutenant, send two men to Norwich Hill. I want signal fires. We'll need to notify the *HMS Halifax* that I have captured a Culper spy." Simcoe grinned, displaying a mouthful of large, rum-stained teeth.

Finn's head was thumping like a piper's drum. He knew not to move, not even to open an eye, remaining unconsciously silent, thanatosis still. In his right ear, which had not quite returned to normal after the rifle strike, he heard a male voice, loud and obnoxious. Listening, he assessed his situation, taking the precious little time to uncloud his thoughts, if that was possible. Desperately wanting to lift his head from the dirt, to spit, to clear his mouth of blood and barnyard dirt. Slowly he opened his right eye and saw a woman's ankle high boots less than three feet away, toe-to-toe with a pair of British officer's boots. Simcoe, he presumed.

Finn was abruptly pulled to his feet by his elbows. His bound hands were tied to a thick rope secured to the back of an open wagon. He noticed Sally standing behind the wagon, next to him. The wagon began to roll slowly forward, out of the barnyard, with Finn and Sally tethered to it by long ropes. Ellis was in the wagon's seat, reins in hand. Simcoe and his dragoons surrounded the procession.

Finn struggled to stay upright, bent forward as he was being pulled along, concentrating on maintaining his balance. The wagon slowly left the barnyard, circled onto South Street, and quickly turned onto West Main Street, where it passed in front of Sally's house. She glanced at Finn with glassy blue eyes, giving him an uneasy smile, sending him an air kiss, before she was struck by Simcoe's cat-o' nine tails whip as he rode alongside her.

Finn desperately wanted to rip that whip from the coward's pudgy little hand and beat him senseless with it, in front of his own men. Let him taste his own medicine. But he couldn't. Instead, he watched Sally as she struggled to walk upright while fending off the biting leather slaps of Simcoe's whip. He wanted to hold her, protect her, tell her he was sorry for bringing all this misery to her. He thought of how Sally had turned his heart: her beauty, her courage, her patriotic devotion to what must have at times felt like a losing cause. Still, she nobly pushed on, rock steady, fully committed to the cause of the American Liberty.

Turning on to West Main Street, he noticed Ellis shift the upper part of his body a little more than necessary to the right, giving a backward glance from his good eye, along with an ever-so-slight nod with a raised corner lip, in an acknowledgement that he would be part of whatever Finn had in mind. Finn had little time to come up with something that would allow Sally to escape unharmed and for him to dispose of the code book. Then he remembered he had the little Toby Queen Anne pistol Ellis had given him, plus his folding pocketknife that he had used to open the back door of the Townsends' house the night before. It had somehow managed to make it through the history hole's energy field. He just needed a diversion to get them out of the deep pockets of the frock coat, and a good plan on how to use them.

He'd only fired a flintlock gun once before, during a Patriot's Day reenactment at Yorktown, Virginia, when he and a couple guys from his sniper unit were on a weekend pass from the Aberdeen Proving Ground in Maryland. The inaccuracy of the flintlock would probably make the Toby Queen Anne almost worthless unless he was within a few feet of his target.

The forced march behind the wagon afforded him precious time to formulate a plan before they arrived at the oak. He was somewhat familiar with the route Simcoe was taking, though it appeared completely different from what he knew. West Main Street was nothing more than a wide dirt coach trail that narrowed to a single track, before meandering through a dense wooded trail along the east side of Mill Pond; this was what he now knew was Mill River Road. The track was uneven and rough, especially under the iron-ringed wheels of an open wagon. The strips of leather were cutting deep into his wrists from the wagon's constant slip-and-tug motion against the rope.

Entering the narrower path of the trail, they lost Simcoe's dragoons. Most had ridden ahead of the wagon. Only four followed in single file in the rutted track behind them, the sides of the trail were too thick with vegetation for their horses to maneuver alongside. "I have the code book," Finn whispered without looking at Sally.

"Oh, bless you, Finn! Thank God!" Sally exclaimed; her tense body muscles softened knowing Simcoe didn't have it. After a brief pause, she added, "It has to be destroyed. We can't let it fall into Simcoe's hands again. I have an idea: we can dispose of it before we get to the encampment. When we cross over the bridge, I'll swing my rope all the way to the left of the wagon, to the edge of the bridge, we'll have Ellis draw the wagon close to the right edge. The dragoons' attention will be drawn to me, as a diversion. That will give you hopefully enough time to dispose of the book in the river. The swift current of the cold water will carry the book away. Even if they retrieve it farther down river, it will be of no use to them, the ink will have been smeared by the water, even wiping clean all the invisible stain," Sally added in a murmured breath.

"I agree, we'll give it our best, we have nothing else!" Finn remarked.

"Whatever happens to us, we cannot let them get their hands on the code book. That ledger is highly confidential, it's the only code book that contains all the specific number codes for all General Washington's Culper associates. Their corresponding identity is written next to each code number, though their identity is written in an invisible stain. It must be protected at all costs; it is most critical for the war."

"Does it list everyone working for Washington?"

"Almost everyone! It doesn't identify the lady with code number three-five-five."

"Why is that?" Finn asked.

"I'll tell you all about that another time."

"Another time? You're a very optimistic woman," Finn said, gazing around at Simcoe's Rangers.

The southern end of the pond was off to his right as they approached the mouth of Mill River. The trail would widen up ahead, where he could make out the clearing of the encampment. Managing a couple quick but painful steps forward, creating a little needed slack in the rope. He pulled the frock coat around the front of his body and fished his folding pocketknife from the left pocket, cupping it from view in his left fist. There were two things that Finn was now really craving, one was to attend to his swollen, bleeding, and blistered feet from the stiff and tight-fitting clog shoes that he'd been forced to abandon at the beginning of the march, the other, maybe more important, was a toothpick.

The encampment came into full view as they were dragged alongside the mouth of Mill River. The slight breeze coming off the encampment carried the strong sent of wood smoke. As they neared the little wooden bridge that crossed over the river into the bivouac area, the clamor of hundreds of soldiers, some drunk, quickly filled the atmosphere. Few if any were interested in Simcoe's party as they approached. Their convoy started across the bridge, with twenty dragoons leading, followed by the wagon, and four dragoons at the rear. Midway across the wooden-planked crossing, Finn saw Sally shift to the left edge of the narrow bridge. Finn swung his rope-tethered body to the right edge, as Ellis's quick action drew the wagon dangerously close to the edge of the bridge.

Sally screamed, and the four dragoons from the rear soon appeared between them. One of them grabbed her rope, pulling her back toward the wagon, onto the bridge. With her diversion, Finn swiftly removed the code book from his waistband and dropped it over the edge, without so much of a splash. No one noticed. The dragoons pulled and hollered at Sally's rope, demanding her to cooperate. Once in the clearing, Finn gave a modest nod to both Ellis and Sally, who both returned slight smiles. Pulling her rope closer to Finn, she whispered, "I'll wait for you!"

"You'll wait for me?"

"Yes, I'll wait for you forever!" she said, sending him one of her endearing smiles.

Simcoe ordered Ellis to position the wagon beneath the oak tree, a Ranger grasping Otis's bridle while guiding the wagon under the thickest branch of the oak, the one that jutted out closest toward the river. Another Ranger cut Finn loose from the wagon, Simcoe ordered two other Rangers to secure Finn while he dismounted his horse, personally cutting Sally loose from the wagon. Simcoe ordered a couple other Rangers to pull Sally up onto the back of the flat platform of the wagon, before placing the hangman's noose around her neck. The other end of the rope was thrown over the extended branch above her head, then looped again over the branch and drawn taut around the trunk of the oak, teetering Sally precariously on her tiptoes in the hanging wagon, her neck stretched painfully tight. She closed her eyes, waiting for Simcoe to give the order for a Ranger to slap Otis's flank, forcing the wagon out from under her.

A crowd of rum-soaked Rangers had gathered about thirty yards behind Finn and his two guards. who'd positioned themselves on either side of Finn with bayonets fixed to their musket rifles held at their sides, less than ten yards in front of the oak. Simcoe took his position front and center at the base of the oak tree to hang the first captured Culper spy in Oyster Bay, and the first captured female of Washington spies.

Assuming an imposing posture in front of those who had gathered, some out of curiosity, others from force, and all out of fear. Simcoe's feet firmly rooted, arms held aloft and stretched wide, he began, *"...To all here today, you are my eternal witnesses to the death of this disparaging Culper wench. Upon her deserving death you will be marked as witnesses to the end of an injustice created by her deceitful betrayal of His Majesty King George III, with his glorious, compassionate, and benevolent practices provided to all here in these colonies. It is for this reason, and this reason alone, that I condemn all those deceitful spies that hath befallen this troubled Townsend house, and for all those who forever take lodging therein. I am bound by a spiritual obligation to express an oath arising from this most vile form of treachery, which has compelled our enemies this very day to hang a most noted and admired Royal British Officer, in a manner not befitting the lowest of a tavern whore. Meanwhile, the real criminal finds sanctuary and comfort within our own ranks. I pledge by all powers of a vengeful spirit to exact an equal and just punishment against every male child that is nurtured within this Townsend domicile from this day forth. Before*

*reaching the rightful age to fight under the colors of this country,
he shall perish before the clock strikes midnight on the day of his
seventeenth birthday."*

There it was, he recognized it immediately: Simcoe's
malediction, his accursed malice, uttered out of misfortune to
cause misfortune. That was the *why* of his murders. It was exactly
as Dr. Seely had told him, at the precise time it needed to be
stopped before the final act. He needed to act before Simcoe's
malediction could be finalized and before Sally could solidify its
utterance.

Struggling to maintain the simplest form of mental alertness,
though still dizzy and disoriented from the countless rifle butts to
his head, and with the loss of vision from one eye, and barely able to
stand upright on blistering raw feet, while everyone watched and
listened to Simcoe giving his vindictive utterance, he'd managed
to secretly open his folding knife. Clasping it hidden in a cupped
fist, he frantically sawed away at the leather straps around his wrist.
Restricted with limited pushing movement of the cupped blade
it was taking longer than he expected. He had precious little time
to save Sally and kill Simcoe, along with any hope of stopping the
malediction. Silently slicing away at the leather straps, he kept his
eyes fixed on Sally struggling in the bed of the wagon, watching
as her neck stretched in excruciating pain from the taut rope that
kept her teetering on the tips of her toes.

Knowing her feet wouldn't have the strength to balance her
weight much longer, before they weakened, before she would be
asphyxiated by her own weight, a slow, terrible death. It would be
quicker, he thought, a more merciful death if the wagon was just
jerked out from under her, with the swift falling weight of her body

she would immediately break her neck, it would be over quickly, less suffering. Finn pushed the knife blade harder and faster, trying not to drop it. It wasn't cutting fast enough, he needed to pick up the speed, to push harder, and faster, it couldn't have much further to go, he thought, but he didn't want to look down at his wrists, he didn't want to take his eyes off Sally as she struggled to stay alive, waiting for him. Is this what she meant by "I'll wait for you"?

Two of Simcoe's Rangers were flanking him, both preoccupied with their commander holding court in front of the oak tree, nearing the end of his rant. Simcoe slowly turned toward Sally, whose colorless face stretched skyward, forced to an uncomfortable angle from the taut rope cutting off the circulation along the right side of her face. Her gasps for breath could be heard over Simcoe's rant as she balanced precariously awaiting her fate. Finn knew Simcoe was about to give the order for the soldier holding Otis's bridle to startle the loyal steed, forcing the wagon forward, plunging Sally to her death. Simcoe drew his saber and held it high above his head in preparation to give the order.

Finn's knife finally managed to cut through his leather bindings. Pulling his hands free, he clutched the folding knife in his right fist with a weakened thumb pushing against the heel of the handle, the five-inch blade protruding from the fatty side of his clenched fist. In a short, quick motion, Finn pivoted his body slightly to the left, bringing his right arm straight out in front of him before pivoting quickly back to the right, carrying the full weight of his upper body. Fueled by adrenaline, rage, and revenge, the momentum of his swinging arm drove the knife blade hard and deep into the throat of the Ranger standing to his right. The soldier's eyes instantly enlarged, in surprised disbelief, as he staggered backwards from the unexpected powerful knife wielding punch to his throat, involuntarily releasing the musket he held perpendicular to his left side. Grasping at his throat with both hands as the knife blade forced out a bubbling stream of gushing blood from Finn's well-placed thrusting blow.

Finn continued his circular motion, managing to catch the soldier's abandoned bayoneted musket with his left hand as it fell toward the ground, the centrifugal force of his uninterrupted pivotal stride continuing onwards to his right. The Ranger to his left realized something was amiss, in a startled gaze and unprepared for Finn's speedy movements, he could only watch the continuing pivoted of Finn's deadly circle before leveling the first Ranger's discarded bayoneted musket at his targeted chest. In an unflinching and power-fueled maneuver, Finn drove the seventeen-inch tri-bladed rifled bayonet deep into the Ranger's chest. Then swiftly retrieved it from the frightened Ranger's chest before the Ranger or anyone realized what was happening, at the same time cocking the musket for fire. Upon completing his 360-degree pivot, he faced Sally at the scarlet oak and deliberately dropped to his right knee.

Right shouldering the butt of the musket, Finn cradled the long-barreled flintlock in the open palm of his left hand. Balancing his left elbow on a bent left knee, drawing quickly, he took two deep measured breaths to control his breathing, slowing his pulse. His actions were a training based involuntary muscle memory, but his need to save Sally was from his heart. Taking a controlled sight alignment on the extended branch above Sally's head, he searched for the rope, his breathing shallowed to that of a hummingbird, then he tuned out all ambient sounds, clearing his mind. He squinted his good eye to a controlled tunnel vision bead on the first loop of rope at the end of the musket barrel, aligning it to the rear just in front of the lock plate and flint. With not an eye blink to spare, Finn squeezed the trigger. The flint fell forward against the frizzen, igniting the powder in the pan.

Through a plume of blue-white smoke, Finn watched the rope untwirl and recoil back against the tree like a frightened snake, dropping Sally's limp body onto the open bed of the wagon. Ellis instantly slapped the leather reins hard against Otis's back. The wagon jolted forward, knocking the Queen's Ranger off balance and to the ground, the wagon kicking up a curtain of dust as it circled around behind the oak tree before heading straight toward the little bridge over Mill River.

Finn let the musket fall to the ground, then stood and pulled the Queen Anne pistol from his pocket. Knowing he needed to get closer for his next shot, his only shot. He watched as the puggy Simcoe had become owl eyed, dropping his Potter's saber to the ground, while stumbling unbalanced backwards, away from the base of the oak as a shroud of dust from Ellis's wagon hung in the air directly behind him. Finn's hearing returned to sounds of chaos: yelling Rangers, the thunder of musket shots being fired, and an iron-wheeled wagon crossing the wooden bridge of the Mill River.

Cocking the hammer on the Queen Anne he set off on a painful, staggering barefooted run straight at Simcoe, who was now grasping the full nature of what was happening, and what he thought was going to happen as he saw Finn charging at him with the Queen Anne cupped in his hand.

Needing to close the distance within six feet of Simcoe for an accurate and meaningful shot, Finn watched terror fill Simcoe's round face as he backed away from a charging Finn. Only fifteen feet from his desired distance, he abruptly stumbled and fell to the ground. Thinking he'd tripped over one of the oak's exposed roots or in a deep hoof track. But when he felt the hot burning pain in his right thigh, coupled with the thunderous reports of a barrage of musket shots, he figured he'd been hit. In a quick glance over his right shoulder, he saw what must have been half of the Queen's Rangers through the smoke-filled field. Scurrying to set up a skirmish line, taking aim at him. Others ran from a 45-degree angle on his right with fixed bayonets, to out-flank him.

Straining, he struggled weakly to his feet, surprised to see that Simcoe had slowed his cowardly retreat. But he was still too far away, dragging his bloody limp leg along the ground, determined to close the needed distance. The pain from the musket shot had surprisingly slowed him, sapping most of his strength, gasping for a needed breath to close the distance for his only pistol shot.

Simcoe stood at the side of the oak, an arrogant smirk hanging on his chubby face, watching a wounded Finn struggling just to stand. Another musket shot hit Finn's left shoulder blade, spinning him around, pushing him a little closer toward Simcoe, who had now haughtily stepped away from the cover of the oak as Finn fell to the ground, landing hard on his stomach at the base of the tree. It was over. He wouldn't be getting back to his feet; he wouldn't be getting any closer to Simcoe. He slowed his breathing to control his heart rate, tuning out any sounds. There weren't any sights on the little pistol, it was a point and shoot kind of gun. The vision in his good eye blurred, he impassionedly struggled just to hold the little pistol steady in the quickening numbness of his hand, his right arm lying lethargic across the ground in front of him. When he felt the presence of numerous Rangers surrounding him as his body lay over the exposed roots at the base of the oak. Finn sensing Simcoe walk closer towards him, then heard him bark, "Kill him!"

Aside from his only thought of killing Simcoe, Finn couldn't help but think as he lay teetering on this side of death, that Simcoe's famous Queen's Rangers had violated the first rules of combat: they failed to search their prisoner and they should have tied his hands behind his back, because, if they had, all this would never would have happened. However, the biggest mistake they had made so far, he imagined, was neglecting to take the cocked Queen Anne from in his right hand, with his index finger still wedged inside the trigger guard, against the trigger.

His semi-conscious attention was painfully drawn to a sudden, intense, white-hot burning sensation felt deep to the middle of his back. The excruciating pain of a tri-bladed British bayonet sent endless ripples of pain throughout his body, like a quivering furrow of circles breaking the placid surface of an alpine lake. He mentally begged his weakening right hand and blurry right eye to stay with him for one last effort, while he willed a final spastic muscle in his twisted, bloody wrist to lift the barrel of the little Queen Anne upward, toward Simcoe's blurred silhouette. He was not six feet away; with every cerebral command he could muster from his disoriented mind he compelled his finger to squeeze the little trigger.

Hearing the metallic snap of the flint striking the frizzen igniting the powder in the pan, followed by a thunderous blast, the little Queen Anne dropped free from his weakened palm. His discontented and exhausted head landed hard against an exposed root at the base of the scarlet oak. He was finished, but not before a final image through a blurred right eye caught the shadowy glimpse behind the lofting plume of blue-white smoke from the little Queen Anne's flash pan, of the overweight tyrant falling backward to the ground like a windblown diseased tree to the forest floor.

Twenty Seven

AWAKE WITH LIFE, MAYBE. He could feel himself thinking, lying dead still, on his back, facing upwards. Mentally surveying his surroundings, trying to place himself. Could he be dead? There wasn't pain in death that he knew of, yet, he had an excruciating headache, his right thigh pulsed in agonizing pain, his lungs burned with each mechanical breath he took, and he was thirsty, so he ruled that out. He rolled his eyes under their lids, refusing to open them or move any body part until he'd assessed as much of his surroundings as possible. Thinking if he were a prisoner, he didn't want his captor to know he was conscious. Where was he? He heard sounds, though his mind believed they were possibly the muffled tones of voices. Was he in a tunnel? Someplace underground? He could smell nothing. His tongue was thick, wedged down by something heavy. He could hear disrupted beeping sounds that were growing louder, closer. And a low rhythmic slurping sound, mechanical, like a pump. The voices remained distant.

He thought he'd take a chance and flutter an eye for a quick assessment, only his left eye wasn't cooperating. His palms lay flat at his sides. Slowly he slid his right index finger over an inch and felt a smooth texture. He moved his whole palm slightly. Smooth, soft.

He was on a bed sheet, he guessed. Most captors didn't provide soft sheets, especially in 1780, he thought.

Taking a calculated risk, he forced open his right eye, his blurred vision taking seconds to bring a clear focus. He was gazing up at a flat, white-painted ceiling and two recessed high-hat lights centered directly above his body, sending a radiant brightness of white light directly into his weakened eye. Outside the lights, he could see a thin silver metal track circling the high hats, gripping a lime green privacy curtain bunched together behind an elaborate configuration of medical monitors, only partially visible when he strained his one good eye. He could hear intermittent beeping. A hospital, he surmised.

His head stiff, immobilized in some type of yoke, why? He could see little, save for a tangle of protruding tubes and colored wires to his left. Moving his right eye slightly, to the inner corner he could barely see two chrome scissored wall mounts extended outwards near his left shoulder, holding an array of wires and two monitors blinking lights and numbers, resembling a dysfunctional laptop computer screen. Two chrome metal floor stands held transparent pouches of clear fluids, flowing through clear thin tubes. He couldn't hold his straining eye long. The head pain! He followed the trail of tubes to his left arm, where they met a webbed mess of smaller clear tubes at his wrist. He still couldn't smell anything, which he thought odd, because all hospitals had that one distinctive smell, a foul antiseptic odor. His mouth was sand dry, and he was extremely thirsty, he couldn't swallow, it was like someone had filled his mouth with cotton?

Then he heard the unmistaken squeak of rubber-soled shoes along a buffed tiled floor. And a muffled voice called out something inaudible. Then more shuffling, quicker now. Two people stood beside him, peering down. One a well-groomed male in a suit and tie, the other a young pretty dark-haired woman in green scrubs. Both smiled, showing lots of teeth. The suit was saying something, but he couldn't understand what was being said, the voice was garbled, he watched his lips move, his voice droned, like he was talking slowly through a hollowed metal container. The nurse turned toward the monitors and was tapping the screen with her index finger. They continued speaking to each other while gazing down at Finn. His hearing began to clear with semi-breaking bursts of audible sounds of their conversation, fading in and out, until his hearing finally cleared. "Nurse, get the doctor!"

He watched the nurse turn and rush off.

"Hey, buddy!" the suit said. "Glad to have you back." He smiled again.

Finn tried to speak. He needed water. Nothing was coming out of his mouth. He tried again, nothing. He realized it was his mind's voice asking for water, his audio voice wasn't working. With his right arm, he reached up and grabbled the suit by his lapel and tugged, then motioned toward his mouth with his index finger.

"You're thirsty, want water?" the suit said.

Finn tried to nod; that wasn't working either. He made a quick fist, stuck his thumb up. The suit said, "Sure, I'll go and get some ice for you. I'll be right back."

By the time the suit returned with a plastic cup of ice, two doctors and two nurses had converged around Finn's bedside, speaking with each other as if Finn wasn't there. They focused their attention on the monitors as they discussed the readings being displayed on the small flat screens, before finally turning to Finn. One doctor removed the bandages from around Finn's head and said, "These stiches can come out. He's healing up nicely on this end." The other examined his right leg. A nurse adjusted the flow of the liquid in the hanging transparent pouches before checking the tube connection at his wrist. Another adjusted his pillows, so his head remained flat against the mattress sandwiched between pillows.

"What do you think, Doc?" Finn heard the suit ask.

"I think he's incredibly lucky guy, Detective."

"Yeah, I should say so. Can he have some ice?"

"As soon as we remove this ventilator." The doctor shone a bright beam of light from his pen light into Finn's right eye, then pulled the sheet back over his right leg. "Then I want him to get some more sleep. The nurse is going to give you something for your pain, Mr. Mansfield, and something to help you sleep." Finn watched as they all retreated from his bedside. The suit was a detective. Finn didn't recognize him; he closed his eye.

Shrieks from an intermittent blast of a cars horn startled Finn awake. Frozen in place by the mesmerizing bright lights of a car's headlights barreling down on him, getting brighter, straight at him, closer, and closer, he couldn't move. Then he realized the horn was the beeping sound of the monitors, and the headlights were the two bright high hats in the ceiling above him.

"How are you feeling today?" the suit asked, standing over Finn's bed.

The tube was gone from Finn's throat. In a dry, raspy whisper, he responded, "Like shit!"

"I'm not surprised. You're pretty banged up. Do you remember anything?"

"Who are you?" Finn asked in a whisper.

"Don't recognize me?"

"No. Should I?"

"It's me, Jimmy Doyle. From the squad. We're friends. We've worked together for years."

"Sorry."

"Remember, we were in the academy together?"

"Sorry, I don't," Finn said, before adding, "I vaguely remember the name, though." He wasn't sure if his head was fuzzy from the rifle butts or the pain killers, or both.

"The doctor said this might happen, that you may not be able to remember much. They said you'll probably have PCS. You've had some serious head injuries."

"PCS?"

"Yeah, post-concussion syndrome. You might remember fragments of some things, with maybe some of your memory being distorted, almost like you're hallucinating. Or you might not remember anything at all. It's from the head wounds. Do you remember anything, anything at all of what happened to you?"

"I remember some things, it's all pretty fuzzy though," Finn said, adding. "Maybe you should fill me in on what you know."

Speaking with Doyle, he'd suddenly remembered him, he was the guy in the office that would unwittingly give up anyone or anything, regardless of how classified or sensitive it was.

"Well, what we've learned so far is this: you were found two weeks ago this past Sunday night, at about 9:20 p.m., over in Oyster Bay. You were on Mill River Road in some private horse farm, barely alive."

"Where am I?"

"You're in the Glen Cove Hospital. You've been shot a couple times with a large-caliber weapon. It appears that you have been stabbed as well, by some odd-shaped instrument, plus you have some serious head injuries. You were found by some high school kid and his friends. They admitted to partying in that horse pasture. Anyway, one kid said he thought you looked like the guy who came into his gas station, looking for a can of gas, when he was closing the station. That was about twenty minutes before he found you. We've ruled him and his friends out as suspects in your shooting. Do you remember any of this? Were you looking for a can of gas?"

"Nah," Finn lied, turning his head toward the window. He began thinking, this kid saw me only twenty minutes before he found me. How was that possible? He knew he'd been back in 1780 for at least twenty-four hours, but then he realized the reality of the time-discrepancy between then and now. But at least he finally had his witness, maybe not to his actual murders but a witness nonetheless for his own recollection. He had Tom and Susanne's friends for the murder investigation, and now this kid from the gas station, plus his own memory. Puzzle pieces for a chain of events, he thought. He'd remembered checking his watch after leaving Dr. Seely's house. The five minutes shown on his watch was vastly different from the time he'd actually spent inside Seely's house, drinking his rum, and listening to his stories.

That time discrepancy would clearly explain the lack of food in Tom and Susanne's stomachs discovered during the autopsy. There must be some extended time difference when time traveling, he thought. Leaning toward the natural time a body needs to digest food, in relation to when their friends claimed they ate together.

It would also explain the coagulated blood on Tom's face, the lividity, and the start of rigor in the bodies, plus the inconsistency in the time of death. He wondered if that alone could establish the longer span of clock time, with a body moving through time, only in reverse. He hoped this wasn't all in his head because it was beginning to make some sense.

"You can't remember anything of what happened? We could always try hypnosis."

"Yeah, that's not going to happen. Hey, did anyone find a small flintlock pistol with me?"

"No. Why would you have a flintlock pistol?" Doyle questioned.

Finn wasn't about to tell Doyle what he did remember, he needed more time to put the pieces together. He wanted to be absolutely certain of what had really happened. Wondering if he'd really met a 236-year-old blind surgeon. Had he really been investigating 238 years of murder associated with 20 West Main Street? Had he really done battle with an eighteenth-century British tyrant? And had he really met a beautiful woman name Sally Townsend whom he'd fallen in love with?

"Finn, you've been in a coma for fourteen days. You're lucky to be alive. The doctor said it's possible you may never totally remember what has happened because of your severe head trauma. The Lieutenant has put all active investigations on hold; he's got the whole police department out looking for leads on the person or persons responsible for your assault. So far, we haven't come up with anything solid."

"One thing I do remember," Finn said, "is 20 West Main Street in Oyster Bay. I remember I was looking into the Buckley murder. Anything new on that?"

"Buckley murder?"

"Yeah, the seventeen-year-old kid and his girlfriend, Susanne White. From Oyster Bay?"

"Sorry, Finn, I'm not familiar with that investigation," Doyle said with a furrowed brow, then added, "You sure about that case name?"

"Yes, I'm sure! The kid was brutally murdered up on Mill River Road. I found both their bodies under that giant scarlet oak in the Cooks' horse pasture, late on Saturday night, the twenty-third of September. Ask the lieutenant. He thinks it was just a fatal auto accident."

"Horse pasture, you mean the horse pasture where they found you?" Doyle answered with a dubious grin. Quickly switching topics. "We did find your car though; it was parked on Orchard Street in Oyster Bay. Your gun, cell phone, and other personal property were recovered from the glove box. The keys were found on top of the right rear tire. Do you remember any of that?" Doyle asked.

Finn had been confronting his own recollection of events, but Doyle was unwittingly confirming vital details that removed any doubt of what he knew, or thought had happened, remembering all of it, but why?

"Twenty West Main Street, Oyster Bay," Doyle said as he fingered his cell phone in search for the address. "Yeah, I thought so, Finn, 20 West Main Street in Oyster Bay, that's a museum, that's Raynham Hall!" Doyle exclaimed with a surprised frown. "It's the Revolutionary home of the Townsend family. Some Townsend family member was alleged to have been associated with George Washington's Culper Spy Ring. I remember passing it on the way over here today, that's why the address sounded so familiar to me."

"Museum?" Finn said.

"Yeah, Raynham Hall, it's the original Townsend family home, built sometime back in the 1700s."

"It's still standing?"

"Still standing? Yeah, sure it is." Doyle laughed. "I just passed it an hour ago."

"It didn't burn to the ground from a fire a couple weeks ago?"

"Nah, I just passed it. It's open. I saw people coming and going."

"Are you sure, Jim?"

"Sure, I'm sure, Finn. I just passed it."

Finn let Doyle's remarks settle before asking, "How long has it been a museum?"

"It's always been a museum. Well, for as long as I can remember anyway. When I was a kid, we'd go there on class trips, and that was thirty years ago."

"Where are my clothes?" Finn asked, knowing that they would also confirm evidence to his recollection.

"They were cut off you by the paramedics up in that pasture, to treat your wounds. You weren't wearing any shoes though."

"Where are they? My clothes."

"I guess they were thrown away. Why?"

"Shouldn't they have been saved for evidence? They need to be tested."

"Tested for what?"

"For trace evidence, and GSR?" Finn said with a skeptic tone. Thinking if he'd been wearing his clothes from 1780, which he believed he was, it would be further confirmation, along with any black powder traces or blood splatter captured in the fabric.

"We didn't need your clothes, or any gunshot residue, we had your wounds as evidence. Plus, the surgeon recovered a small fragment of bullet lead from your femoral shaft when they put the titanium rod in your leg."

"They recovered a partial bullet?"

"Nothing worth saving, just a solid piece of round lead lodged in the femur. There were no rifling or markings of any kind, just a smooth piece of round lead lodged in the badly splintered bone of your leg. Useless for any ballistic comparisons. And there was nothing found in your left shoulder wound. Looks like that was a clean in and out shot."

"How about testing that bullet for metal composition?"

"Yeah, I don't think they'll be doing that, Finn," Doyle said shaking his head.

If what Finn could remember was real, he knew they weren't going to find anything. The shooters were long dead.

"You've got some pretty nasty abrasions around your wrists. Any idea how you got them?"

"Not really," Finn lied. He sure as hell wasn't going to share what he did know with Doyle until he knew all the facts.

"So that's it?" Finn said.

"Yeah, pretty much. Like I was saying, you have two extremely large gunshot wounds, caused by an unknown, large-caliber bullet. And a puncture wound in your back that is totally something else. It went all the way through your chest, passing right through your rib cage. It missed every bone but the sternum, which it fractured, nicking part of your left lung, somehow missing every vital organ along the way, except your sternum, which it fractured, like I said. Oh, and you've got some nasty lacerations and contusions on the bottoms of both feet, with some serious skin infection from all the blisters. You're extremely lucky to be alive, Finn! But it's going to take many months of rehab to rebuild that right leg. Even then, the doctors say you may never have a hundred percent use of the leg again, especially when it comes to police work."

"What are you saying?"

"Looks like you got hit with the silver bullet, my friend! If you can't come back to full duty, which doesn't look likely to happen. They'll pin a couple medals on your chest and put you out to pasture. It could be a good thing, Finn. It'll give you plenty of time to do all the things you've always wanted to do, on full disability pay."

"What, like running a marathon?" Finn replied

"Yeah, I guess that's out. You'd better get some rest. I'll have the nurse give you something stronger for your pain, and I'll be back tomorrow. In the meantime, there are two uniformed officers stationed outside your door and will be available if you need anything."

"Uniformed officers?" Yeah just in case whoever did this to you wants to finish you off. If you need anything, just ask them."

"Thanks, Jim."

"Oh, and Finn. We still haven't found your police badge. Do you have any idea where that is?"

Twenty Eight

AFTER HEARING THE *GOOD part* about being disabled, Finn heard little else of what Doyle had to offer. Gnawing on a plastic hospital straw, he crawled deep into reflection. The marble in his mind rolled around, banging into everything he could possibly remember about Tom Buckley's brutal murder and the crime scene that everyone treated as an unfortunate fatal auto accident.

Looking back, at his visit to the ME's office, to the county records department with Langdon Foster, and his discovery of 238 years of unexplained deaths associated with that house. To the *House of Fredrick* and Lawrence Joseph with his friendless, and suspicious behavior, the missing spadroon above the fireplace. To the revealing phone conversation with Tater, along with the invaluable electronic forensics provided by Detective Rhoads, and old Dr. Seely's odd tails of Simcoe's malediction mixing with his wild theory of time travel. To the dinner party at the Stackhouse's, getting the can of gas at the station in East Norwich, setting fire to 20 West Main Street—which didn't burn, according to Jim Doyle. Then somehow arriving back in 1780 at the Townsend house, with Ellis, the brutal Simcoe, his ragtag Rangers. And, of course, the beautiful Sally Townsend. The thoughts were painfully tiring.

Did any of this occur, or was it just a reaction to being heavily medicated? Finn knew it was medically possible, he'd known assault victims who struggled with this very same thing. Victims who remembered nothing of a violent incident, some who remembered only a limited variant or a distorted version of an incident, due to the severe trauma. It was the mind's way of blocking a memory of pain, self-protection. But that wasn't him, if that were the case, he thought, the very things that suggested why he shouldn't remember anything, was the very reason he did remember, because he knew he'd been musket shot, rifle butted, bayoneted, and bound by the wrists along with the blistered and bloody feet. He had the physical evidence.

Another week passed before Finn was moved out of the intensive care unit, though he remained hospitalized for another three weeks before being transferred to the veterans' hospital in Northport for an additional six months of extensive rehab for his damaged right leg. His visitors were few, soon fading to just Detective Doyle, who made the drive once a week to bring a fresh box or two of toothpicks, informing him that as soon as they received any credible leads, they'd reopen his attempted murder case.

For the next twelve months, Finn's heart and mind stayed on Sally, though his struggles persisted, not because of his health———but with his memory. He'd finally come to accept that 20 West Main Street was a museum and had been for several years. He had no reason to doubt Jim Doyle, which could only mean one thing: he'd been successful in stopping Simcoe's malediction. Then he thought, if he'd stopped the malediction, there couldn't have been any murdered Tom Buckley, because he'd never have lived at 20 West Main Street. And if he'd never been murdered, his girlfriend Susanne White could never have died from witnessing his brutal murder.

Another thing that he couldn't dismiss or pass off was the explanation for his wounds, they were consistent with the smooth bore of a Brown Bess British musket rifle. He couldn't fault anyone from not knowing that, even the forensic pathology report indicated that the piece of bullet removed from his right thigh was an unremarkable smooth piece of lead fired from an unknow large caliber weapon, which only he knew was from a .75 caliber Brown Bess musket. Because he wasn't shot on October 2, 2018, he was shot on October 2, 1780, from a firearm of the times. It was no wonder they couldn't come up with any credible leads on who shot him, or why.

Once again, he was fighting the clock, finally accepting what the crazy Dr. Seely had told him, though mostly from things he witnessed firsthand. Even so, he'd have to believe what Dr. Seely had said about the restrictions of time. And logically thinking––if there weren't any murders, there wouldn't be a killer. But he distinctly remembered Seely telling him.

"Just for the record, Detective, and you must listen very carefully to me now! You have victims that have yet to be discovered, yet to be identified, they are not the result of some unknown serial killer, however they share the same reason, or what you'd call a motive. You'll find one person responsible for the mastermind of these mysterious murders, and only you can sort it out, because only you will have discovered the why for these murders. But remember, time is not your friend here, Detective, as you will be limited until the stroke of midnight, exactly 365 days from tomorrow, October 2nd,

to apprehend your killer, but only if you are successful in stopping Simcoe's malediction, will you learn the identity of your killer."

Still, there were other independent facts to corroborate what he'd remembered, like his car being found exactly where he'd parked it, with his gun and cell phone in the glove box, the keys over the wheel, just like he left it. In addition, there was the kid from the gas station who thought he recognized him, and Dusty's voice message, along with his email. All facts not to be ignored, from murders that hadn't occurred.

For Finn, his unofficial homicide investigation had just moved to another level. He had the *how* of the murders that didn't occur, and the *why* of the murders that didn't occur. Now he needed to find the *who* of a murder he had no knowledge of. Nevertheless, he had a very good idea where to begin. He just needed to do one last thing: he needed to pay an unannounced visit to J. Barrington Cook at the *House of Fredrick.*

Glancing at his watch, it was 6:05 p.m., the fading light of a blood orange autumn sun sank deeper in the sky over the western edge of the little hamlet's fourth hill, bringing an end to a warm, sunny, breeze free afternoon, promptly replaced by a thick, rat grey cloud cover sending the early evening into premature darkness on the second day of October 2019, exactly 365 days from the day he'd stopped Simcoe's malediction.

Driving south along Mill River Road, passing the southern tip of the Mill Pond, he slowed, his eyes scanning the narrow grassy edge of the roadway, for a place to leave his car, just short of the first deadly curve. With the car off the roadway, he limped the remaining 500 feet alongside ridgeline of the dry ravine to the location of his old crime scene. Crossing down and through the dry ravine, then up through the thick inkberry holly hedges, stopping at the horse fence. Resting his folded arms over the top railing of the fence, he paused to survey the giant scarlet oak tree in the pale light, and the vacant pasture that lay beyond, pondering how he was going to gain access to the Cook estate without being detected.

The murky light of the pending darkness gave the sedate horse pasture a tranquil air of silence and calm, until four large ghostly shadows trotted slowly out from around the far side of the scarlet oak, toward the fence line. A majestic, chestnut gelding pulled up short at the fence just in front of Finn, while the other riderless horses remained guardingly close behind. With a soft nudge of the animals large nose, the gelding knocked Finn's arm from the fence railing, then flaring back his large supple lips, displaying a set of tightly clenched teeth, giving a loud whinny, as if suggesting something. Finn stepped back from the fence into the hedges and took a good long look at the chestnut steed, who stared back with large, telling, glassy brown eyes. The gelding gave another short whinny, before turning his right flank toward the fence, sidestepping his majestic body against the slats of the fence.

Hastily Finn scaled to the top of the fence, quickly pulling himself across the gelding's warm, smooth, muscled back. Without commands, all four horses trotted across the pasture to the paddock gate at the southern end of the pasture. Remembering Joseph's intrusion-detection system, Finn reached down and pulled up the long metal latch that opened the tubular gate at the pasture entrance, just behind the estate's gatehouse. The gelding assumed the lead as all four horses trotted in single file silently behind and past the well-lit gatehouse, straight up to the main house. Allowing Finn to prepare for any sudden surprises through the darkened landscape. He was surprised he hadn't set off any of the elaborate security alarms Joseph had previously bragged about, and without any of the armed goons chasing after him.

Making it to the rear of the mansion he quickly dismounted the majestic gelding, watching as the four horses calmly trotted back into the evening dusk toward the stable like they'd just tactically executed a perfectly maneuvered plan. Quickly but silently, Finn moved along the north side of the mansion, hidden from view by the smoky shadows of an early night, checking the oversized double-hung ground-floor windows, all locked. Scaling a four-foot-high rock wall, he found an unlocked set of French doors in the English style courtyard in the rear yard. Entering the lightless, deserted room he quickly recognized it to be the library. A fifteen-foot-high mahogany bookshelf with ornate molding was located to his right, swiftly passing a large oak desk, complete with an imported antique Mongolian high-backed leather armchair sat in front of a wall of glass to the right of the French doors. Two dark leather antiqued wingback chairs sat purposely positioned in front of the desk like silent sentries, resting on an expensive oval Oriental rug covering the highly buffed, Italian marble floor. Crossing in front of the wide-hearth fireplace, he made his way to the far side of the dark but spacious oak-paneled room to its entrance door. Pausing, he opened the door a crack and gave a focused listen. Not hearing anything, he quietly stepped into a grim light of the hallway.

His intend was to surprise old man Cook, to catch him off balance, because he'd had that gut feeling that Joseph and his heavily armed security goons weren't just protecting some lavish

North Shore mansion, with an oversized iron gate and its nicely landscaped property, he wanted to know what and why.

He hadn't made it twenty feet down the thick carpeted runner of the gloomy hallway when he came upon an intersecting cross hallway that was dimly lit by a flickering glow of a soft light coming from an opened doored room at the far end of the hallway to his left. Pausing, he listened, waited, it was eerily quiet, then he started across the intersecting hall when suddenly he felt the cold, hard steel of a gun barrel pressed tight against his right temple and hearing the unmistakable metallic click of the hammer being cocked.

A whispering, confident voice stated, "Welcome back, Detective! Oh, that's right. You're not a detective anymore...Too bad." Finn recognized the voice, Joseph. "What did I tell you the last time you were here? This place is impenetrable. When will you cops ever learn?" Joseph then added in a disappointed tone: "I would love to kill you right now, but the boss wants to do it himself. So, we'll have to wait, but not here, my friend. Someplace where we're all familiar with."

Finn's face was pushed hard and flat against the hallway wall, then searched. His hands pulled and twisted behind his back, and handcuffed by two of Joseph's security goons, his head covered with a soiled cloth hood smelling of tobacco smoke and body odor. He wondered if Joseph's security goons carried this blindfold on their person to be readily available, thinking it was probably standard security equipment for the *House of Fredrick.*

He was frog-marched down a long hallway that led to an outside door on the south side of the house, then across the graveled driveway for a short distance to an idling car. Forced into the backseat, landing face first across the seat, pulling his legs in between the seats before hearing the door slam behind him. He heard the front passenger door slam, thinking there must be two in the front. He heard another car's tires crunch slowly over the gravel up alongside, hearing Joseph's voice. "Stay close behind and follow me."

He couldn't be sure, but he thought the short car ride covered three of the local hills before it came to a stop, figuring that would put them atop Anstice Street hill. Without speaking, they jerked him from the backseat and pulled him along an uneven sidewalk for a short distance. Hearing the metallic sound of rustling keys, then the rattle of a chain, before he heard the chain fall to the concrete ground. One of the goons grunted loudly before pushing Finn into an area that echoed with the sounds of their every movement. The stale, but musty odor couldn't hide the hundreds of years of incense and candle wax embedded in the walls and flooring. Finn knew immediately where he was: His limping footfalls re-echoed loudly as they crossed the wooden floor of the baren and abandoned cathedral high ceiling of the large dining room of Saint Xavier's. He knew where they were taking him. Passing the abandoned kitchen, he sensed they were making their way past Father Dom's old office and sleeping quarters before stopping again. Hearing someone open the basement door, then shoving Finn hard from behind toward the first step. Quickly finding his footing he descended to the subterranean floor.

Anxiety immediately began to percolate with the forethought of where he was being taken. His brow beaded with sweat, his stride slowed, his heart raced. But he still had his toothpick. The goons pushed, punched, and dragged him by the arms through the hollows until they stopped at the alter box door. He heard them remove the unlocked padlock from the hasp, then pulling open the heavy wooden door before forcing him inside. Stumbling forward, he fell face first, landing on his chest next to the small wooden bed pushed tight against the outside wall.

Joseph gave a throaty laugh. "We'll be back as soon as the boss returns. Don't go anywhere, Detective." The other two security goons laughed and slammed the wooden door. Finn heard the dreaded sound of the large padlock fall against the door, then their footsteps fading as they returned to the stairway.

Frozen with fear, never believing he'd ever be back in Father Dom's alter box again, he managed to sit upright against the wooden wall, his feet extended out in front of his body towards the bed, his gimp leg throbbing with a dull pain. With his eyes locked tight, his teeth clenched, he could feel the perspiration dripping from his forehead, running down his face under the smelly clothed hood. Tasting the salty flavor of his own sweat dripping on to his lips, his chest tightened, his breathing labored. He was one short breath away from absolute panic, as he guided a mental curse at Father Dom's alter box. He sat and waited, with no idea how long he'd waited for his body and mind to reach a thinking level of composure, but he knew it'd been a long time, too long.

It was all Father Dom's fault, he reasoned to himself, for all the anxiety, the crippling claustrophobia, all the emotional fears, the constant need for a toothpick. In his mind he could hear the echoing voice of Father Dom's broken English, as though he were standing just outside the door, like the first time he'd been put in the alter box, when he was eight years old. *"Remember, my son, whenever you need help, look to the heavens, to God."* He'd always wanted Finn to pray, like prayer was the answer to everything. Then hearing Father Dom's voice again, saying. "*Remember, my son, whenever you need help, look to the heavens.*" Look to the heavens? What did that even mean? Why did he always want him to look to the heavens? Did he really think prayer was the answer for everything? Finn silently said himself. "Guess Father Dom never thought I'd be back in his alter box with a smelly hood covering my head, unable to look toward heaven, if there is such a place as heaven."

Sitting in the middle of the alter box, waiting in total darkness, between a soiled old bed and a coal-stained wall, knowing he had to do something. He had to at least get the smelly hood off his head. Mustering the physical strength to sit up straighter, he pulled his bent knees up close to his chest, with his feet flat to the floor, he forced his handcuffed wrists down along the small of his back until he was almost sitting on them. He laid the open palms of his hands against the cold damp floor, then using his flattened hands for leverage, he forced his butt up off the floor, just enough to give his handcuffed wrist a quick jerk forward while pushing his hips backwards. Thinking it was the farthest he'd rolled his left shoulder since he'd been shot. Forcing his handcuffed wrists into a new position, under his bent knees, against the heels of his shoes. Pausing for a second while he prepared himself for more leg pain, he pulled his legs hard and tight up against his chest, closing his eyes, he used all the inner strength he could collect to push his knees as high into his chin as the pain would allow. With a piercing sharp pain to his crippled leg he squeezed his handcuffed wrists out from under the heels and soles of his shoes until his hands were finally in front of his ankles. Reaching up he pulled the hood from his head and took a few deep breaths of stale air, waiting for his eyes to adjust to the darkness of the alter box.

Tipping his head backwards on a deep inhale he gazed up at the ceiling. For all the times he had spent in Father Dom's alter box, he'd never once noticed that the ceiling held two pieces of coal-stained lumber running perpendicular across its upper beams.

Looking at his watch, it was 11:25 p.m. time was running out, when he heard the hurried footsteps above, crossing the dining room floor. Three of them, walking fast. They flung open the stairway door.

Quickly, he pulled the mattress from the bed, tossing it to the another corner. He stood the wooden bed frame on end against the stone wall, using the thick burlap lattice as a ladder he did the only thing he could do.

The moving footsteps clicked hurriedly along the stone floor of the basement, then the alter box padlock fell to the stone floor. The door swung open with a loud thud; a shadowed figure hesitated in the doorway. It was uncommonly dark for anyone without a flashlight, who hadn't let their eyes adjust. Finn heard Joseph bark. "Get in there and drag him out!"

Twenty Nine

THE FIRST SECURITY GOON moved cautiously, at the pace of a blind slug through the blackened open doorway with his gun extended at an arm's length, he was instantly overtaken by Finn dropping like a bag of falling rocks from the coal-black ceiling, securing the goon's gun from his frightened fingers and outstretched arms, before swiveling the unsuspecting goon's body around to face the open doorway, using him as a human shield.

With control of the goon's gun, Finn squeezed off two quick shots into the chest of the second security thug standing disorientated in the darkened open doorway, sending him flying backwards to the floor, clearing the way for Joseph's returned fire aimed toward the fire flashes from Finn's commandeered pistol. Joseph's three thunderous rounds struck Finn's struggling human shield. The illuminating flashes from Joseph's shots gave Finn the silhouetted target he needed to return fire, with two rapid rounds to Joseph's chest, hearing him fall to the floor. The dead goon in Finn's arms slipped from his grasp like an underfilled water balloon. Rushing to Joseph's side, Finn grabbed him by his tie, pulling the dying man's head from the floor. "Where is he?" Finn demanded. Joseph's cold, dilated eyes glazed wildly, with a halfhearted smile crossing his face.

Finn yelled again, "Where is he?" In a calmer tone he added, "You're circling the drain, my friend. Just tell me where he is and make your peace with God!"

"He's waiting for you!" Joseph coughed, revealing a thin trickle of bubbling blood seeping from the corner of his parted lower lip, flowing over his chin on to his neck. "He's waiting to kill you, Finn!"

"Where is he, Joseph?" Finn demanded through clenched teeth.

"At the oak!" Joseph said with a frothy gurgle before his head fell limp, to the floor.

Frantically searching in the darkened hallway for a handcuff key among the three dead bodies, Finn finally found one on the car key ring tucked into Joseph's suit jacket pocket. Unlocking the handcuffs, he quickly checked the remaining rounds in the clip of the gun. Pausing for a split second to pull out a fresh toothpick from the stash in his shirt pocket, he limped from Saint Xavier's to Joseph's waiting car, parked in front of the home. Re-checking his watch, it was 11:35 p.m.

Racing down Mill River Road, he sped along the east side of Mill Pond toward the pasture, slowing only when he came to the first curve, then driving off the apex of the curve until the car teetered precariously at the top edge of the dry ravine. He quickly jumped out and limped to the ravine, then up and out the other side before pushing through the burly inkberry holly bushes, vaulting over the horse fence he limped toward the giant scarlet oak. Pulling his gun from the waistbands of his pants he held it low against his lame leg as slowed to a calming gait, then seeing the shadowed figure of a man standing in the far distance on the other side of the darkened oak.

"Hey, Finn, what took you so long?"

"I was busy, Tater," Finn managed to answer catching his breath, tucking the pistol tighter to the outside of his limping leg.

"Hey, Finn. Don't call me Tater."

"Why? You'd rather I call you Riley Russet? I don't think that's going to happen. You're nothing but a Tater! You've always been a Tater."

"Where's Joseph and the other guys?"

"They couldn't make it," Finn said, slowing his pace, widening his circle as he walked away from the front of the oak, hoping to pull Tater in closer, for a better target.

"That's too bad. I wanted them to hear what I had to say to you before I killed you."

"Nobody wants to hear what you have to say, Tater," Finn said as he fingered the trigger of the gun tucked against his leg.

"Don't you want to know the real story?" Tater asked as he moved closer toward the front of the oak.

"I know enough."

"Well, maybe then you can tell me now that you're not a detective anymore. How'd you know it was me?" Tater asked, maintaining his distance from Finn.

"Sure, I'll tell you, it wasn't just my gut feeling, or the evidence, or lack of evidence, actually it was the way the pieces came together," Finn said as he shortened his steps crossing over the sweetgrass, keeping his body bladed with the massive oak tree, his face looking over his left shoulder, eyeing Tater's shadowed movements as he moved toward the front of the oak, while Finn slowly widened the distance between him and the tree. "For one thing, it was all those phone messages you left for me, wanting to get together. I knew you were up to something, Tater. Looking back, I figured you wanted to pick my brain about some murder case. You haven't changed, you've always wanted something from somebody! Then when I called you about Cook's damaged fence, you threw Joseph under the bus, which was typical Tater. But when you said Father Dom suddenly died of a heart attack and his family wanted him cremated, well, that was a sure giveaway. All those years at Saint Mary's hadn't taught you a thing, Tater. Don't you remember the church frowns on cremation, especially when it comes to a priest? That would be a huge sin. Then when you wanted me to meet your wife and family––well, that was another giveaway. Tater, I checked. You don't have a family; I knew you were setting me up for something."

"What damaged fence are you talking about?"

"That's not important anymore, you're not expected to remember any part of that conversation, because it never happened. Which makes me wonder, Tater, why'd you pick this scarlet oak to have your shown down?"

"I'm not really sure! Maybe because old man Cook told me all about its history. Or maybe because I felt like it was calling me. Besides, how would you know what Father Dom's family wanted?"

"Your pure evil, Tater, that's why it's calling you! Besides, Father Dom never had a family. He was an orphan, like us. You should at least remember that. Why do you think he established Saint Xavier's?"

"Doesn't matter, he was a weak old man," Tater added, with a tone of disgust. "He wouldn't listen. He was going to destroy everything."

"So, you had to kill him?"

"There's a lot of money at stake here, Finn. I think he had a guilty conscience; he was thinking of just giving it all back, some kind of atonement or something."

"What are you talking about, Tater?"

"You don't know anything, do you?" Tater laughed. "The money, this estate. How do you think Father Dom kept Saint Xavier's alive all those years?"

"From some anonymous donor, I believe."

"Finn, Father Dom was the anonymous donor! He kept Saint Xavier's going. He was working with James Barrington Cook the Fourth, the owner of this estate, helping to smuggle diamonds from Europe. They'd been smuggling for years, that's all Cook does. Father Dom had a connection in the Vatican, who would middle uncut diamonds from some unidentified politician in the English parliament. Who'd acquired them for next to nothing from some native mine workers in Africa, the skinnies, they'd call them. It was foolproof. Everything moved through diplomatic pouches. J. Barrington Cook the Fourth has been smuggling forever, and before him it was J. Barrington Cook the Third, all the way down the line to the first J. Barrington Cook. Before they smuggled diamonds, it was gold, the King's gold."

"How do you know all this?"

"Because a few years ago, I was up here doing some fence work. I happened to overhear Father Dom, who was visiting with old man Cook, a business meeting of sorts. Anyway, I heard him tell old man Cook he was having some problems with the courier at the Vatican. The courier had a change of heart and wanted to bail on the diamond gig. Said he wasn't going to move any more diamonds into the United States. Father Dom called it ice, but I knew it was diamonds. Anyway, old man Cook tried to persuade Father Dom into pressuring his courier to continue with the scheduled shipment of diamonds a little longer until they could find a replacement. Father Dom said he couldn't, his courier some American bishop assigned as an attaché to the Vatican, had been found that morning murdered inside the Vatican walls. That's when Father Dom told old man Cook, he wanted out, said he was getting too old, it was getting too dangerous, he'd never wanted people being hurt in the first place. Not being one to pass up a good business opportunity, I convinced old man Cook that he didn't need Father Dom anymore, that I could provide his courier service between Europe and the United States."

"A fence installer turned smuggler. You've never been the brightest, Tater."

"Look who's talking. You couldn't even make it as a cop. I had a little help from one of our old X's—we X's stick together. Well, most of us do anyway. Except for you. You've never been a team player, Finn; I knew you wouldn't be. Everything will be better once you're out of the way."

"So, that's when you killed Father Dom?

"Oh, I didn't kill him. Butch did that. He was getting old anyway. His conscience was weak. I didn't need him running off to confess his sins to the cops. Though I did think Father Dom had told you everything; that's why I was reaching out to you."

"Who's your new courier—Joseph?"

"You're absolutely correct, Finn," Tater said, laughing.

"Yeah, I suspected he was up to something, I could tell by the way he was acting when I first met him at the estate."

•❦•

But the nails for the coffin came when he'd found the blank photocopy, the one he'd dug up from his home copies of the Buckley murder investigation, the grainy-green infra-red photo image of the Buckley boy's car passing by the *House of Fredrick,* the one Joseph had force fed him during his visit. Only now, that copy had nothing more than a date and time stamp, 09-23-2018 at 23:30 hours at the bottom right-hand corner, nothing else. That was all the proof he needed.

There were too many signs not to ignore, or maybe it was his cop instinct again, he just needed to keep looking, to dig deeper. Even Detective Rhoads's discreet satellite images of the horse pasture between 11:30 p.m. to 11:40 p.m. on the night of the twenty-third of September revealed nothing but a vacant horse pasture with one giant scarlet oak tree, which he now understood, it was to be expected. Along with the parking lot images of the Syosset diner's CCTV on the night of the twenty-third, there was no Buckley car leaving the lot.

•❦•

"Everything was working beautifully," Tater gloated. "We even secured some privileged connections, with Butch being established as a member of Her Majesty's Diplomatic Service and a bona fide courier, through a private security contractor. Everything was running smoothly, Butch made the scheduled deliveries in the secured diplomatic pouches that aren't checked by Customs and took them right back here to old man Cook, who had the uncut stones passed off to some discreet cutter in Manhattan. The finished stones were then laundered on the international wholesale market through a bogus diamond company. I never touched a stone. Shit, I never even saw a diamond, but I was making a good cut from them, no pun intended." Tater laughed, as his unwitting path crossed between Finn and the scarlet oak.

Finn stopped, turned, and squared his shoulders to face down Tater, taking a couple short steps toward him. "So, what happened to your brilliant plan, Tater?" Finn said sarcastically.

"Well, a couple weeks ago, old man Cook decided he'd had enough too. Must have been in his eighties. He was getting stupid, or maybe it was Alzheimer's, he was old anyway. He'd never married, had no children that I knew of, but he had connections: the cutter, the international wholesalers, the contact in London, someone from their secret feudal society the old man had never even met. He called him Nigel. At any rate, I had the old man tell Nigel that I was going to be the new point of contact here at the House of Fredrick for all further deliveries. Then I had him plug me into his cutter and the wholesaler. It was simple, really," Tater added with a devilish laugh.

"So, then you killed James Barrington Cook the Fourth?"

"I had to. Well, I mean, Butch had to. How else was I going to acquire this beautiful estate for myself? Don't get me wrong, Finn. It's all legit, I wouldn't have it any other way." Tater laughed. "Get my drift?" He laughed again, adding, "I had the old man sign the estate and all the property over to me before we killed him. No one's going to miss the old man anyway. Who even knew he was alive? But on a lighter note, did you know that this property has been in the Cook family since 1780? The first recorded deed was to a James Barrington Cook the First."

"Did you cremate Cook as well?" Finn asked.

"Yep, sure did. You never know when you'll be needing a trusted mortician. Cremation is the only way to go: no mess, no hassle, no evidence. But you know all that, don't you, Finn?"

"Where're the ashes?" Finn asked, facing Tater as he closed the distance to within fifteen feet, quickly checking the illuminated dials on his wristwatch: 11:59 p.m.

"In the dumpster. Same place yours are going to be, Finn!" Tater said as he suddenly wheeled his right arm around from behind his back and fired two quick rounds from his 9 mm Glock.

Finn never heard the Glock's thunderous reports echoing through the darkened horse pasture, but he did see the blinding muzzle flashes laser past him as he felt a single sledgehammer like blow to his chest, the other shot going wild. His legs immediately jellied, he collapsed to his knees, his head bent low from the pain. Consciously, he managed to draw a needed breath to slow his heart rate. Lifting his head, he emptied his mind, and guided his arm out as far as he could manage before giving the trigger on Joseph's 9 mm three rapidly controlled squeezes, sending two well-placed rounds center mass to Tater's chest. The final round found the center of his forehead.

Finn slumped forward, his head falling sideways into the sweetgrass, while he eyed the giant scarlet oak and watched Tater's silhouetted dead body fall backwards against the raised knobby roots at the base of the massive tree.

Thirty

THE AIR WAS CALM, serene, he felt no pain, breathing was effortless. Yet he would wait to open his eyes, he needed to place his surroundings, mentally envisioning who was near, watching him, guarding him, if anyone. Lying on his back, he sensed his head resting on something warm, something smooth. He began a mental assessment. Living life on the edge taught him to be consciously alert of his surroundings, to be aware, to sense immediate danger. Training taught him to use sound, touch, smell, sight, then, if needed, taste. Mental preparedness was paramount for survival.

He suddenly felt the comforting warmth of a soft touch, feathered fingers slowly combing through his thick dark hair. Followed by a sensitive soft pressure against his forehead, matched by the pleasurable feeling moving evenly down the side of his face. Then came that exhilarating aroma, that alluring scent, lavender. There was no need to wait. He immediately flashed open his eyes to see he was staring straight up into seductive deep blue eyes of sheer beauty. "Sally!" Finn said.

"Finn!"

Sally's lips quickly met Finn's as he lifted his head to meet hers. The warming softness of her tender touch refilled Finn's heart. After a long-desired kiss he asked, "Where are we?"

"My house," Sally said happily, revealing her warm smile.

"Oyster Bay?" Finn asked, sitting up.

"Yes. Twenty West Main Street."

"What year is it?" Finn questioned, as he gazed around the parlor in the front room, a place he remembered so well.

"Any year you want it to be, silly."

He glanced down at his clothing and ran questioning hands across his chest with a puzzled concern on his face. "I remembered being shot," he said with a wide-eyed look at Sally.

"Yes, you were. But not anymore."

"What happened?" he said as he rose, confused, moving around the parlor, studying the eighteenth-century furniture. Pulling the floor-length curtains aside he peered out the window at the darkening street. "It looks no different than yesterday!"

"Actually, it's our tomorrow."

Turning back to her, he asked, "When was I shot?"

"According to your living life, only moments ago."

"Moments ago? My living life?" Glancing down at his wrinkled clothes, he pulled open his blood-stained shirt to see a bullet hole in his chest, next to his heart. He stared at Sally's welcoming blue eyes and whispered softly, "Am I dead?"

"Not to me," Sally answered with a soft smile. "But you don't have to whisper. No one can hear us or see us."

"They can't see us?"

"No, silly. No one can see or hear spirits, unless of course we want them to. Now come over here and sit next to me." She said, patted the fabric of the sofa with a soft palm. "Remember, you were going to tell me all about that killer from Oyster Bay?"

"I'm a spirit?" he murmured, his disbelieving eyes focusing towards the floor with a sensation of sudden awe. What will happen with me, my life, he wondered silently if I'm dead? Pausing to reflect, then realizing he wasn't really leaving anything, he had nothing, no family, no job, no loved ones. Only now he had Sally, his heart was immediately filled with something he'd only ever dreamed of, something he'd never thought to be real, or possible.

Suddenly brimming with an unimaginable feeling of pure contentment, knowing he would be with the only woman he'd ever loved, and who loved him. With a crested smile of pure excitement crossing his lips he took a seat next to his beautiful Sally. "Yes, I did, didn't I," he murmured, kissing her soft lips.

Finn told her everything, his complete story. He told her about finding young Tom and Susanne's bodies by the scarlet oak, of informing their parents of their tragic deaths, then learning of all the unexplained deaths linked to 20 West Main Street from Langdon Foster. He told her about meeting Dr. Seely, and Simcoe's malediction. Sally smiled, saying, "Yes, I like Dr. Seely. He is a very smart man, and he was very good to my sister Phoebe." Finally, Finn told her how he'd stopped the 238 years of murders, which was the key to uncovering Father Dom's killer.

"But how did you know you'd stopped Simcoe's malediction?" she asked.

"Remember when we had the unfortunate or, as it turns out, the fortunate encounter with Colonel Simcoe at the scarlet oak, when he was going to hang you for being America's first female spy. Well, that's when he uttered his malediction. Only for his malediction to be put into play it needed to be facilitated upon your death. You see, for a malediction of misfortune to befall any intended, it can only be uttered by an aspirant who believes himself to have suffered a grave misfortune, in this case Simcoe, who believed he was deprived of his just rewards from King George III, with his plan of Arnold's treasonous betrayal. Then, only after he was successful in causing the death of the person who either caused the aspirant's misfortune or took an active part of that misfortune, which in this case was you, one of General Washington's Culper spies who undertaken the dangerous mission to inform his Excellency of Arnold's subversive plan of betrayal, to surrender the vital Hudson River Fort to the British, along with their plan to capture him as well. Only then could Simcoe's demonic malediction be inaugurated. Until I successfully disrupted it by preventing your death, something that could only have been done by someone with a direct Arnold bloodline."

"Yes, I do know of your blood line. But how did you know I wasn't dead?"

"At first, I had no way of knowing. I learned later, while in the hospital recovering from my wounds, when Detective Doyle said your house was a museum and it had been for years. That's when I knew Simcoe's malediction hadn't been completed, I'd been successful in stopping him, plus, knowing that 20 West Main Street hadn't burned. But more importantly to me, was that you hadn't died at the hands of Simcoe."

"You don't have to worry about any of that anymore. And you won't be needing that toothpick either," Sally said, pulling the tip of the wooden spear from his lips as she wrapped her arms around his waist.

"Though I do wish I had the answers for a couple of other things, before I died," Finn said with a dejected tone.

"Maybe I can help you with those questions." A familiar voice rang out as Dr. Seely's translucent image suddenly appeared in the high-backed upholstered chair directly across from Finn and Sally.

"Dr. Seely?" Finn blurted out in a surprised tone.

"Hello, Finn! I think I can help you with any questions you may have," Dr. Seely said with his milk-glazed eyes fixed straight ahead––without turning his head he added, "Just for the record, not that there will be any record of your achievements, as history is recorded only by those who know it and is not always accurate. Anyway, your initial suspicions were correct. Tom Buckley's car didn't plunge through that fence. It was J. Barrington Cook the Fourth who had his security team detour the Buckley car off NY Route 106, forcing the kid to take the Mill River Road home. Once they passed the entrance to the *House of Fredrick*, other members of Cook's security halted the car and forcibly removed the young warrior and his pretty girlfriend from the vehicle before they lashed him to the scarlet oak. Four generations of Cooks kept Simcoe's malediction active, though only one or two had the opportunity to use the history hole at the scarlet oak. J. Barrington Cook the Fourth took advantage of it.

Had you been at the scarlet oak on the twenty-third of September 1780, just ten days prior, you would have been an eyewitness to the Buckley boy's execution by Simcoe's Rangers, by the same method you witnessed similar executions at the oak before you took the opportunity to stop Simcoe's malediction." Dr. Seely momentarily paused, slurping back a small amount of drool from his sagging lower lip, before adding, "Susanne White is what they commonly refer to as a casualty of war; her death wasn't meant to happen. However, sadly, it did, though she was shown the solemn respect of a warrior's bride, laid out in reverence, as you had also witnessed. The car accident was staged, all the physical evidence professionally removed. But you figured all that out.

"Anyway, it's all a moot point now because none of it happened. There never were fourteen unexplained deaths from our house, because you changed the future by stopping Simcoe's malediction. Although you cannot take credit for killing one of America's infamous enemies, you did give him some lasting pain, along with a lifelong prominent limp. I hope that has answered your questions."

"As usual I didn't get to ask one. Though I would like to know what would have happened if I hadn't stopped Simcoe's malediction?"

"That was never an option, Finn. Remember your bloodline. You were ordained by birth as the only one who could stop him. I knew you'd be triumphant, it's all history now. I will however answer your question. If Simcoe's malediction had continued because you were unsuccessful in stopping it, then you would have never recognized that it was essential for you to travel into the past to change the future, to stop Tater. Remember what I said? *'Only if you are successful in stopping Simcoe's malediction will you learn the identity of your killer.'*"

"Yes, I remembered you saying that, but it didn't initially fit, especially knowing that I had stopped Simcoe's malediction, and since there weren't any murders. How could there be a killer? I struggled with that for almost a year, until it finally dawned on me after seeing Lawrence Joseph's blank photocopy of the

Buckley kid's car, and Detective Rhoads's blank satellite images, why would I have blank copies of something that never happened? Then I remembered the phone call with Tater about Father Dom's sudden and unexpected death along with his cremation, it all came together, and I knew it was Tater. But why was it necessary for me to stop the killer—Tater—by the stroke of midnight on the second of October, exactly one year from the time I stopped Simcoe's malediction?"

"Though James Barrington Cook the Fourth was a prolific smuggler and a diehard loyalist, he wasn't stupid. You must remember his family has been in the smuggling business for 238 years, long before some matricidal post hole digger came along."

"Matricidal post hole digger?"

"Yes, the reason Tater was an orphan was because he pushed his mother into the path of that westbound express to Manhattan."

"I'm not surprised," Finn said.

"In any event, Tater was never going to learn of Cook's diamond connection in London. Nigel was a fictitious person. So was the name of his wholesale diamond cutter, as well as the international wholesaler. Plus, Tater never learned J. Barrington Cook the Fourth and Father Dom shared an equal partnership in the House of Fredrick, along with its vast fortune, which Father Dom kept hidden in a charitable foundation. Father Dom used all the profits from any diamonds ever smuggled into this country to provide support for countless children's hospitals and orphanages throughout America. Oh, and the House of Fredrick, with all its holdings and property, that is financially sound for many years to come. Going forward it will be known as the *House of Fabiano*.

"Ending 238 years of smuggling," Finn suggested.

"Well, that remained to be seen," Dr. Seely snickered, before continuing. "Though the estate will be used as a shelter for orphaned military children, thanks to Father Dom. Tater's quick-claim deed from J. Barrington Cook for the House of Fredrick expired a short time ago at twelve midnight on the second of October, with Father Dom's irrevocable charitable foundation set in motion a few seconds ago at triple oh one on the third of October, providing that Tater and his quick-claim deed were nullified, which you saw to that. Father Dom bequeathed the entire estate, along with all its holdings to ASAMC."

"ASAMC?"

"Yes, the American Society to Aid Military Children. Now are you satisfied?"

"Yes, thank you, that answers most of my questions. Though I do have one other rather small question, Dr. Seely, since you say you know everything there is to know about me, who is my real family?"

"We all have but one biological mother and father, and as a talented sleuth, I'm sure you'll sort all that out. Perhaps you'll need to travel to the past again for some help." Seely chuckled, then added, "Though isn't that also a moot point? Aren't we now your real family?" Seely gave Finn a large smile, then vanishing quicker than a burst water bubble.

Finn thought for a second, he did it again, he answered a question with a question. But Seely was right again, he was more than satisfied with his new family, just being with Sally.

"Finn, I have something I want to show you," Sally said, excitedly.

"To show me?"

"Yes, I think this is something you have been looking for," Sally said as she held up Finn's detective badge.

"Oh yeah! Where did you find it?"

"Right here, by the door, right where you left it, remember?" Sally said as she walked toward the hanging wall mirror in the parlor holding Finn's detective badge up toward the reflective glass. "Your badge number is five-five-three. Look in the mirror, what number do you see?"

"I see 355."

"Yes, that's me! I told you I'd tell you all about myself. It seems we even share the same numbers," Sally said, handing the police badge back to Finn, before adding, "Now don't get too comfortable, there is so much more we must do, I think TR is in need of our help!"

About The Author

Thank you for choosing The Scarlet Oak, I hope you've enjoyed the story. Though the story and behavior of the characters are purely a fictional account of my imagination, actual historic events and locations, specifically in Oyster Bay, New York, did inspire the lore. An underlying theme to this story was meant to expose the dangers and sacrifices suffered by the few dedicated patriots who despite the unsurmountable odds of an occupying foreign army, helped shape the core of this great country. Those few, who either chose to remain anonymous due to the era's cultural nonacceptance with the methods of covert warfare, or whose identities have faded from the American spotlight of history. Or perhaps their stories and activities have been intentionally omitted from the annals of the American Revolution, forever protecting the identity of those who deliberately placed freedom and liberty above their own safety and comfort for a future America.

If you've enjoyed The Scarlet Oak, and would be so kind to leave a short review with an online bookstore, such as Amazon, Goodreads, Barnes and Noble, or BookBub, I'd be more than appreciative. For any comments, questions, or suggestions you

can contact me through my website or email me at my contact
information listed below. I would enjoy hearing from you.

website: www.jerryaylward.com

email: jerryaylwardauthor@yahoo.com

Regards

Jerry

Acknowledgments

I've always been a bit curious about the everyday people from our American past, specifically the average man and women who had a direct hand in shaping the course of our present way of life. Often wondering if they were aware at the time of their bold behavior that it would dramatically change the course of America. While many lived long enough to witness the fruits of their endeavors, along with seeing the retreating invaders, some did not. I would like to acknowledge the actions, efforts, and sacrifices to all the nameless colonial patriots who waged that victorious war against the mightiest of the world's army, and to all those brave and noble warriors since who have fought the continuous fight to protect our freedoms, and our way of life. I would also like to thank Anita for her keen eye on proofreading and encouraging support with this project along with all my writing projects, and of course her delicious lunches. I would also like to recognize my devoted Katie, who rarely left my side.

Also By Jerry Aylward

Nassau County Police Department

Francis "Two Gun" Crowley's Killing's in New York City & Long Island

Made in the USA
Middletown, DE
22 June 2022

67543356R00194